THE BEST DAYS OF OUR LIVES

HELEN ROLFE

B
Boldwood

First published in Great Britain in 2025 by Boldwood Books Ltd.

Copyright © Helen Rolfe, 2025

Cover Design by Alexandra Allden

Cover Images: Shutterstock

The moral right of Helen Rolfe to be identified as the author of this work has been asserted in accordance with the Copyright, Designs and Patents Act 1988.

All rights reserved. No part of this book may be reproduced in any form or by any electronic or mechanical means, including information storage and retrieval systems, without written permission from the author, except for the use of brief quotations in a book review. This book is a work of fiction and, except in the case of historical fact, any resemblance to actual persons, living or dead, is purely coincidental.

Every effort has been made to obtain the necessary permissions with reference to copyright material, both illustrative and quoted. We apologise for any omissions in this respect and will be pleased to make the appropriate acknowledgements in any future edition.

A CIP catalogue record for this book is available from the British Library.

Paperback ISBN 978-1-83561-111-1

Large Print ISBN 978-1-83561-110-4

Hardback ISBN 978-1-83561-109-8

Ebook ISBN 978-1-83561-112-8

Kindle ISBN 978-1-83561-113-5

Audio CD ISBN 978-1-83561-116-6

MP3 CD ISBN 978-1-83561-115-9

Digital audio download ISBN 978-1-83561-114-2

This book is printed on certified sustainable paper. Boldwood Books is dedicated to putting sustainability at the heart of our business. For more information please visit https://www.boldwoodbooks.com/about-us/sustainability/

Boldwood Books Ltd, 23 Bowerdean Street, London, SW6 3TN

www.boldwoodbooks.com

For all the wonderful writing friends I've met along the way...

1

MALLORY

Mallory thanked the kennel assistant and closed the front door behind her. She scooped her dog, Cedella, into her arms. 'I missed you. It's good to have you home. Did you have fun at the boarding kennels? I bet you did, ten whole days with your doggy friends.' She sounded like a loon but it was either that or bawling her eyes out and she'd cried so much over the last week and a bit that she could really do with a break. She also needed to hold it together for when Jilly came home. Her teenage daughter had been staying with a friend while Mallory was away on what her daughter thought was a course – it wasn't, but she couldn't share the real reason for her absence, not yet.

'You'll have to do for cuddles for now,' she whispered into Cedella's white fur. She'd better not mention Jilly by name or the dog would be leaping all over the place, far too excited. They'd save that for when Jilly came in through the front door.

Mallory sat down on the sofa with Cedella on her lap. Jilly would be home from school soon, and reality and normality would resume.

Except how could it? Everything had changed, the extent of which she hadn't really known until a couple of days ago, when her world had changed forever.

She thought back to the relatively carefree existence she'd been living up until that life-changing moment. She thought about the wonderful weekend break in the Cotswolds with her cousin, Penny, celebrating their fiftieth birthdays, just five days apart from each other. The person she'd been then, only four weeks ago, felt like it was someone else entirely.

Penny wasn't only Mallory's cousin, but her best friend too, and despite the family tension and their mothers' estrangement that could've easily kept them apart, they'd only grown closer over the years. Mallory wasn't sure what she'd do without Penny and vice versa, and that weekend, the champagne, the good food, the laughter and the memories they'd created, had been wonderful. But almost as soon as Mallory returned home, reality had hit with a bang she hadn't heard coming. And she was still ricocheting from it.

Funny how she'd thought she had so much to worry about before – last year, in the final year of her forties, the signs of ageing creeping up on her, Mallory had worried about her appearance. She'd whitened her teeth to brighten her smile and get rid of discolouration, probably due to too many coffees in an attempt to stay awake on shift as a rheumatology nurse. She'd had her hair coloured to cover the few greys that were creeping in – she didn't want to look old just yet! And she'd not been happy until she'd lost the three kilograms she put on after a holiday in Florida.

How stupid, the things she'd obsessed about back then.

Those were the little things.

As if they really mattered.

They didn't, not any more, not now this boulder of a worry

had come along and threatened to destroy everything in its path.

Her thoughts were interrupted by the sound of the front door opening and Jilly's voice calling out, 'Mum, Mum! You've got to look at this!'

She went out into the hallway, careful not to let an overexcited Cedella trip her up.

Thirteen-year-old Jilly had hold of her phone and her long dark ponytail swished as she let her school bag drop from one shoulder onto the floorboards, then swished again as she let the holdall on her other fall to the floor too. Whatever was on her phone that she couldn't tear her eyes away from was even distracting Jilly from Cedella and nothing ever did that.

'I'm not looking at anything until I get a hug from my girl.' Mallory held open her arms for Jilly to step into. Jilly, her beautiful girl, whose life was about to be detonated beyond belief when Mallory told her the horrible truth.

Jilly beamed. 'I'm glad you're home.' But she giggled soon enough. 'You're squeezing me a bit tight. And I think Cedella is getting annoyed.'

The little dog was most perturbed that she wasn't the centre of attention for once and Jilly passed Mallory her phone to free up her arms to make a fuss of Cedella. 'Did you miss me?'

'I did,' said Mallory, knowing full well she was asking the dog.

'Mum, look at what's on my phone.'

Mallory lifted the phone to check the screen. 'Okay, what am I looking at? Wow, nice dress.' She was looking at a social media post of a woman wearing a beautiful wedding gown. 'Whose Instagram post is this?'

Jilly rushed through her answer as though that was secondary to what she'd found – she followed a singer slash actress whose mum had been very famous in the sixties, seventies and eighties and had been in 'a ton' of movies before she passed away a few months ago.

'Mum...' Jilly pressed on urgently. 'Look closer.'

She did.

'It's not just any dress,' said Jilly. 'Mum, *the* actress Norma Monroe wore *Granny Gigi's* dress in a movie!'

Mallory frowned and looked closer at the famous actress in the black and white shot of a movie scene. The wedding dress certainly looked a lot like her mother's. In fact, it was uncanny. But why would this actress be wearing Gigi's dress? It didn't make any sense.

'Jilly, there are a lot of wedding dresses that must look just like Granny Gigi's.' But she humoured her daughter and looked at it some more. She swiped right to see the actress in the same dress, this time walking away from the camera and turning her head over her shoulder. The back detailing certainly looked the same too. She tried to pass the phone back to Jilly but Jilly urged her to look again.

'Read the wording below.'

Mallory wasn't in the mood, she didn't want to read a tribute to someone who had died. But she would do anything for Jilly so she read the blurb accompanying the photographs.

The write-up covered an overview of the life of Norma Monroe, a famous actress whose career began in the sixties. The first movie she'd been in had shot her to fame apparently, so a lot of the focus was on that time period. The actress talked about the dress saving the day after a terrible storm ruined the filming company's costumes for that particular movie. But it was next part of the write-up that told Mallory there was every possibility this was the same dress her mother had made, the same dress Gigi had worn to marry Mallory's late father,

Hector, the same dress that was still boxed up in the attic of her mother's house. The movie had been filmed in Saxby Green and Norma Monroe's daughter was quoted as saying that her mother never forgot the generosity of two sisters from the quaint English village who provided the dress for one of the most important events of her entire life. The date the film was made also coincided with the time Mallory knew Gigi had lived in the village with her sister, Rose. All the details seemed to fit.

Mallory took Jilly's phone over to the framed photograph of her parents that sat on the windowsill. She compared the images of the dress side by side. Reminiscent of the 1930s era, the cream, ankle-length heavily sequinned gown with tulle sleeves and hand sewn details was one of a kind, a thing of beauty.

'Is it the dress, Mum?' Jilly urged.

'I think it is.'

'So they made it together? Granny Gigi and her sister, Rose?'

'It looks that way.'

Eighty-one-year-old Gigi had always batted away any questions about her older sister, Rose, and to this day Mallory had no idea why.

She had always told Mallory that she'd made the dress, which was true, but it sounded as though Rose had been integral to its creation too, which made sense given Aunt Rose still lived in Saxby Green and owned a wedding dress boutique.

Mallory's mind rushed with information, too much information today, she felt on overload. Gigi had always been so tight-lipped about the falling out and so had Aunt Rose, Penny's mother, because if Penny knew about this she never would've kept it from Mallory.

Now she'd seen the Instagram post, Mallory had a growing

suspicion that the sisters' estrangement had a lot to do with the dress.

She had a sinking feeling in the pit of her stomach. 'Did you comment on the post, Jilly?' Letting her teenager have social media was something Mallory would've liked to refuse but given all her friends were on it, she had had to settle with monitoring what Jilly did when she was on there and keeping her aware of the risks.

'No.' Jilly shook her head. 'I really didn't, Mum. I just follow the actress. I saw the post when I was walking home and came straight in to tell you about it.'

'You should put your phone away when you're out and about. I've told you that.'

'Sorry.'

Mallory hugged Jilly. Telling her off about anything right now felt impossible. She kissed the top of her head. 'Do me a favour – don't mention anything to Granny Gigi about this.'

She frowned with confusion. 'Okay.'

'I mean it, this is important, and delicate. I need to work out where to go from here so we don't upset anyone unnecessarily.'

'Fine. Now can I get something to eat? I'm really hungry.'

Mallory, distracted, didn't answer straight away.

'Food. Mum, I need food.' She was already on her way to the kitchen.

Mallory snapped out of her trance and called after her, 'There's a fresh loaf of raisin bread in the bread bin.'

While Jilly was out of the room, Mallory picked up the phone to call Penny. She had to tell her what she knew.

But the phone rang and rang, no answer, and so she left a message to say it wasn't urgent, that she'd call later on.

Mallory welcomed Cedella onto her lap while Jilly was in the kitchen. What would Penny make of all of this? It was the first hint either of them had ever got as to why their mothers didn't have anything to do with one another.

Mallory closed her eyes and transported herself back to the Cotswolds and the time spent with her best friend celebrating their fiftieth birthdays.

They'd kicked off their stay with a dip in the hot tub out the back of the cottage they were renting and talk, as it often did, had turned to their mothers.

'How's Aunt Gigi doing?' Penny had asked as she swished her hands through the water in front of her.

'I think she's keen to get the cruise over with, she promised Dad when he died that she'd still go on it even though it was supposed to be the two of them.'

'It'll be hard, but having you there with her will help.'

'I hope so. How's Aunt Rose?'

'As stubborn as ever.' Penny reached for her glass of champagne. 'She's eighty-two years old and still refusing to retire, still living in the flat above the shop and saying she's not budging. I know she loves Rose Gold Bridal, it's been her life for so long. But I can't ignore how much she's struggling. She made a couple of mistakes on bridal gowns – luckily her assistant, Michelle, rescued the situation and no harm done, but it upset her, you know how she values her brides and wants the very best, every time.

'Anyway, I'm going down to Saxby Green to see her, work out for myself how she really is and perhaps talk to her about the future of the shop if she'll let me.' She knocked back the rest of her champagne. 'I'm getting shrivelled; let's go have that cake.'

Mallory carefully climbed out of the tub, steadying herself on the side for a moment. The heat, or perhaps the glass of champagne, had made her a bit wobbly.

Penny handed Mallory a big white fluffy towel and plucked the other one to wrap around herself.

'Penny, do me a favour?' Mallory dried off a little so they wouldn't take the water inside.

'Anything.' She picked up both of the empty champagne flutes between her fingers.

'Don't ever let anything come between us like Rose and Gigi did.'

Penny hooked an arm around her cousin's shoulders as they made their way in through the back door. 'I promise I won't. I'm afraid you're stuck with me. For ever.'

Once they were dressed, they walked to the fish and chip shop and strolled back to the cottage with their parcels, the scent of vinegar and salt so tantalising they wasted no time emptying the food onto plates.

Penny went to top up both glasses of champagne but Mallory shook her head. 'No more for me, not just yet.'

'Oh come on, this is a major celebration!' Penny tried again but Mallory covered the top of her glass.

Penny sighed. 'Looks like I'll have to take one for the team. Or several. This is only our first bottle.'

'I might have some more later.'

'Glad to hear it.'

Mallory was tired; she'd done a few extra shifts lately and was really feeling it but she hoped that after this time away she'd return home and the fatigue would pass so she could get back to feeling like herself.

'I think I need glasses.' Mallory winced as she momentarily saw two big cakes, not one, while Penny pushed the sparklers into the top of the iced sponge. Surely the alcohol hadn't gone to her head that quickly, although her tolerance had lowered somewhat since perimenopause came knocking at her door.

She would've thought those fish and chips might have at least soaked some of it up, but it appeared not.

Penny tutted. 'Book your eye test and get it sorted.'

'Bossy boots.'

'You know you'd nag me if it was the other way round.' Penny found a box of matches in the fourth drawer she tried. 'Go sit down, I'll bring in the cake.'

Mallory turned out the light when Penny yelled through the instruction from the kitchen.

Penny came through with their joint birthday cake – bright yellow with flickering candles, sparklers and a big number fifty in gold lettering on top. She positioned the cake on the coffee table and sat down next to Mallory on the sofa. 'Ready?'

They launched into the traditional song, smiles on their faces, giggles in between the words. 'Happy birthday to us,' they chorused, 'happy birthday to us, happy birthday dear Mallory and Pe-nny, happy birthday to us!'

Mallory lifted up her glass of water and passed Penny her glass of champagne. 'To us,' she said, clinking her vessel against Penny's. 'Fifty and fabulous.'

Penny beamed. 'Fifty, fabulous and friends forever.'

In her own home Mallory's thoughts of the celebrations quietened as Jilly came back into the lounge with a couple of slices of raisin toast. Cedella had her eye on the food already.

Mallory savoured her daughter's laughter as she tried to bat her dog's attentions away.

When Cedella finally leapt off Jilly's lap Mallory put an arm around her shoulders, pulled her against her. 'I really did miss you. Did you have fun at Sasha's?'

Mallory vaguely took in the details of Jilly's ten-day stay with her work colleague and close friend and for now, the keeper of her secrets.

She watched her daughter when Cedella came back demanding her attention once again. This girl was only just getting started – the girl who had the same dark skin as Mallory who had inherited it from her Jamaican father, the girl with the soft brown eyes just like Mallory's, the girl with the world at her feet. A world that she wouldn't recognise when the truth came out.

Mallory wished she could go back to being that woman who'd sat in the hot tub chatting away with her best friend, the woman who'd eaten two massive slices of cake. She wished she could go back to being the woman who worried about the trivial things like piling on the pounds on holiday, or keeping the house relatively clean; she wished she could be the mother who sat and laughed with her daughter without a huge weight looming over them both. She wanted to be the woman she was before she knew what she knew.

But she couldn't be.

She never would be again.

And where did she go from here? At some point she'd have to share the truth but when she did, it wouldn't only be her world that would collapse.

2

PENNY

Penny finished up her yoga session. She'd taken up yoga about ten years ago when workplace stress had almost got the better of her, and had kept it up. It was versatile, which was part of what she loved – she could roll up her mat and take it wherever she needed to. She'd done the session in her apartment and she left her mat by the door ready to take with her to her mother's.

After a shower she had a quick FaceTime call with her twenty-five-year-old son, Marcus. Six months ago he had been made redundant from his computing job and was using the funds to travel the world before he settled into another position. Penny couldn't blame him. Lately she'd been feeling that perhaps there was more to life than the corporate environment and the demands it made.

Penny had graduated with a degree in Business Management and gone on to get her MBA. She'd got a job in project management after finishing her studies and finally became a management consultant. Most recently she'd worked for a company who provided professional services to banks. She provided advice, identified scope for risk mitigation, supported strategy development. She managed several large-scale projects in what had been a demanding, high-pressured role, way beyond a nine-to-five job. She'd had a lot of responsibility – sometimes hundreds of thousands of pounds or even millions in the form of the client's resources – and expectations had understandably been high.

But Penny had got to the point where work had become pretty much her everything – she was still seeing Carlos, a colleague who, much like her, gave work his full attention, but other than time with him, which was usually snatched and rushed and very casual, she had little time for friendships. She squeezed in yoga because she knew she had to for her mental health, but really she had no proper time to relax, she was barely at home given her work hours and she couldn't even remember the last time she'd read a book from start to finish.

On the other hand, without her job as a management consultant she probably wouldn't own her two-bedroom apartment in Notting Hill and she wouldn't have had the security her job had given her as a single mother. She likely wouldn't drive a brand-new Audi A5 Cabriolet either, and she definitely wouldn't stay in the nicest hotels all around the world whenever she felt the need to have a break away or extend her time in a place she'd been sent to with work.

She finished her call with Marcus with a smile on her face. He was currently bumming around – his phrase not hers – Thailand without a care in the world and he looked relaxed, the way he should do in his mid-twenties. She needed to channel some of those chilled out vibes herself.

She texted Mallory to say she was sorry she'd missed her call yesterday but she'd been in a meeting. She said she'd give her a call later – that was another thing she didn't spend enough time doing, chatting with her best friend who just so happened to be her cousin. They'd had a weekend away in the Cotswolds just over a month ago but since then they'd both been so busy. It wasn't right, was it? You worked say forty years up to retirement and then had ten to twenty really good years left if you were lucky. Was that really what she wanted? Did she want to be doing the same thing when she was in her mid-sixties, to still be on the work treadmill with one demanding project after another, relentless demands, copious amounts of pressure, and not even having the time or the energy to return a phone call?

Within an hour Penny was on the road, yoga mat in the boot along with her suitcases, the car roof down, the breeze lifting the waves of her hair as she headed for Saxby Green, the village her mother had lived in all her life. She was going on an open-ended visit too, hence all the luggage. She'd taken leave from work – she'd accrued a lot of holidays given she rarely took any and if she did they were short and sweet, and this trip would not only give her a chance to see whether her mother was coping and perhaps talk to her about the future of the shop, it would be a total break for Penny away from her corporate demands.

Penny loved London, had done for years ever since she landed a great job shortly after Marcus's dad left her for the final time – a blessing in the end. But ever since Marcus had moved out and done his own thing, Penny's job and lifestyle hadn't quite given her the same euphoria as before. And she was getting old. Fifty! Half a century, yup, old!

As she drove she sang at the top of her voice to the radio station replaying favourites from the eighties. Nobody could hear her – a few drivers gave her a look but she could be talking to someone on Bluetooth for all they knew and why should she care what they thought? She shouldn't. And singing relaxed her, so she did it most of the way until she turned off the main road and slowed her speed as she drove into the village.

She pulled up outside Rose Gold Bridal, the shop her mother had established over forty years ago. But Penny didn't need a toot of the horn to announce her arrival because Rose was already coming out of the front door.

Penny got out, ran around to the passenger side and hugged her mother. 'It's so good to see you.'

Rose beamed. Her flame-red hair had faded but there was still a hint of it in the grey tresses piled on top of her head in a haphazard bun. Somehow it didn't look messy on Rose, it looked right. 'I'm glad you're here.'

Penny drove them to the country pub where they'd be having the legendary afternoon tea and where they would be able to talk better than they could at the bridal boutique or in the flat above.

'How's my grandson?' Rose asked after they'd placed their order and taken the round table in the bay window, the best table and the one Penny had requested.

'He's having a ball.' Penny recounted their call earlier, the things Marcus had been up to. 'He's already been thinking about what he'll do when he gets back.'

Rose took off the light weave cardigan she'd put over a white high-necked blouse. 'Don't worry too much about him.'

'Except I do.'

'You're worried he'll take after his father.'

'Is it that obvious? On the one hand I'm glad he's taking time for himself, on the other I want to see him settled again with a good job.'

'He takes after you, Penny, not Russell. At least not in any ways that I can see. I have a feeling he'll be just fine.'

Marcus's father, Russell, had been in a band when he and Penny got together and he'd played in whatever venue would have him. It wasn't that Rose hadn't liked the man, it was more that she saw him as the Peter Pan he was. He didn't want to grow up, he didn't want responsibility. Penny hadn't really seen that part of him until it was too late, until after they got married in Vegas and she fell pregnant with Marcus. But she'd never been sorry about that part – Marcus was a blessing from day one. It was the relationship with his father that wasn't. The cracks soon began to show – Russell didn't contribute in any way to the household, nor to parenting, and eventually she'd told him to leave.

Marcus rarely had contact with his dad these days – he said he had enough people in his life who cared about him more than his own father ever had. To hear him say that had made Penny so sad, but somehow, despite the absence of his father, Marcus had turned into a well-rounded, lovely young man; he was kind and Penny was lucky to have him.

In the pub Penny poured some water into the big glasses the waitress had brought over with ice cubes clinking inside. 'Have you been busy at the shop today?'

'Steady, not too bad.' Rose smiled. 'And I knew it wouldn't be long before you mentioned my business.'

'Am I not allowed to ask about it?'

Rose frowned. 'I'm not ready to leave it behind.'

'Oh, Mum.' Penny put a hand over Rose's. She didn't want her mother to leave it behind either, but they had to face the fact she was getting older. 'I'm not here to badger you. But I do worry. Having a business is a lot to cope with.'

'At my age you mean.'

'At any age. It's demanding, and you've worked hard for so many years.'

'Do something you love and you'll never work a day in your life. Isn't that what they say?'

Penny smiled. 'It certainly worked for you.'

'It's a shame neither you nor Stephen share my passion. I could've handed over the business to you or your brother and stayed on the sidelines.'

'Maybe you still can if whoever takes it over wants that.'

Rose laughed. 'I doubt anyone would want to have a woman in her eighties who is making more and more mistakes anywhere near their business. And as for the paperwork side of things…'

The shop occupied a prominent corner position in Saxby Green. It was beautiful, warm and welcoming. Established in the early 1980s with windows wrapping around its sides, its displays showed the elegance and sophistication locals had come to associate with Rose Gold Bridal. Penny could still remember watching her mother work day and night on the beautiful gowns that hung on the racks, on the accessories that would make a wedding day extra perfect.

'I can help you with the paperwork,' said Penny.

'I've let things go in that respect.' Rose leaned to the side so the waitress could deliver the three-tiered afternoon tea that made Penny realise she hadn't eaten anything since breakfast. That was another thing she did – sometimes she was so busy at work that it was coffee on the run, a grabbed snack here and there. Home cooking was for people with time, not for someone with her job, and she was growing tired of takeaway and restaurants. She would never admit it to Carlos but coming here wasn't just about helping her mother, she needed to take a break from the routine that she'd been caught up in for so long she barely knew who she was any more.

'I can't bear the thought of selling up,' said Rose when the waitress left them to it. 'What if someone buys my shop and turns it into a café, a dog grooming parlour or an Airbnb?'

'One step at a time, eh. We need the business to be doing well, for all the books to be up to date, to make it appealing as it is, so someone might buy it and continue on with what you've built so brilliantly.' She didn't add that even then it wasn't a given that someone wouldn't buy Rose Gold Bridal and do what they liked with it. And usually Penny would be pragmatic, it was business after all, but this felt different. The thought of Rose Gold Bridal ceasing to exist didn't please her either. She'd never dreamed of being a dressmaker – she hadn't inherited her mother's talent or patience for anything involving a needle and thread, but the shop was such a huge part of the family's identity.

Once their tea was poured Penny asked her mother, 'Is the actual business doing okay profit wise?'

'Oh you know, so-so. And Michelle is a gem of an assistant. It's a shame we can't clone her.' Rose plucked a little cheese and pickle sandwich from the bottom plate. 'The pandemic had a real effect on both me and my business. The shop was my sanctuary and I clung onto it.'

'I'm glad you had the shop during that time.'

'I don't know what I would've done without it.'

Penny had hated not being able to see her mother during those months of lockdown but she'd been incredibly glad that Rose was busy doing what she loved. It wasn't quite the same – there were no walk-ins, no fitting appointments for a while, but Rose had continued to make or adjust wedding gowns. She'd had a purpose and had thrown herself into it the way she always did.

'I can't say I ever got on board with virtual ceremonies,' said

Rose, 'but some of my brides had no choice during the pandemic.'

'Oh, I don't know, virtual ceremonies would be a hell of a lot cheaper and easier when so many families are separated by miles. Take Stephen and Delta for example. It cost a fortune to put on their wedding in Boston. My wedding in Vegas wasn't something I'd ever appreciated until Stephen revealed just how many thousands he and Delta and her parents shelled out.'

'It was a bit over the top.' Rose spoke in a voice that suggested they might be overheard and reprimanded for their criticism. 'She had ten bridesmaids and Stephen and Delta covered the cost of all the dresses plus their accommodation, their wedding favours, and the little bottles of locally produced wine, which cost more than some brides would spend on a dress. I'm glad we went though.'

'I'm glad too.' Penny cut a warm scone filled with plump sultanas in half. 'I think it would be a good idea to give Rose Gold Bridal some online presence. Let me look into it for you.'

'You'd do that?'

'Of course.' It was why she was here. Rose would never have asked for help so she'd made the decision for her mother and come here on her own steam. 'I can create a Facebook page for the shop, an Instagram account, and sort out getting you a basic website. I promise there will be no extra stress added to your plate.'

'I never needed to be online before.'

'Things change, Mum.'

'Don't I know it.' She looked at Penny. 'Before the pandemic I was considering announcing my retirement. I was going to put the shop up for sale.'

'You never told me.'

Misty-eyed, Rose said, 'The thought of letting it go became

impossible during that first lockdown. Without it I knew I would be even more lonely and cut off from the world.'

Penny stood up and went to her mother's side, wrapped her in a hug. 'You'll always have me and Stephen.'

'I know I can't keep going in the shop forever. Making those mistakes broke my heart.'

'Well, luckily I'm here for a while. I'll get you online, sort your paperwork, then let's take it from there. Nobody will make you do anything you don't want to do.'

Penny sat down again and poured them some more tea after she handed her mother another tissue to wipe her eyes.

'This really is beautiful crockery, isn't it?' said Rose. 'Especially for a pub.'

'It's definitely more akin to some of the fine dining places I've been to.' In the ten months she and Carlos had been seeing each other they'd been to no end of restaurants but today's afternoon tea was something else. 'This afternoon tea is one of the nicest I've ever had, I think I'll come here again.'

'Your Carlos is missing out. On the china and the afternoon tea.' Rose had met him once when Penny took Rose up to London for a few days to get her away from the shop over a bank holiday and she'd thought him aloof and not really Penny's type. He was exactly like Penny was – ambitious, hardworking with little time for anything other than his job, which, according to Rose, was the whole problem. 'I bet he wouldn't be seen dead somewhere like this.'

Penny grinned. 'You're probably right.' The pub had that lingering smell that couldn't be covered up no matter how many times it was cleaned – the unmistakable smell of beer, of pints enjoyed long into the evening by crowds of punters, locals who came here because it was their habit. The floor wasn't level either and Penny had had to push a couple of napkins under one of the table legs to stop it from wobbling. Things weren't perfect here but they had character and it was comforting.

'What sort of thing would I put on a website?' Rose asked.

Good, she was talking about it. It was a step in the right direction, letting Penny get involved. 'Anything, and it wouldn't need to be fancy. You could have photos of the gowns, brides who've bought from you and are happy to share pictures of their special day, maybe one or two shots of the interior of the shop and the area where you and Michelle work.' She paused. *Tread carefully, Penny,* she reminded herself. 'One day – even if it's not for a long while – you'll want to sell the business. And as a buyer, the first thing I'd be looking at with a business such as yours would be its online presence.'

'You seem to know a lot about it.'

'I don't know bridalwear but I do know business basics.'

Rose selected a piece of quiche. For a petite eighty-two-year-old she still had a good appetite. 'I'm glad you're going to look at the paperwork for me. Michelle is wonderful, but her talents are with a needle and thread, talking to clients, advising about colours, sizes and styles. She, by her own admission, hasn't got a head for the books.' She fussed with the napkin on her lap. 'Do you have the time to do this, Penny?'

'I've taken some extra leave.'

'You have? How long?'

'A while. I accrued lots of holidays.' And she hadn't committed to a return date yet either. She was at burnout point, something she had seen happen to others and she didn't want to fall apart. She wanted to take action before that happened, so here she was. She'd reached the end of a contract with an external company and had put the brakes on before her boss lined her up with anyone else. She'd told him she'd let him know when she was ready to return, when she was ready for the work demands to come at full pelt all over again.

'If you'll have me in the flat, I'll stay a month perhaps, maybe longer.'

Rose's words rushed out. 'Stay for as long as you like. Oh, this is a wonderful surprise, Penny. You're a good daughter.'

'Don't let Stephen hear you singing my praises, he might get jealous.'

Rose laughed. 'You're my favourite daughter and he is my favourite son. I can't be any fairer than that.' Her eyes narrowed. Even though she had a lot going on herself, she was still tuned in to her children and how they were feeling. 'Are you really here to help me? Or is this an escape for you?'

Penny smiled. 'Busted. It's a bit of both. I'm here to help but I need a break from work.'

Rose let out a sigh. 'About time too. You work far too hard.'

'I wonder where I get that from.'

'But you love London still, don't you?'

'I do, but I don't always love the pace.'

'And Carlos? Where does he fit in to all of this?'

'I think Carlos is part of the problem. We're so similar, which worked for a while, but he never slows down and alongside him I don't let myself either.'

'Well, that doesn't sound like much of a love match.'

Penny shook her head. 'I like him a lot.'

'But you don't love him.'

Penny answered honestly. 'I've no idea. I just think that it would be good for me to be somewhere quieter for a while, somewhere where people stop and talk in the street, where I can take a breath.'

'I didn't know you were so stressed.'

'That's because I have your work drive. Admitting to myself

that I was tired wasn't easy.' And Rose was doing exactly the same, hanging on to the shop no matter what, but at least now she'd accepted some help Penny could see how things were working and this arrangement would be good for both of them.

Penny and Rose spent the afternoon in the shop. Penny loved watching her mother chat to customers, the same sparkle in her eyes as there had always been when she talked to a bride about her special day, but she could see that by the time they sat down to dinner in the flat after closing her mother was exhausted.

When her mother excused herself to get ready for bed Penny went into the bedroom that had once been hers. There was something so comforting about closing the door and being in the space where you had always felt so safe and loved. It never seemed to change, no matter how old she got.

She sat on the edge of the bed, tapped on Mallory's contact in her phone hoping for a chat but when Mallory didn't answer Penny felt determined to carry on with this idea of a total change now she was in Saxby Green. She put her phone on silent, got into her pyjamas and went into the lounge to see whether there were any books on the small bookcase that she could read.

She couldn't remember the last time she'd felt this relaxed.

3

MALLORY

Mallory had been in to the hospital briefly today, but she wasn't on shift. Instead she'd seen one of the doctors. She'd sat in the waiting room, toyed with the straps of her bag, done her best to ignore the information leaflets pinned up on the cork boards around. There was so much of it. Was it helpful? Or was it overwhelming? She didn't really know. All she knew was she didn't want to look but it was like a road traffic accident. You knew as you passed that you shouldn't let your eyes be drawn to the wreckage or, heaven forbid, the victims, and yet you couldn't help it.

Over a week had passed since Mallory returned home from the fictitious work course she'd had to conjure up as an excuse to be away from home for a while. She'd lied to her daughter, to her mother and she'd lied to Penny every time they texted – lies by omission – and she hated every minute of doing it. But, sometimes, lies had to be told, for everyone's sake.

Unfortunately, one lie often led to others. One lie she could cope with, she could justify, but multiple lies ate up at her insides. And she'd had to tell another enormous fib to get out of the cruise she'd agreed to go on with her mother. She'd told Gigi that she had forgotten to officially book the time off work and at this late stage nobody could cover her shifts. Gigi, being Gigi, had said that Mallory shouldn't feel guilty, and with a stiff upper lip she'd told her daughter that she would go on her own and perhaps it would be good therapy for her grief. Mallory had cried when she left her mother's that day, waiting until she turned the corner at the end of the street so there was no danger of her being spotted if Gigi was looking out of her bay window to wave her off. She knew her mother didn't want to go on the cruise alone – Gigi hadn't really even wanted to go on the holiday she'd booked with the love of her life before he passed away, but she was doing it because she'd promised Hector.

Hector had asked Gigi to go on the cruise but the day he died he'd asked Mallory to do something too. He'd asked her to get Gigi to talk to her sister, Rose. They'd smiled at each other when he made that request, as Mallory stroked his head and promised him that of course she'd try. She'd thought it would be impossible, she thought she wouldn't have any idea how to go about it, and then Jilly had shown her the Instagram post about Gigi's dress. Now, she had a plan. It was a long shot, perhaps a little bit crazy, but anything was worth a try. She, and everyone else, was running out of time.

Mallory emerged from the hospital into the sunshine a couple of hours after she arrived for her appointment. As she made her way to the bus stop she tried Penny again, desperate to tell her her plan.

'At last. It's good to hear your voice.' Mallory smiled.

'Yours too. We keep missing each other.'

'Are you in the village?'

'I am, and I just had a bubble bath, at 11 a.m. How wild is that!'

Mallory laughed. 'It'll do you good to take your foot off the pedal for a while.'

'I'm not sure there'll be much of that here at the shop.'

Mallory frowned. Penny worked too hard – had she merely swapped London stress for village stress? Surely not – she was having a bath; that told her something about her friend. Saxby Green would be good for her, Mallory just knew it.

'I have something I wanted to discuss with you,' said Mallory as she got to the other side of the zebra crossing.

'It sounds serious.'

'It concerns our mothers.'

'Wait, I need to sit down in that case.'

As Mallory walked she told Penny what Jilly had found online and the information she'd read about the actress, the movie, the reference to the sisters.

'I can't believe it.' Penny sounded as shocked as Mallory had felt when she'd discovered there was more to Gigi's dress than she'd ever realised. 'They must have made it together. But the dress fitted your mum and she ended up with it.'

'She did. And yes, it fitted perfectly.'

Penny gasped. 'You know, I *do* remember something. Mum didn't talk about Gigi at all but she did mention a dress that was supposed to launch her bridalwear shop. I overheard her saying something to my dad once, something about it being stolen. I'd forgotten all about it until now. You don't think…'

'That my mother took it? Well yes, I do now.'

'Shit.'

'That's one word for it. It would explain the fallout. Listen, Penny, I've got a plan. Hear me out though before you say anything.'

'Why do I get the impression you're going to tell me something insane?'

Mallory took a deep breath. She needed family in place for Jilly, she needed to honour her dad's last wish, and there weren't many ways to do that so she just hoped her idea worked. And she'd already made a start with it.

'I went to Mum's house and I took the dress,' she admitted to Penny.

'Mallory!'

'I had to, while she was on her cruise.' Her words tumbled out. 'I've lined up a house sitter and dog sitter. I'm going to come to Saxby Green for a month – Jilly and I need a holiday but we can't afford much so I've found a lovely cottage for us – and me and you will get Rose and Gigi talking about the dress if it's the last thing we do.'

Penny let out a long breath. 'I'm not sure this will work.'

'We have to try something.'

'You know doing this might well be the last thing we ever do. They'll kill us with their bare hands when they both know what's going on.'

'You think it's a terrible plan?'

Penny paused. 'Actually, I don't. Now I'm here I'd say my mother is bloody lonely. It breaks my heart. And I know Aunt Gigi is sad and more alone than she needs to be since your dad died. It's high time they talked. Even if they don't make up, it's worth a shot. I mean, it's family.'

'It's family,' Mallory repeated, the words so poignant now more than ever.

'It'll be really lovely to have you here in the village,' said Penny, brightening. 'I'm intending on staying a while so we can see a lot of each other.'

Mallory smiled. 'I can't wait to see you too. Now I have to

go. I'm about to get on the bus to collect the dress from the dry cleaner's. I accidentally trailed it through dust in the attic.'

'Shit, Mallory!'

'It's all good, it'll be pristine by the time it arrives in Saxby Green.' She held her phone against the card reader as she boarded the bus. 'I'll text you with more details about where I'm staying, exactly when I'm coming, but it'll be soon.'

She took a seat towards the middle of the bus. Stealing her mother's dress from her attic had been such a low act and she'd felt even more dreadful that it got dirty. Dry cleaning it was the only option even though it was a pain having yet another thing that needed doing, especially when she was reliant on public transport.

In the town, Mallory got off the bus and made her way to the dry cleaning shop. No matter whether their mothers were going to be furious with them, this was a way to get everyone she loved, everyone she needed, in the village together for what was about to unfold. And thinking of the dress as well as making plans with her best friend worked like a reprieve in some ways. It stopped her obsessing about the thing she needed to obsess about but would rather not.

4

MALLORY

Mallory's positive spin didn't last. When she got to the dry cleaning shop she handed over her ticket and it wasn't long before the assistant brought out a dress and laid it onto the counter. She felt a feeling of foreboding sweep through her body as she stared at the garment in its plastic wrap. 'This isn't my dress.'

The blonde-haired assistant stopped midway through the spiel she'd launched into about removing the garment from the plastic and storing it according to the instructions on the leaflet enclosed. 'Not your dress? But...'

Mallory's chest tightened, her emotions threatening to unleash at any second. 'I'm telling you: this... is... not... my... dress.'

'I'm so sorry.' Flustered, the young woman checked the tag, went to the computer, wiggled the mouse and presumably tried to find out what had happened. 'There's been a mistake. A dreadful mistake.'

Mallory couldn't believe it. Taking the dress was bad,

trailing it in dust was awful, but losing it altogether? That was unforgiveable.

The owner of the dry cleaning store, an untidily dressed man with a paunch beneath his striped shirt, a man who looked like he was used to throwing his weight around, barged in on the conversation. 'What seems to be the problem here?'

Mallory held up the covered wedding dress she'd been given. 'This isn't mine. I need my dress. I *really* need my dress.'

'Ma'am, I'm sure we can sort this out.' Sweat beaded on his brow and upper lip as his own stress levels began to rise at the error. 'We will find you your dress.' Although he didn't look all that sure to Mallory.

'This is... this is unimaginable.' Her heart thumped with her mounting fury and utter devastation. She caught sight of herself in the mirror on the wall. The scowl was something she wasn't proud of, the drained complexion due to the overwhelming stress she wished she had an easy way of putting a stop to. A few weeks ago she probably would have come in with a smile on her face and a willingness to listen. Mind you, a few weeks ago she might not have done anything as crazy as using a key given to her for emergencies to enter her mother's house and steal something so precious.

'Rest assured, we will rectify this.' The owner garbled on, his tone with an edge that suggested once Mallory left, all hell would break loose. He disappeared too, presumably to speed up the search.

The dress is out back, I know it is. I'll have it in my arms soon enough, Mallory told herself.

Her mother would be devastated if the dress was gone. All Mallory had wanted to do was to help Gigi, to get her talking to her sister, Rose. Ever since her father's death sixteen months ago, Gigi seemed to have lost her happiness and her hope. Mallory truly believed, especially after Hector's request that she get the sisters talking again, that Gigi needed Rose back in her life. She wanted Gigi to have people, family, to have stability, to be ready for what would sooner or later come her way like a tsunami about to hit. She wouldn't see it coming, not unless Mallory warned her, and she couldn't do that. Not yet. Not until everything was in place.

When the young blonde-haired woman emerged from the back she came empty-handed. And she looked terrified.

'I'm so sorry, Mrs—'

Snippily Mallory corrected, 'It's *Miss* Templeton.'

'I apologise. Miss Templeton. I'm really very sorry. Someone else came to collect a wedding gown this morning. I don't know how I did it, but I must have mixed them up.' She snatched up the phone from its cradle. 'Don't panic. I have the number of the other customer. I will call them now. I'll exchange the dresses myself, deliver yours to you. I really can't apologise enough.'

She was already dialling.

What if this other person was happy with the mix-up? What if this other person wanted to keep the dress they'd been given? Could they do that?

'There's no answer,' said the young woman nervously.

Through gritted teeth Mallory told her, 'Try again.'

The boss of the store hovered, every now and then giving Mallory a tight smile as he drummed his fat fingers on the countertop right in his assistant's line of vision.

Was the young woman shaking? She was. But this was all her fault. She'd done this.

And then the young woman's face brightened as she got an answer on the other end of the line. She introduced herself as Skye, gave a run-down of what had happened today but

Mallory couldn't stand it any longer and held out her hand to take the phone herself.

Skye didn't resist and Mallory quickly had it arranged that she would go to the address in the next couple of hours before the woman's shop closed and she would make the exchange herself. She didn't trust anyone else to do it properly. Sod what she had going on in her own life, she had to do this.

The second the call ended the owner insisted he send Skye. 'It was her mistake, we want to do everything we can to—'

'No thank you. I think the pair of you have done quite enough.'

He tried to thrust a booklet of vouchers at her before she left but Mallory wasn't interested. She needed to get outside. She felt like she couldn't breathe in here.

She hated the person she was becoming – weak and tearful, quick to anger, petrified about what came next. A month ago she never would've behaved like this. A month ago she had the usual stresses and strains of a fifty-year-old woman – menopause, getting older, a few niggles and creaks – but other than that nothing so out of the ordinary. She'd ticked along just nicely. She would have said to the dry cleaner that mistakes happened, been nice to the young woman. But no, today she'd been the sort of person she dreaded facing at the hospital – irate patients or relatives who were so caught up in their own emotions that they took it out on whoever was in front of them. She felt terrible. That poor young woman in the dry cleaner's had been at the mercy of her behaviour. Her own daughter, now thirteen, would be out in the big wide world eventually, taking on responsibilities, engaging in conversations with people she may or may not know and it was terrifying to think a single person might have the power to make or break her day.

She went out of the opened-up glass door, around to the

side of the building and leaned against the brickwork. Tears snaked down her cheeks.

When she heard the owner's voice she froze. She needed to cross the car park to get to the nearest bus stop on the road beyond but she didn't want him or the young woman, Skye, to know she was still here.

And as a result she heard their entire, mostly one-sided, conversation.

'I can't have mistakes like that happening again,' he said.

A timid voice replied, 'I'm very sorry.'

'Yes, well you may well be sorry, Skye, but I'll have to let you go.'

'But—'

'I'll pay you until the end of the week. And you're of good character, I can't deny that. You're honest, a good employee in many ways. But I can't afford to risk my reputation. This is my livelihood.'

'Please...'

'I'll give you a reference without referring to today's little incident. That's all I can do.'

Silence apart from footsteps across the gravel car park. Mallory didn't dare look over to watch the young woman leave, the woman who had lost her job because of her and the almighty fuss she'd made.

She waited until she was sure the coast was clear, fished in her pocket for her bus ticket and made her way to the high street to catch the bus almost home except rather than going to the house she'd detour and head in a different direction to rescue her mother's dress and return this one.

The summer sun cast a beautiful glow over Marlow town centre, the town she'd settled in because it was near to her parents and her place of work, but it did little to lift her spirits.

Today it seemed that the country was finally getting one of its first real summery days but it was bittersweet. Joyful but also a big reminder that nothing was permanent, seasons changed, people changed, lives altered and nobody had forever.

She slumped into a seat at the back of the second bus and gazed out of the window, catching her reflection. To others she still looked like the same person with the petite build, her delicate features with her tiny nose and cupid lips she'd got from her mother, and her dark skin, hair, deep brown eyes she'd inherited from her dad. And yet, she was an entirely different person now. There was the Mallory before the life-changing news and the Mallory afterwards.

The bus rumbled on its way, belching its noxious fumes every time it came to a stop, creaking and hissing as it got moving once again. She kept her sunglasses pulled firmly down; it felt like a little way in which she could hide herself from the world.

'Beautiful day today,' the next passenger boarding the bus said and Mallory smiled in return. On any other day she might have engaged in conversation, recognising that perhaps that person was lonely and she might be the only person they saw that day. But Mallory wasn't up to exchanging pleasantries right now.

The bus stopped for so long at the next stop that passengers were leaning around each other to see what was going on.

'He probably needs a rest stop,' the same woman said, leaning forward almost over Mallory's shoulder. 'Oh wait, they're swapping drivers, we'll be on our way soon.'

Mallory thought of the bench near her mother's house where there was a sign for people who wanted to sit, have a talk to anyone else who turned up. She wondered whether you could get bus seats that had a clear message that she wasn't in the mood for conversation. That was another thing that was changing for her. She was always the woman anyone could talk to, any time of the day, about whatever they needed, but she was transitioning into someone who desperately needed time with her own thoughts so much that she was closing herself off to others.

The bus was finally on the move and joined a steady stream of traffic she would've avoided by using her car and taking a different route if this had happened a month ago. Rather than being stuck on a bus doing its own thing she should be in her car, her slap-in-the-face-orange, less-than-a-year-old Honda Civic right now, going to rescue the dress, windows down, sunroof open.

But the DVLA hadn't wasted any time taking away that privilege, had they? And the Honda had been sitting idle for the last couple weeks since her life changed beyond all recognition.

Mallory no longer felt fifty and fabulous, the declaration she and Penny had made in the Cotswolds, just over a month ago, the declaration she had believed.

Now what was she? Fifty and nearing her expiration date?

Mallory had had a seizure at work a few days after that weekend away. It had been a regular Wednesday morning, she'd been walking from one ward to another and it happened. Just like that. She lost consciousness.

When she'd come round her friend, Sasha, a fellow nurse, had explained what was happening. She didn't hear much at all, she was confused, she was tired. So tired.

'Everyone wants to be on the safe side, do the necessary investigations.' Sasha's voice broke through her sleepiness. 'You're popular around here.'

Mallory had been taken for a CT and because the doctors

were concerned, an MRI followed. All the while Mallory had felt almost like it was a bit of an out-of-body experience. She was the nurse, not the patient. This was all wrong.

What followed had been the terrifying news that she had been dealing with ever since.

She had a brain tumour.

When she heard the words, 'I'm very sorry, Mallory, but you have a brain tumour,' the sentence had floated around, then settled on her shoulders with no other candidate in the room.

This was all about her. This was *her* diagnosis.

Sasha held her hand the whole time the neurosurgeon informed her about the biopsy they needed to perform, the burr holes that would be made in her head – in her head! – so they could take a small piece of tissue from this horrific thing growing inside her.

She'd sobbed against Sasha. Sasha had cried too; she didn't let go of Mallory. She'd called her mother to come sit with her kids, let the dogs out, make the dinner because she was with a friend and couldn't leave her side. Mallory had texted Jilly – she hadn't trusted herself to call because she knew she wouldn't be able to speak – and told her she would be late home from work and to go ahead and reheat the pasta dish they'd had last night. She'd make herself something when she got home, she said.

Sasha had taken her home, chatted to Jilly, told her that her mum had overworked so much she had a migraine and led Mallory up to bed where she'd stayed. Sasha had sat with Jilly until Jilly's bedtime; she'd asked Mallory again whether she could call someone for her. But Mallory was adamant. Not yet. The fewer people who knew right now, the calmer she could be to think about what happened next.

Except she had no clue.

Sasha had come up with the plan about the supposed training course to cover the time Mallory would need in hospital for the biopsy and subsequent recovery. She had come over the next day when Jilly was at school and Mallory had unleashed her sheer panic on her, along with her denial and disbelief. Sasha had patiently listened to it all. Mallory was adamant that neither Jilly or Gigi would be told yet. 'I can't do this to them until I know more,' she'd said and, as a mother herself, Sasha understood why she didn't want to tell Jilly in particular until she really knew what was happening.

Mallory knew the deal though. A patient's support system was incredibly important. But right now she had to do this, she had to get things sorted before she broke the news, make sense of it herself.

And who knew, perhaps the biopsy would come back and show that something could be done? It wasn't impossible, was it? She'd tried to keep the same positivity as a patient that she had as a nurse. She was often applauded for her ability to lift people's spirits when they were having their worst of days. Would someone be able to do that for her now that the roles had been reversed?

Sasha had been there for her again when the news Mallory didn't want was broken. The tumour was a grade three oligodendroglioma and because of its location it was inoperable.

The news was bleak.

When she got the diagnosis, Mallory had felt herself gasp for air; she couldn't breathe. Sasha's hand was on her back, Mallory's head was on her knees, she didn't want to sit up. She didn't want this to be real.

Except that it was.

Teams of experts got to work on her case. They decided the most appropriate course of treatment. Chemotherapy and radiotherapy could buy her time, she was told. The treatments could stop the tumour from growing, but the tumour couldn't be removed. The treatments weren't curative. She was given anti-convulsant drugs to control the seizures. She asked for a prognosis, but doctors couldn't commit – the five-year survival rate for patients like her wasn't fantastic, but some could live for up to ten years. Maybe that would be her.

But maybe it wouldn't be.

Mallory had hated being a nurse in the days following the biopsy. She'd seen and heard so many stories of a similar nature, seen what a terminal diagnosis did to a family, never mind the patient. She wanted no part of this, and yet, she had no choice.

Sasha was by her side as much as she needed and Mallory was grateful. She knew and trusted so many of the doctors and nurses she'd seen so far. They were like her, they wanted the good outcome. Their faces might be grave but they would look after her.

Except there was only so much to be done. Without surgery the tumour was still there, an imposter in her brain, unwelcome and not going anywhere. Over time the symptoms would worsen – she might lose her balance, her co-ordination, the ability to swallow, speak, see!

It was too much to cope with and yet, what choice did she have?

As a nurse she knew that there were over a hundred different types of primary brain tumour. Each could grow in different parts of the brain, they could intrude on others.

The brain was a complex organ. Why didn't the doctors know more? Why hadn't they found a way to stop tumours in their tracks?

Since she'd found out about her tumour there were days

when Mallory had cried so hard she'd worried she may never stop. There were days she tried to be grateful for making fifty when so many didn't. There were days she walked around in a state of disbelief. And then there were days when she got so angry with the universe at doing this to her.

She'd surreptitiously observed her thirteen-year-old daughter, Jilly, as she went about her usual routine – eating her breakfast, scrolling through her phone, lugging her school bag upstairs – and wondered how many more years she could be by her side. Or would her time be measured in months, weeks, days?

What her life was like from now on was partly up to her but did she really have the power to change anything at all in the long run?

Mallory never prioritised herself – patients came first at hospital whether she was exhausted, needed a pee, hungry; she didn't stop until they were ready. If her mother needed her at her place to help her with something – mow the lawn, take her to an appointment because she didn't want to go alone – she was there, never mind if she'd worked a long shift or had household chores of her own to get through. And if Jilly needed her, Mallory jumped right to it. She was always way down the list. And she couldn't change the path she was on... she couldn't alter her health... all she could do was take each day as it came, wring the most out of every single moment.

The bus came to its final stop and Mallory got off.

She'd have to put herself first at some point. But not yet. Soon she would have four weeks in Saxby Green to sort everyone out first.

And right now the first stage of that was to rescue the missing wedding dress.

5

PENNY

Penny was used to international travel in her work as a management consultant, as well as long hours in the office, pulling all-nighters save an hour or two of snatched sleep when she could. She'd taken phone calls whenever they demanded her attention, multitasking with vigour, but since she'd left London less than a week ago and come on an open-ended visit to Saxby Green, a sleepy-ish village in the Surrey countryside to help with Rose Gold Bridal, she'd quickly got used to a different pace of life. She'd even found a copy of *Rivals* by Jilly Cooper on her mother's bookcase and read half of the book already.

The adjustment meant that when her phone rang that evening she didn't immediately dive to get it from the coffee table when she saw that it wasn't Mallory. She was waiting for good news about the wedding dress that according to Mallory's text had somehow gone missing! There'd been a mix-up at the dry cleaner's and Penny only hoped that when the call came it would be good news.

She stayed right where she was, her legs curled snugly

beneath her on the squishy sofa in the flat above the shop. The call was from her boyfriend, Carlos, and this time he was going to have to wait. She couldn't deal with talking to him right now, not since they'd talked last night and he'd suggested they should move in together.

Penny had almost dropped her glass of wine when he'd said it because they'd been together ten months and in all that time she'd thought they were on the same wavelength, that they enjoyed each other's company, had great sex, understood each other from a work point of view, but that was as far as it went. It sounded callous thinking in those terms, but it was an easy way to be, stress-free and without the risk of anyone getting hurt.

Penny had left her mother watching her favourite game show and had taken her phone into the bedroom.

She closed the door behind her. 'Move in together?'

A hard-edged businessman and a careful, thorough lover, Carlos wasn't one to chase a woman, certainly not in all the predictable ways, which was why his proposal knocked her somewhat sideways.

'It's what couples do.' He laughed and she imagined him loosening his tie, kicking off his shoes, making his way into his sleek kitchen with its black cabinetry and quartz worktops, the kitchen he rarely used to make anything from scratch.

'We're good as we are, aren't we?' She was almost out of wine; she should've brought in the bottle rather than her glass.

'Think about it, Penny.' He didn't wait for a response. 'When are you back at work?'

She hadn't told him her leave was open-ended. 'Not for a while. I accrued a lot of holiday. And I need to make sure Mum is all right.'

Carlos hadn't understood why she was coming here in the

first place when her mother ran a successful business and had never expressed a wish for her daughter to step in. He had a good relationship with his parents but they saw little of one another. His mum and dad were forever travelling around Europe or America but Penny couldn't even remember the last time Carlos had mentioned them. When Penny tried to tell him about the significance of the wedding dress, the sisters' estrangement and how she and Mallory really wanted to reunite them, he'd told them that they were messing with something they should leave alone. What he said had made her wonder how well he actually knew her even after all this time if he thought she could ever turn her back on family.

Carlos had cut their call short to take a meeting online. He, like her, had never said no because they were in a different time zone. Their clients were UK based and international, it was part of the gamut of their job. They were both successful management consultants, they understood each other. Or at least that's what she had once thought.

Her phone rang a second time, echoing in the quiet of the flat above the shop. Carlos again. Rose was still downstairs working – much too hard in Penny's opinion and far too late.

She ignored the call. He wouldn't call too many times – he'd told her last night that tonight he was visiting a fine dining establishment he'd been on a waitlist for months to get into. Eating at those places was like a hobby to him; she was surprised he didn't get fed up of it. She wondered whether, if they moved in together and got married, he'd start wanting to spend more time at home. Perhaps he wasn't quite the pipe and slippers person yet, but wasn't that what couples did when they were properly together?

She set down her glass of wine on the coffee table, the same coffee table they'd had here since she was a girl. There were plenty of other items from the same era: the kitchen table complete with the dent in the wood at one end where her dad had dropped an enormous saucepan onto it and it hit at just the right angle; the wrought iron bed in Penny's old bedroom; the freestanding wardrobes in Stephen's. Rose had bought some new furniture over the years too. She told Penny she loved to shop at the McGregor's furniture shop as they had some lovely things. The McGregors had been running their furniture business for years and it didn't surprise Penny that her mother was loyal to another local.

When Penny's phone rang again and she saw that it was Mallory she snatched it up and answered the call without preamble. 'Tell me you have good news.'

'I have the dress.'

'Thank goodness for that.'

'I really thought that was it, Penn.' She gave a sigh of relief. 'I didn't think I'd see the dress ever again, I was starting to panic.'

'Okay, breathe. You have it now. But I hope you gave the dry cleaner absolute hell.'

'I wasn't very nice.'

'And yet you sound remorseful. Don't be. Losing people's clothing, never mind a wedding dress, is absolutely no way to run a business.'

'The assistant got fired because of me.'

'Was it her fault?'

'Well... yes. But the owner was awful to her, I mean, mistakes happen.'

'They do, but I also know you're way too nice and understanding. You'd never make it in the corporate world.'

'And you'd never make it as a nurse.' They often had this back-and-forth banter. Total opposites in personality, it was sometimes surprising the cousins were so close and had become best friends. With their mothers estranged it had only been coincidence that they'd got to know each other at all.

Mallory and Penny had met for the first time when they were eighteen. Mallory's mother, Gigi, had come back to the village with the sole reason of helping her ailing father and when she came she brought Mallory. Mallory, quiet and studious, had been sitting down by the river reading a book and when Penny went for a jog along the towpath she'd been startled by a swan but kept on going, whereas Mallory had been so scared by this enormous white bird that she'd climbed up onto a picnic table, her book clutched to her chest.

'It's fine, he's just showing off,' Penny had assured the darkskinned, beautiful girl who she was sure didn't live in the village and yet looked vaguely familiar. But she definitely wasn't from around here – if she was, she'd be used to these swans by now as they kind of ruled the towpath whenever they felt like it. 'Off you go, Norman.'

The girl clambered down only when Norman was back on the water cruising along as if he hadn't a care in the world, his question-mark neck and head turning every now and then to make sure he didn't have anyone else to teach the rules of the river. 'You've named him?' she asked.

'I have, but come to think of it, it could be a girl.' Penny had shrugged, tightening her low brunette ponytail where it poked out from beneath her cap. 'I don't know how to tell the difference.'

'It's something to do with the male's knob.' The girl had said it in all seriousness but as soon as the words were out, she locked gazes with Penny and the pair of them had begun to giggle.

'I'm Mallory by the way.' The girl smiled at her.

'Good to meet you, I'm Penny.' And then it clicked. 'Wait, I knew you looked familiar. I've seen photographs of you at my grandparents' house.'

Mallory's jaw dropped. 'You're Rose's Penny? I've seen pictures of you too. School pictures.'

'Same. The grandparents seem to love memorialising us in our uniforms, don't they.'

'Wow, we're cousins, and we barely know each other.'

Penny took charge. 'Why don't we change that? There's a coffee shop just up the street, would you like to go there?'

'That would be lovely.'

From that moment on, they'd been friends and over the years had grown closer and closer. Penny had never had a best friend. She'd had friends but they'd come and gone through school, she'd floated from group to group not quite gelling with anyone and then with her career she'd had little to no time for friendships. Meeting Mallory had changed all that and now, she didn't know what she'd do without her.

Penny enjoyed hearing Mallory laugh on the phone when Penny suggested her cousin should have strung the dry cleaner and his assistant up by the short and curlies. Laughing wasn't something Mallory had been doing a lot of over the past few weeks, not since their time in the Cotswolds, in fact, and she hadn't been her usually high-spirited self then either. Perhaps she needed a decent break. And she'd get it here in a quiet village, although maybe not when their mothers found out what they were up to.

'So when are you coming?' Penny asked.

'By the end of the week.'

'I can't wait.' Penny put the call on speaker, unscrewed the bottle of red wine and topped up her glass. 'I had another swan confrontation this morning. I swear this one was

Norman reincarnated. His wings were flapping, his body lunging at me. I was out for a walk, I knew I should've done yoga instead. Make sure you warn Jilly about them, won't you.'

'About what?'

'Swans! Mallory, are you even listening?' She looked into the mirror above the sideboard and put her fingers on her forehead. Much more frowning and she'd need Botox for her forehead. Already she had a deep crease in the centre she blamed on too many stressful days at work. She didn't want it to get any worse.

'Sorry, yes, they're pretty scary,' said Mallory. 'I'll warn Jilly to be on the lookout if she goes for a walk along the river.'

'I can't believe she's happy to come to a little village for a month. For a teenager that's a lifetime.'

'I think she'd rather somewhere more exotic,' said Mallory. 'Maybe next year.'

'Yeah, maybe next year.'

Perhaps Mallory had a man and that was why she was holding back, why her words weren't tumbling out as they chatted. 'Did that surgeon – what was his name, Parker? – did he ask you out again?' The day she'd returned to work after their trip to the Cotswolds Mallory had texted Penny to say she'd been asked on a date by an orthopaedic surgeon. Penny had looked him up online and he was gorgeous!

'We only had the one date.'

'What was wrong with him? He was very, very sexy.'

'And very, very up himself,' said Mallory. 'How's Carlos?'

'His usual self.' Apart from the small matter of asking her to move in with him. But Penny didn't want to think about that for now. 'How are things with Jilly going?' Thirteen-year-old girls could be a challenge – she should know, she'd been one.

'School isn't going as well as it should be – I know she hasn't done particularly well on any of her tests lately.'

'Urgh. Tests. Far too many of them in my opinion. Don't worry too much, she'll get there. She's a good girl. She'll settle down.'

'What if she doesn't?'

'Then you're in it for the long haul, my girl.'

Penny was usually quick to probe or delve into an issue when she required a bigger understanding of it; she was known for quickly evaluating pros and cons and for making firm decisions right off the bat. She wasn't one to dither, not usually. But there was something going on with her friend. She'd suspected it when Mallory said she'd had to cancel the cruise with her mother because of a failure to notify the powers that be of her holiday in time. That wasn't like Mallory at all, the usual on-the-ball nurse who never let details slip through her fingers.

And now Mallory had gone very, very quiet and whatever was going on with her, Penny got the feeling she needed to tread lightly.

Penny probed gently. 'Are you sure it's only Jilly you're stressing about?'

'You're one to talk about stress.'

'Hey, I'm dealing with mine. I've got wine, I'm reading a book, taking baths during the daytime.' She heard a low laugh. 'You're really okay?'

'I'm just tired. Long hours at work, parenting, then what with the dress going missing… Honestly, I really thought that was it, it was lost. I thought Gigi would come home after her cruise and murder me with her bare hands. She might well still do that when she finds out what I've done.'

Mallory's dog barking madly in the background had all the attention for a moment.

'I'm going to have to go,' said Mallory above the din. 'Jilly just got back from taking Cedella for a walk and the dog is going crazy. It's like she hasn't seen me in days rather than an hour.'

'Mallory...'

But her friend had already hung up. She kept doing that, cutting chats short or not taking calls at all. Mind you, Penny wasn't one to talk; it was something she intended to improve upon though. She longed to natter for hours, the way they had years ago in their twenties and their thirties before they both got so busy. But Mallory had gone, back to her own life.

So Penny got back to hers, although lying back on the sofa and picking up her book once more, she wasn't really sure what that was supposed to look like these days.

6

MALLORY

Mallory had thought the missing dress was bad enough but that had easily been rectified despite the unexpected bus trip. It had been a smooth swap and a bit of a laugh with the other customer. What came mid-morning two days after the dress debacle topped that with a gold star and made Mallory want to climb into her bed, pull the duvet over her head and pretend none of it was happening.

Mallory had just got back from walking the dog and as Cedella curled up on the rug in front of the fireplace, she answered a call from the head teacher of St Neven's High to let Mallory know that Jilly's slipping grades weren't the only issue her daughter was having at school.

'Vaping? Jilly?' Mallory said once Mr Cull had finished his spiel. 'There must be some kind of mistake. Jilly doesn't smoke or vape. I'd know if she did.'

He must have heard that one a thousand times and reiterated the facts. Jilly had been caught vaping in the girls' toilets at lunchtime and had been suspended for the remaining week of term. The suspension was effective immediately and as a consequence, he informed Mallory, Jilly would be missing out on end of term activities.

Despite the gravity of the situation Mallory almost laughed. Jilly might well have done this on purpose – she'd recently declared the end of term activities *totally lame.*

Mr Cull said that Jilly needed to be collected immediately and all Mallory wanted to do in that moment was go to her daughter, hug her and tell her she loved her, to shake her and reprimand her for being so silly. She wanted to tell her that there were bigger things to worry about than grades and misbehaving, but of course she couldn't do that. She had to teach her right from wrong. It was her job as a mother. But she was torn between losing her temper and folding her love around her daughter to make all her problems go away because that was exactly what she wanted someone to do for her.

'Miss Templeton, I trust you will address the vaping issue. I suggest you talk with Jilly so we can work together on this and ensure there's no repeat behaviour come September.'

'I will talk to her,' she assured the man. 'And I'll be there to pick her up as soon as I can.'

The problem was, when she checked the bus timetable, buses were few and far between at this time of day in the direction of the school.

She'd have to take an Uber.

Was life out to get her right now? It seemed that a cascade of things was happening and every single one of them wanted to take her down.

But her daughter was her priority. Looking after people was what she did, and she did it well. At some point she'd need to reverse the roles, but not yet. She couldn't do it before everything was in place.

She checked on her Uber app and found it was a forty-five-minute wait.

Had the whole of Marlow and its surrounds hung up their car keys for good like she'd had to?

She went next door to Mr Rafferty who a couple of evenings ago had brought her home from the supermarket – she'd made something up about the car having dodgy brakes and needing to get them checked – so she didn't have to explain why she hadn't taken herself there and back.

But Mr Rafferty wasn't in. He would've taken her, and she could've said the car wasn't fixed and that Jilly was sick.

She called her friend, Sasha, who had been an absolute rock lately and was the support Mallory would rely on until the time was right to tell everyone else in her life the truth.

Mallory swore at the top of her voice after Sasha's phone went to voice mail. Even the dog flinched.

She was going to have to call Mr Cull back and tell him that she couldn't get to the school for at least another hour, and Mr Cull was going to just have to lump it.

She snatched her phone from where she'd left it on the windowsill and winced as the sun bounced off the windscreen of her blazing-orange Honda and made straight for her line of sight until she moved to the side. Mallory hadn't been keen on the colour at first but she had embraced the bargain price. *And it'll be easy for me to find it in the car park,* she'd joked, making her daughter laugh and reply with, *No kidding.* Jilly might not have liked the colour of her mother's car either but she'd always jumped in for a lift to school rather than take the bus when it fitted around Mallory's shifts.

The car had been idle for weeks now and to explain it away whenever Jilly asked, Mallory had had to cite car pools for the benefit of the environment, using the bus to keep the public service going, not being able to get out of the driveway because someone had parked across it. Her white lies would eventually need to alter so that the horrendous truth could emerge. But right now she wanted to cling on to every ounce of normality she could as she felt the walls of the house, the world, closing in on her. Already she could touch the sides and couldn't push them away.

She called a taxi company but the phone rang out, she googled another but before someone answered she glanced out to the coat rack in the hallway, the shiny bunch of keys that hung at the end.

And she made a decision.

Probably a stupid one.

She had to get to Jilly. She could drive perfectly well, had done for years. Just because she wasn't supposed to didn't mean she was incapable. And it was only this once.

She'd get Jilly, bring her home, and that would be that. It wasn't far, she'd be fine.

She grabbed her bag and locked up the house before she could change her mind. She wanted, she needed, to get to her daughter, she had to be there for her while she still had that privilege.

The car's interior was stifling from the summer sunshine. Her hand shook as she put the key in the ignition. She pushed away the voice in her head telling her this was wrong.

She took a deep breath and set off. Slowly. She'd be there and back in no time, and her vision had been fine, the recent headaches mild. And she had medication to help her as well.

Two minutes after she left the house, only just out of the thirty miles per hour zone, her eyes filled with tears as she crawled along at barely twenty miles per hour. It was another minute before the first tear dared to track its way down her cheek, two more minutes until huge wracking sobs took their place and she came to a complete stop at a give-way sign.

A horn beeped from the vehicle behind. Once… twice…

She couldn't move. Her head resting on the steering wheel, she unleashed the emotions she'd tried to keep in check even though that wasn't the advice from anyone who knew what was happening.

More beeping.

She covered her ears. She shouldn't have done this. She shouldn't be here. She never should've got in the car. She could've caused an accident, hurt herself or worse, some other innocent party.

And then as well as beeping, a thudding, a loud noise coming from her left.

She nearly jumped out of her skin when the passenger door flew open.

'Are you all right, lady?'

She couldn't answer the young woman's question, she continued to sob.

'You really need to move,' said the voice, but Mallory had her head against the steering wheel again as if closing her eyes might stop all of this.

The beeping was relentless. When did people get so angry? So impatient? So unable to understand when someone was having one of the worst bloody days of their life? She was having so many lately that she was beginning to lose count.

'Lady, you have to drive! You're holding up all the traffic.'

Mallory turned at the vaguely familiar voice.

She blinked away her tears as she realised it was the young woman from the dry cleaner's, the woman she'd managed to get fired. 'Skye?'

'Hey.' Skye winced at one long continuous beep from an angry driver behind.

Mallory looked in her rearview mirror. The man in the vehicle behind looked ready to kill someone.

'I can't drive,' she said to Skye. 'I shouldn't even be behind the wheel.'

'You're banned?' Skye was leaning in the passenger side, hands on the seat, observing the crazy woman causing local mayhem.

Mallory wished she could stop her tears; they weren't going to solve anything.

A man roared an expletive from somewhere and the next thing Mallory knew, Skye had leapt in to the passenger seat.

'My boyfriend just got out of the car behind!' Skye yelled. 'For God's sake, drive!'

The urgency in her voice had Mallory putting the car into gear and pulling out onto the next road as her new companion fastened her seatbelt.

She wasn't this person. She was sensible, played by the rules, she certainly didn't break the law – and yet that was what she was doing, wasn't it?

Mallory took the next street on their left, then left again until she was back to the main road she'd driven up and frozen on. She turned right this time and headed for home. When she saw a police car up ahead her hands tightened on the wheel, she held her breath, but he turned the opposite way to her street and in a few minutes she'd parked up on her drive.

She'd never do this again. What a total cock-up she'd made

of everything. This wasn't the way to do things, she knew that much.

Skye hadn't said anything between when they started on their journey back to the house and now.

Mallory turned off the engine. 'I need to book an Uber.' She got on with the task with Skye still quiet in the passenger seat.

'Did you get the dress back?' Skye asked once Mallory was done.

'You remember me.'

'Hard to forget.'

'I'm sorry I got you fired. I heard your boss when I was still outside the dry cleaning shop.'

Skye shrugged. 'Didn't love the job anyway. And I've got a bit of tutoring work on the side; I do dog walking, that sort of thing.'

'Good. I'm glad. And yes, I did get the dress back.'

'Well that's a relief.'

'Yes, it is.' She looked across at Skye, suddenly registering that the young woman had got out of her boyfriend's car and into hers. Mallory was good at picking up clues about the back stories of patients when they came into the hospital, especially women who were afraid. 'Your boyfriend has a bit of a temper.'

'He does.'

It could explain why Skye had been so quiet as Mallory drove; she'd probably been checking the wing mirrors the entire way to make sure they weren't being tailed.

It was nice sitting here on the driveway, a breeze drifting in through the windows and filling the car with a freshness Mallory welcomed. She still had to get to the school, face the drama there, make up a reason why she'd taken so long to get Jilly and why she hadn't just driven herself.

'Thank you again,' she said to Skye, who seemed as reluctant to get out of the car as she was. There was a certain contentment that came from simply sitting here and the Uber was still ten minutes away. 'I froze today. But that's what happens to a rule follower when they do what they know they shouldn't.'

'Want to talk about it?'

'Not right now, but thank you. And once again, I'm really sorry about getting you fired, I feel terrible about it.' Skye couldn't be much older than her mid-twenties and Mallory really hated knowing she was responsible for her losing her job. She thought of all the times she'd been yelled at by patients – imagine if those altercations had resulted in the same outcome for her and she'd been given her marching orders.

'Like I said, I have other sources of income. And this will give me some free time to study.'

'What are you studying?'

'I'm not... not yet. I want to do a teaching assistant training course but had to defer my start date as I couldn't fit it in what with my hours at the dry cleaning shop. I suppose I'll have some more time now so perhaps I'll try to get going with it sooner rather than later.'

Mallory knew the boundaries at work, but given she'd lost this girl her job and Skye had leapt to her aid despite that, she felt a level of concern that might not be warranted given they were virtual strangers.

'That man...' she began.

'It's fine, honestly.' Skye smiled, albeit a weak smile. 'He just has a temper. We'd been in a traffic jam already, he was running late.'

Mallory just nodded. It wasn't her business after all. 'Listen, I need to go.' The Uber was only a couple of minutes away. 'But stop by some time, you know where I live now. Can I drop you anywhere on my way?'

'It's fine, I'll walk from here, I'm not far.'

And that was where they left it. Briefly, worrying about someone else's welfare worked like a form of therapy, a distraction.

At least it did until Skye went on her way and Mallory got in the Uber to go fetch Jilly.

* * *

'We're over there.' Mallory pointed to the Uber idling in the car park as they emerged from the school. Jilly had been waiting in reception when she arrived, bags on her lap, ready to go. She at least had had the good grace to look guilty and remorseful for what she'd done.

'Where's the car?'

'Just get in, Jilly. We'll talk about this when we get home.' Brain tumour or not, she still had to be a parent; she couldn't just stop the world because she wanted to get off.

Mallory made them both a cup of tea when they got back to the house.

When Jilly came downstairs after putting her bag in her bedroom she said, 'I don't understand why you wasted cash on an Uber today, Mum.' She was probably eager to put off their talk about what happened at school for as long as possible and was therefore going for normal conversation; she had no idea this wasn't normal for Mallory, that it was all part of the lies she'd found herself tied up in – the car, the supposed work course, the wound on her head she'd said was a result of a workplace accident. None of it was true. But all of it was necessary.

Mallory had used most excuses about the car already and she was running out.

'Mum, why didn't you take the car?' Jilly asked again once Mallory had brought both mugs of tea over to the table.

She had to think on her feet. 'I'm not allowed to drive... I have a ban. I was caught speeding.'

'You? Speeding! Well, I never thought I'd see the day.' A grin spread across Jilly's face and despite the situation Mallory could've bottled the feeling it gave her seeing her daughter beaming, whether at her expense or not. How many more smiles would she get to see?

But she couldn't enjoy the moment for ever, she needed to parent. 'I think we should focus on you, not me. Vaping? Really?'

Jilly blew across her tea. 'All the girls in my year do it.'

'*All* of them?'

'A lot of them then.'

'Doesn't make it any better. You're thirteen, five years younger than the minimum age to buy a vape. Where did you get it from?'

'A girl at school. I don't know her really. I wasn't smoking, Mum. Vaping is safe.'

Mallory set her mug down so hard a bit of tea slopped over the brim. 'Safe? Really? It might be less harmful than smoking but it certainly isn't safe.' She took a tissue from her pocket and wiped up the spill. 'I could get some photographs of lung damage if you like, tell you stories of young kids who have vaped, stories that would make you feel sick to your stomach. Those vapes contain toxins and in years to come, I bet we'll be seeing studies of their harmful effects.'

Jilly's lips twisted and she lost the edge she'd started the conversation with. 'I didn't really like it. I did it because the other girls were.'

She reached out for her daughter's hand and for once Jilly didn't drag hers away. 'You're not that girl, you're not a follow-the-crowd-for-the-sake-of-it person.' She studied Jilly's face which was torn between contempt for her mother's rules and wanting to fall into her arms and be a little girl all over again. 'I had a call from your form tutor recently too, your grades aren't so good.'

Jilly's shoulders fell some more. 'I find some of the work hard.'

'You're more than capable, Jilly, that's what I don't understand. But over the last year or so you haven't been putting the effort in, I know you haven't.'

Tearfully, Jilly told her, 'I miss him.'

Mallory was about to ask who she missed when she realised. She put down her mug, went around to the other side of the table and embraced her daughter. 'You miss Pappy. Oh, Jilly, I know you do. So do I.' Mallory would've fallen to the floor and cried if she didn't have to stay strong right now. But she did. It was up to her, only she could help Jilly prepare herself for what was to come.

'I don't have a dad,' said Jilly with a vulnerability to her voice that Mallory sometimes missed when it felt as though her daughter was pulling away from her more and more with every passing month. 'Pappy was like a dad to me as well as a grandparent.'

Jilly's biological father hadn't been interested in a baby. She'd contacted him – they were no longer together – but she might as well have told him she was welcoming a new pet into her life. He didn't offer any support, didn't request to be in their child's life, and Mallory had known in that moment that she was better off without him.

Hector had fallen for Jilly the day she was born and he came to visit them in the hospital. He'd scooped her up, soothed her crying, and as she got older he was the one she went to as soon as they arrived at the house for a visit. Gigi used to laugh that there was a clear favourite. Jilly loved her granny too, but Pappy had a way with her that felt a little like magic.

'I don't like that things are changing, Mum.'

Mallory closed her eyes, her head resting against her daughter's. Jilly was almost as tall as her now, another reminder she was growing up so fast. 'I don't like it much either.' And there was an even bigger change coming, one none of them had much say in.

'I'm sorry… for the vaping.'

'I know you are. Promise me you won't do it again, please.'

Jilly burst into tears. Unable to speak, the flood gates were open and all Mallory wanted to do was jump into the water after her.

Once she stopped crying and sat leaning her head on Mallory's shoulder, Mallory stroking her hair, Jilly said, 'Can I ask you something?'

'Anything.'

'What is Granny Gigi's dress doing upstairs?'

She hadn't bothered to hide it. She was taking it to Saxby Green with them so Jilly would have to know; Mallory couldn't very well shove it in a suitcase.

'I have a plan,' said Mallory. 'A plan for when we're in Saxby Green, and a plan your granny probably won't like.'

'You took the dress from her house?'

'I did.'

Jilly sat upright. 'Mum… speeding and theft? You're a rebel!'

'I'm hardly that.'

'So do you think your plan will work? Do you think Gigi and Rose might make up?'

'I've no idea.'

It was a long shot, but anything was worth a try. And what choice did she have but to give the sisters a little push? Time was running out. For all of them.

7

GIGI

'Look what I found!' Rose came into Gigi's bedroom without knocking – something Gigi hated and would usually reprimand her sister about but Rose had already thrown herself down on the bed next to her.

'What is it?' Gigi looked at the newspaper thrust across at her, covering the book she'd been reading.

Rose ran her finger along the print of the headline halfway down the page. 'It's a competition. It says it right there in black and white.' She implored Gigi to read the details. 'Contenders have to make a dress and first prize is a £200 fabric bundle, *plus* a brand-new Singer sewing machine.'

Gigi pulled her book from beneath the newspaper and bookmarked her page. If there was one thing she knew about her sister it was that once she got an idea in her head it was hard for her to let it go.

'So what do you think?' Rose was up and pacing now as if they were two professionals whose livelihood depended on this rather than two sisters who got their dressmaking talents from their mother and enjoyed it as a hobby.

'I think this might be a stretch for us.' She handed the newspaper back to her sister.

'A stretch...' Rose smiled. 'But not impossible.' She clutched the newspaper against her chest, her forehead in a frown that told Gigi she was thinking hard. 'We have to stand out. If we're going to do this then it has to be something really special.' She clocked her sister picking up her book again, gingerly, in case she could squeeze in a few more pages, and threw the newspaper over to her again.

Gigi obliged and read the piece once more. 'Rose, I know we love making things, but all the experimenting we'd have to do with fabric to get something perfect for this competition, it might be a bit too much.' She pointed to the photograph running alongside the article. 'Look, the winner last year made a christening gown. It's incredibly intricate.'

'Don't you think we should at least try?' Rose slumped down on the bed.

Gigi knew her sister well enough to know that she was serious. 'Do you have anything in mind?' She got up, opened the bedroom window even wider. It was summer in Saxby Green and the top of the house where both of their bedrooms were was stifling. She was sure as evening descended it was getting even warmer.

'I do as a matter of fact.'

Gigi smiled. Much as she thought this a crazy idea, something about Rose's passion for it had her feeling a fire too. 'Out with it.'

Rose pulled a folded-up page from a magazine from her back pocket and handed it to Gigi.

'Oh you're crazy.' She handed back the photograph of a beautiful wedding gown.

Rose, hands on her hips, refused to take the magazine page.

'It's not crazy. And we won't be making that dress – which I don't particularly like by the way – we'll design something ourselves. Something sophisticated, one of a kind. We've made dresses, fancy ones too, we tried making wedding type gowns out of cheap material. Okay, so they didn't work, but it was practice. And we made a little bridesmaid dress for Heather down the road at Easter, and that was using fancy material, remember?'

'That was a good dress. But her mother paid for the material; we'd have to supply our own.'

'So we make it out of cheap material first, get it right as far as possible before we use the more expensive fabric.'

Gigi looked again at the article about the competition. 'Do you really think we'd be in with a chance?'

'I think we can do anything we set our minds to, Gigi.'

Gigi's lips twisted together in thought. 'I suppose there's no harm in entering.'

Rose leapt up from the bed. 'So you'll do it?'

Gigi laughed. 'Sure, let's do it.' She went over to stand by the window but there was no air and she complained to Rose.

'If only we had a river to cool off in,' said Rose, with more than a hint of mischief.

Growing up in Saxby Green, a picturesque English village, the river was always a temptation.

'We can't.' Gigi flapped at her T-shirt. 'Mum and Dad are downstairs.'

'We'll sneak out, they'll think we're busy with one of our projects, and we'll be quick.'

Gigi grinned and turned to pull her bathing suit from her bottom drawer. 'Let's do it.'

Within fifteen minutes Gigi and Rose had snuck out of the family home and Gigi closed the door quietly behind them.

They ran down to the river, hushing each other as they went. Strictly speaking you weren't supposed to swim in the river unless it was from a particular spot that was on private property owned by the McGregor family. But if they went and asked, the McGregors would be sure to query whether their parents knew what they were up to so they agreed they'd go for it, leap in from a different spot just to cool off for five minutes, and then they'd run home.

'Three, two, one!' Rose leapt in first, Gigi soon after, the freezing water making them laugh so hard that even treading water was almost impossible.

But it worked. They ran home, dripping wet and cool, and sneaked upstairs without their parents being any the wiser.

Two sisters, two best friends, who would always be there for each other no matter what.

* * *

The next day they walked home from secretarial college and Rose closed the garden gate behind them.

'Do you really hate it?' Gigi asked.

'Hate what?'

'Typing, shorthand, all of that stuff.'

'I don't hate it, but I don't love it either,' said Rose. 'It's not where my passion lies.'

Gigi was about to put her key in the front door when her sister let out a squeal. Rose was peering down the street.

'Is that a...' And now she was walking back down the path towards the gate again.

Gigi followed her sister. The couple from the end of the road, who hadn't lived in the village for long, were selling up and moving away, Gigi already knew that. But she hadn't expected to see loads of their old stuff left out on the grass verge – a washing machine, a radio, a stool, an old desk, and… a mannequin, which was what had got her sister excited.

'It's an omen!' Rose declared. She bent down to pick it up.

'You're taking it?'

'Sign says we can.'

The mannequin was with a heap of other stuff alongside a sign that read, 'Help Yourselves'.

'Feels like we're shifting a corpse,' said Rose as they carried the mannequin back to the house, Rose at the head, Gigi at the feet.

Gigi almost dropped her end twice she was laughing so hard at the peculiar looks from passersby.

Their dad just smiled when he saw them come in through the door. He was the softer of their parents, their mother a lot more serious and expectant of them doing the right thing.

'Make sure you give it a good clean,' their dad said with a wink as he took his pipe into the lounge. Pipe tobacco was always a smell that reminded Gigi of their dad; it felt like coming home.

Rose stood the mannequin in her bedroom. She had the largest room and a big wooden table onto which they could lay out their materials, do all their pinning, their cutting, and another table for the old sewing machine their mother let them use.

'What should we call her?' Rose grimaced at the dirt on the cloth she'd been using to wipe the thing down.

'What about Naked Nellie?'

Rose inspected the slight blush to the doll's plastic cheeks. 'Bashful Bertha.'

'Motionless Mona.' Gigi was laughing hard now.

'Silent Sally!'

'Helpful Harriet!'

Rose looked closer at the mannequin. 'She could be a Harriet...' She addressed the doll. 'Helpful Harriet, are you going to help my sister and me become the most successful dressmakers in the whole of England?'

Gigi used one of the rags Rose had found to dry Helpful Harriet. 'She's plastic, she might not be quite capable of performing miracles.'

Rose had the biggest smile on her face. 'Having her in here makes me feel like we are professional dressmakers. She'll really help us in the early stages of making the wedding dress. But... one of us will need to be photographed in the dress for the competition. And you have the better figure.'

'Stop that nonsense. You are gorgeous. Tommy Hardcastle thinks so.'

'I have no intention of getting involved with Tommy or any other boy I went to school with. They're all so immature. None of them have thought beyond chewing gum, cigarettes and getting a girl into bed. Now, are you happy to model the dress or not?'

'I'm happy.' She leaned past her sister and grabbed her pillow, whipped out the pillow and put the pillowcase on her head. She plucked the three fake tulips from the little vase on the windowsill and hummed, 'Here comes the bride,' as she walked down the centre of the bedroom, pretending she was walking down the aisle.

When they stopped messing around it was down to business. Rose took Gigi's exact measurements, Gigi giggling every time Rose wrapped the tape measure around her waist.

'I'm ticklish, I can't help it.' She squirmed yet again and Rose had to remeasure.

'Whatever you do,' said Rose, 'don't get any thinner or fatter while we make the dress.'

Gigi grimaced. 'Thank goodness the competition closing date is early November. I won't be beholden to the weight rules come Christmas because you know me and—'

'Mince pies!' Rose laughed. 'Oh yes, wouldn't want to get in the way of you and the mince pies. Heaven forbid.' She put down her pencil and pulled out the band from her red hair now she didn't need it away from her face so she could focus. 'Come on, let's go get some milk and cookies. Then we'll have another practice with the material and the machine.'

* * *

For the next couple of weeks the sisters worked on their design whenever they had a spare moment. They were both at secretarial college – Rose had worked in a flower shop for a year after school and without any opportunities to make a start in dressmaking she needed a skill and so secretarial work it was.

During that month the sisters researched styles of wedding gowns, materials, techniques, they practised on any fabric they could get their hands on. They went into London on their day off to visit a sale at one of the haberdasheries and came back with armfuls of material to practice on. They both spent the money they'd earned working alternate shifts in a newsagents and Gigi was glad her sister had pushed her to make the dress with her and give the competition a go.

Eventually they were ready to buy the actual material for the dress and so they took the train into London to visit their favourite haberdashery.

As the train trundled along the tracks they talked excitedly about the dress, the competition, their hopes and dreams.

'We could open a shop one day, Gigi.' Rose fished in her school bag and pulled out a brown paper bag filled with rhubarb and custard sweets. 'A bridalwear shop. There isn't one in Saxby Green; there isn't one for miles.'

'We shouldn't get carried away. We're making one dress. I'm not sure we could make a shop full.' Gigi took a sweet from the bag Rose proffered. 'Although I suppose every dressmaker had to start with a single dress.'

'Exactly.' Rose's sweet clacked against her teeth as she spoke. 'And women can work outside the home these days.'

'I know, but having our own shop? It feels like an out-of-reach dream.' And she wasn't sure she was quite as daring as her older sister. Rose was only older by eleven months, but she seemed so much more confident and worldly than Gigi felt.

'We need dreams, Gigi. And it *will* happen. The question is, are you with me?'

Gigi grinned and put her hand out for another sweet. 'I'm in,' she said.

As the train pulled into Waterloo, Gigi knew she'd do anything for her sister and vice versa, and she couldn't think of anything better than having Rose by her side every single day.

She was still thinking about the infinite possibilities when it came to dressmaking and two sisters making a start in the world as they disembarked, linked arms and all chatter and laughter, walked the length of the platform that would take them into the station and to the big city beyond.

They both turned at the sound of, 'Hey, miss! Miss!'

A man was running towards them, the most beautiful man Gigi had ever seen with skin the colour of ebony, a smile that was nervous, a hesitation in his demeanour that suggested he wasn't entirely comfortable addressing them.

The man spoke with the deep velvety voice and a hint of a

foreign accent that Gigi couldn't identify. He was holding out her neck scarf. 'You dropped this.' He refused to meet her gaze, as if he thought it wasn't his place to be talking to her.

She put a hand to her neck. In all the excitement, the talk of dresses and being working women one day, she hadn't even realised it had slipped off.

She took the scarf from his outstretched hand. She clasped it against her chest, her fingers lost in the soft material of the turquoise garment. 'Thank you! This is my favourite, I'd have been devastated if I'd lost it.'

Rose tugged at her arm. 'Gigi, come on, let's go.'

But Gigi couldn't stop staring at the man and she wanted to stay here talking to him.

'Do you work here?' Gigi asked him.

'I'm a cleaner. For the railways.' That explained the shirt and trousers and clumpy boots rather than smart dress that so many folks wore if they worked in the city.

Rose had a firm hold of her arm and the way the man looked at Gigi now suggested he'd also picked up on some of the other disembarking passengers watching their interaction. Because he was black, Gigi knew that was why. And it made her want to stay here on the platform with him all the more, never mind what anyone else thought.

She looked the man right in the eye. 'Thank you for picking up my scarf. How silly of me to drop it. I really should be more careful,' she rambled. Why did boys, and men, make you talk so quickly? Before you could think about your words.

'My pleasure, miss.' His accent wasn't strong; he must have lived here in London for a while.

'What's your name?' Again she ignored the tug of Rose's arm, which was linked through hers, attempting to pull her away.

'Hector.'

'Hector,' she repeated.

It would sound silly to a lot of people, Gigi was sure, but she was convinced she felt a spark, a connection with this stranger.

Somehow, standing on that platform, she sensed that her life would never be the same again. And all because of a turquoise scarf.

Rose tugged her arm a little harder this time and Gigi finally relented, letting herself be led away.

But she turned around once more to find the man watching her go.

'I'm Gigi!' she called out.

And the smile he gave her was something she'd never forget.

8

MALLORY

The house was quiet when Mallory woke up. In fact, it was silent apart from a bird perched in the tree outside chirruping away its happy song. It was a small thing but she was learning to appreciate those, even though things kept going wrong. She'd had everything lined up – the house sitter who would double as a sitter for Cedella – ready for her month in the village, but last night the house sitter had cancelled. It couldn't be helped, she'd broken her leg, but it left Mallory stuck. She desperately needed to get to Saxby Green but so far no news from the house-sitting agency about a replacement.

She ventured downstairs and the quiet came to a close when Cedella scampered out of the kitchen.

'Good morning, you.' She scooped the dog up into her arms. Cedella had been Jilly's tenth birthday gift – their bond had never been questioned, but Mallory hadn't expected to enjoy having a dog in the house quite as much as she did. Cedella was loving; she was good company when Mallory was tired and just wanted a cuddle.

She set the dog down so she could give her her breakfast in

the bowl near the back door. Cedella slept well in here – her favourite spot come winter was by the radiator, same in summer, perhaps because of the coolness of the steel. Mallory unlocked the doggy door, a handy addition to the room because it meant that Cedella could take herself out to the toilet as and when she needed to during the day if nobody was home.

She looked out of the window and peered up at the sky, wondering what the weather was like in Saxby Green right now.

She picked up her phone to check she hadn't missed a call. But of course she hadn't, she would've heard it. She'd give it another couple of hours and if she hadn't heard anything she'd call the agency again. It was still quite early for them – Mallory found it next to impossible to sleep in with what she had going on inside her head, quite literally these days – so maybe they'd have good news when they clocked on.

There was nobody else Mallory could ask to step in either. There was no way she was asking Sasha for this favour because Sasha had already done so much and besides, she had young kids, two dogs of her own and a full-time job.

She was fast running out of options.

Dark clouds in the distance beyond the glass hinted that it might not be the nicest of days, but Mallory would take any day she could get. Rain, hail or shine, gale force winds, ice, snow and slush, all of them were welcome.

Cedella came in through the doggy door as Mallory flicked on the kettle. While she was waiting for it to boil she reached for her medication which she kept at the very back of the cupboard behind the mugs they never used, where Jilly wouldn't see it.

She closed her eyes for a moment. She had a niggling

headache from the lack of sleep, or from the tumour, she wasn't sure which. She put a hand to her head. An area had been shaved for the burr holes but her hair hid some of it – they'd lifted some hair out of the way, shaved what they needed to. She'd told Jilly she'd had an accident when she was away on her course, that she'd hit her head, and that's what she'd tell anyone else who asked about the injury. It's what she had told Penny in a text message.

She took a couple of painkillers. She wondered how much of her current head pain was because she was thinking about the biopsy, the throbbing that had happened right afterwards. Every time she felt a twinge in her head since her diagnosis, Mallory thought the worst – that this was it. She hadn't known the tumour was there after all, it had been growing without her even realising, so what was to say it wasn't still doing that? The bastard was going to take everything away from her, from her loved ones, and she could do nothing to stop it. All she could do was put a few obstacles in its way. Her chemotherapy was scheduled and fitted in with the date she planned to return from Saxby Green. And by then, she'd assured Sasha that Jilly and Gigi, as well as Penny, would know the whole truth. She'd have her support system in place.

The thing about a diagnosis was that life didn't stop the moment you got it. It changed, sure, it shifted gears, but you had to carry on. Mrs Denton from next door but one didn't know when she waved over to Mallory every time she saw her, Mr and Mrs Simpson were none the wiser when they nodded their heads and smiled as they walked their dog past her driveway. The world was still normal but her world had shifted to something unrecognisable.

And not only for her. For everyone else in her life. Especially Jilly.

One of Mallory's dad's favourite sayings – which he'd adopted early on in his time in England along with a bit of cockney rhyming slang he thought hilarious – was *get your ducks in a row*. And that was exactly what Mallory was trying to do. She needed to get to Saxby Green with her daughter and the dress, get everyone sorted, all their ducks in a row so that she, and everyone else in her life, was ready for her next step in this absolute nightmare.

She thought she heard Jilly stirring in her bedroom above the kitchen and double checked her medication was pushed to the back of the cupboard before she told Cedella she'd be back – she didn't mention the word *walk* or the dog would get too excited – and she went upstairs to get dressed.

* * *

Mallory took Cedella on a walk into town. She spotted the same coffee cart on the street near her favourite book shop. It wasn't always there but cropped up on random days and did the best cappuccino she'd ever tasted. Its popularity seemed to be shared by plenty of others given there was such a long line, so she joined the queue.

In the days following her seizure at work she'd been frightened of it happening again, but it hadn't. The doctors had said that as long as she took the anti-convulsant medication then those should keep any seizures under control, but it had taken over a week to believe it. She still didn't, not really, but she tried to push away the thought and enjoy the bright sunshine, the loving dog at her side, Jilly at home snug and warm and safe.

Cedella was doing her utmost to sniff the dog in front of them and the owner seemed unimpressed so Mallory tugged Cedella backwards a step and the dog sat obediently beside her feet. If she behaved like this every time they went away then she'd be most welcome, but she got over excited or overwhelmed in a new place and Mallory needed to focus in Saxby Green. She took out her phone and checked again, willing there to be a text message, an email, a missed call. But there was still nothing from the house-sitting agency.

The woman two in front of Mallory tutted, none too quietly. 'Oh, for goodness' sake, some people.'

'Come on,' another man groaned from behind the moaning woman.

Mallory felt like she should tell them that there were bigger things to worry about than whether they got their coffee in two minutes or ten.

She leaned around the bellyachers to see someone at the front of the queue and the cart owner shaking his head.

The cart owner called out, 'Anyone for a cappuccino?'

And that was when Mallory saw an embarrassed Skye, the young woman from the dry cleaner's, backing away from the server.

'I'll take it!' Mallory bustled her way forwards. 'Plus another one please.' She didn't give a crap at all the tutting behind her either. 'Here, take yours,' she said to Skye gesturing to the cup the barista had left on the counter.

'I'll pay you back,' said Skye, once Mallory had her coffee too and they left the line of moaners and non-understanding citizens behind.

'No need. You helped me the last time we crossed paths, today I stepped in for you.'

Cedella had taken an interest in Skye and Skye bobbed down to make her acquaintance after Mallory introduced them.

'She's gorgeous.' Skye was giving Cedella a fuss all over, the way she really liked, especially the top of her head and around her ears.

'She is. But she's also trouble a lot of the time, mischievous.'

'She seems pretty perfect to me. And so clean.'

'You haven't seen her in the winter – this white coat is more grey; she loves to find the muddiest parts of our walk.'

'Sounds like fun.'

'Actually, she is.' And she was glad Cedella had become a part of their household.

They walked along the high street and Mallory led the way towards the Thames Path. 'So what was that all about back there at the cart?' she asked. 'Did you forget your card?'

'Something like that.' It was at least another five hundred steps before she added, 'My card got declined; think I'm at my limit until my final pay goes in.' She looked out at the water, the rowing team and the blades cutting their way through the current. 'I applied for other jobs.' Skye volunteered the information and Mallory was happy to listen as they started walking again, Cedella not happy to stay still for too long.

'Any luck?'

'Not yet. I applied to be a part-time worker at the supermarket but I didn't get an interview. I applied to a couple of shops along the high street but have heard nothing, and I was going to apply for a delivery driver job but I don't have my own car and the jobs advertised require it.'

'It sounds difficult.'

'It's stressful.' The young woman's smile faded.

'Can your parents help you for a while?'

Skye kept her gaze ahead. 'I don't have any parents. I was in foster care for years, then on my own once I was out of the system, then I met Dean.'

The poor thing. Mallory couldn't imagine not having Gigi and Hector when she was growing up.

Skye dropped her empty coffee cup into the nearby recycling bin and Mallory did the same as they turned back the way they'd come.

'Do you live on your own?' Mallory asked, more for conversation than anything else.

'I live with my boyfriend in his mother's council flat. Nothing is in my name; I was hoping to get a place of my own some time but...'

'It's expensive.' And now she felt bad for being so nosey. 'I'm sorry, I shouldn't be asking you so many questions.'

'It's fine.' She crouched down to fuss over Cedella again. 'I don't mind.' She looked up at Mallory. 'I won't stay with him forever you know. I just don't have many options right now.'

As she watched Skye with Cedella, who was lapping up all the attention, something came to Mallory – an idea that would help her and would help Skye and stop Mallory feeling so awful for losing this young woman a job she clearly needed.

She almost began to laugh because her brain was working quite well considering the tumour that had taken up residence.

'How are you in the garden?' she asked Skye, whose attention was still on the dog.

Skye stood up. 'Why, do you know of a job going?'

'Kind of. I'm going away for a while and my house sitter slash dog sitter has let me down at the last minute.'

'You mean...'

'Would you like the job? It's for a month, starting tomorrow. You'd live in, you'd look after Cedella, take care of the garden – I'll leave instructions. I'll pay you what I would've paid the house sitter.'

'You're serious? But you don't know me.'

'I heard your ex-boss say what a good character you were, that he'd give you a reference. I'll have to go by that for now. And as I said, you were kind to me when I needed it.'

'I don't know what to say.'

'I do have a request though, should you accept the job.'

'Anything.'

'I'd rather your boyfriend didn't know my address.'

Skye hesitated. 'Fair enough. But he won't like not knowing where I am.'

After a pause Mallory said, 'Do you really want him in your life forever?'

She didn't seem surprised by the pertinent question. 'I don't. But I have a roof over my head, company, you know. I'm not alone.'

Sometimes there were worse things than being alone. Mallory had seen it enough times in her job – women who put up with emotional abuse never mind physical, but felt they had no choice and even if they did, what was the alternative?

Gigi always said Mallory took in strays wherever she went. When she was eight years old she'd taken a young boy under her wing at the playground when he fell off the swing and his older sister had gone off to get ice-creams – she'd told him they'd take him home if his sister didn't come back soon, he could have some of Gigi's homemade pineapple upside down cake. She'd tried to adopt a tabby cat when she was ten years old – the cat had leapt into their window one day and kept returning; she was convinced it wasn't being looked after by its owner until they saw a poster in a shop window with its picture to say that the cat was missing. She and Gigi had taken the tabby, called Tiggy, back to her owner and Mallory had flat refused the reward but had asked to stop by now and then to see the cat. She wanted to check on it, make sure it was being looked after, but of course she didn't tell the owner that.

'You need to have a plan in place,' said Mallory. Cedella sat down as she'd been trained to as they waited for the cars to stop at the pedestrian crossing on the high street.

'To leave him?' Skye didn't look upset, rather she looked scared at the unknown if Mallory had read her reaction right. 'I don't have anyone else.'

'You have me now. We don't know each other all that well but we've already helped each other so how about we keep doing that? You'll have a whole month away from your boyfriend and when I'm back I'm happy to rent you my spare room for a while if that works.'

'Mallory, I—'

'Think about it.' She had savings, she owned her house, but money would be tight given her prognosis. This might help both of them out.

Skye stopped walking. 'I don't need to think about it. Do you really mean it about your spare room, once you're home?'

'I do.'

'Because once I leave Dean, there's no going back.'

'Good. That's the best thing I've heard this morning.'

Her comment was met with a smile that warmed Mallory right through. Helping other people always did.

As they took the path back up to the high street she felt a sense of calm now she knew she was going to Saxby Green as planned.

She thought of the bright yellow ducks Hector had bought his granddaughter when she was first able to sit up in the tub. Even then his analogy of getting all his ducks in a row had been something he wanted to pass down and Mallory understood it now more than ever. She wanted to get everything in place –

for herself, for those she loved, and that included getting to the bottom of the issues between Rose and Gigi, getting them talking after all these years.

Mallory wasn't ready to leave this world, but if she had to she wanted everyone around her to be prepared. She wanted them to know their own path, to have each other, and she knew that she was going to need them all to be there for her.

It would soon be time for Mallory to be the one who was cared for rather than the other way around.

9

PENNY

Penny woke up in bed in a hotel room and sat up as Carlos emerged from the bathroom. Bare-chested with a mass of dark hair she'd laid her head against often enough, he wore the jeans he'd travelled down to the village in, and a lazy smile. 'Good morning.' He came over and planted a lingering kiss on her lips which made her body respond.

He headed for the machine on the long table beneath the flat-screen TV. 'Coffee?'

'Please.'

Carlos had turned up last night to surprise Penny and whisk her away to the hotel. She hadn't been overly impressed at his arrival, she had thought that by coming here to the village to help her mother she might also find time to think about what she really wanted out of life, but she hadn't wanted to argue with him so she didn't protest.

He'd no sooner put his bag down in the hotel room than swept her into his arms and they'd tumbled into bed. Their chemistry couldn't be faulted, but still something held her back, the sense of permanence he wanted that just didn't feel right to her.

As Carlos made the coffee she picked up her phone and looked at the Instagram post that had fuelled Mallory's plans to come to Saxby Green. The dress was stunning, the dress she'd never realised her own mother had played a very big part in creating. Gigi had talked of the dress being hers but going by the write-up this had to be the same dress that Rose had once talked about as being stolen from her, the dress she'd wanted to use when she first opened the shop.

The sisters' feud had gone on for years, and had it not been for a chance meeting in Saxby Green, Mallory and Penny might not even know each other despite being cousins. Mallory was dead right – enough was enough. Rose and Gigi needed to talk, even if they screamed at each other, they had to move forwards.

'You're obsessed.' Carlos set down a cup of coffee for her on the bedside table and looked at what she was doing on her phone.

'I'm not obsessed. I... *we*, Mallory and I, think it's high time our mothers sorted this out.'

'They won't thank either of you for interfering.'

The coffee tasted too bitter. She probably should've waited until later to have a cup, she didn't usually have one this early and her taste buds hadn't quite woken up yet. 'We're trying to help.'

'So you've said.' He swigged from his own mug.

Penny sighed. 'They might well murder us for what we're doing.'

'Don't say I didn't warn you.'

'I won't.' She grinned. 'You love being right.'

'I do, but in this case I hope I'm not, for your sakes.' He kissed her again. 'How long are you staying with your mum?'

After another polite gulp Penny took her coffee into the bathroom and discreetly poured the rest away. 'I'm not sure yet.'

'Don't you miss your job?'

Actually, less than she thought she would. 'It's been good to spend time with Mum, she needs help sorting out her books and getting organised. I'm going to help her get the business online, talk to her about ways we can boost sales because she'll only ever be ready to take a step back if she knows she can sell it to someone who might fall in love with it as much as she has.'

'You can't mix—'

'Emotion with business,' she finished for him. 'This isn't the same as the big corporations you and I deal with, this is a small business started by my mother; it's her pride and joy.'

'Tread carefully, Penny.' He was well aware of how attached her mother was to Rose Gold Bridal.

'I'm not going to make her stop, but she needs to ease up at least. She's made a couple of mistakes lately, and mistakes on a bridal gown at the eleventh hour can spell disaster.'

He put his wash bag into his overnight bag and zipped it up. 'I'm going to have to go. But before I do, have you given any more thought to my suggestion?'

'Not yet. But I will. Promise.' She was surprised he hadn't mentioned it last night.

Carlos dropped her back in the village and after a brief hello to her mother who was talking with a client in the shop, Penny went upstairs to do a yoga session before she started trying to organise some of her mother's paperwork.

Following her session which had enforced the sort of

breathing that left her calm and ready for the day, Penny filled a glass of water from the tap and it overflowed when she was distracted watching what was going on in the street below. Nothing special was happening, but she still appreciated the rear view of a sexy tradesman, plaid shirt and all. It was fun to watch the way the muscles in his arms tensed when hauling out the ladder from his pick-up truck. Mr Sexy Tradesman was the antithesis of a corporate guy like Carlos. Men like Carlos seemed out of place here in Saxby Green. This guy seemed right at home.

Penny hit the shower and before she went downstairs she gave Mallory a quick call.

'Oh, I'm sorry,' Penny said as soon as her friend answered. 'You were asleep.' She had that telltale groggy voice that gave it away.

'I was napping, that's all.'

'Not working today? I thought you might have shifts right up until the last minute, that I'd call and you'd be zipping from ward to ward.'

Mallory let out a gentle chuckle. 'That does sound like me. But no, not today. I didn't get much sleep.'

'Are you still worrying about Jilly?'

'Yeah. Always. You know what it's like. Parenting.' She recapped about her drama with her house sitter and dog sitter.

'You could've just brought Cedella here, couldn't you?'

'The place I'm renting doesn't take dogs, not that Cedella would cope anyway, strange thing, she doesn't do well away from the house. Remember that time we went to Cornwall? She was tearing around all night like she was on speed.' Mallory had been waiting for her dog to calm down as she got older but so far it hadn't happened.

'So who is this Skye person?'

'She's the assistant from the dry cleaner's.'

Penny gasped. 'The one who mixed up the dresses?'

'Yes, and the one who got fired because of me.'

'It wasn't your fault, she got fired be—'

'Penny, it's fine. She's honestly really lovely and she's great with Cedella too. I trust her. I overheard her boss when he told her she no longer had a job, he said what a good person she was but he couldn't tolerate mistakes.'

Penny wasn't convinced. 'Hmm... well if you're sure she's up to the job.'

'She is, and it means I'm still coming, more to the point. She'll look after the dog and my garden while we're in Saxby Green.'

'I can't wait to see you, but I'm nervous.'

'Me too. The dress...'

'The dress,' Penny repeated.

Penny thought about the shop down below, the shop which, illuminated beneath beautiful lights, was a little girl's dreamland with all the pristine white dresses. Was one dress the answer to Rose and Gigi's fallout? Was it going to help or make things so much worse?

'I was looking at the Instagram post again this morning,' said Penny. 'I had a bit of a thought.'

'Go on.'

'I'm here, right, I'm here in the shop. From what I've seen so far the business is doing okay but Mum, if she's ever going to retire, would love someone to take this place on and keep it as a bridalwear shop. There's no guarantee of course but the more profitable it is the more likely it is to attract someone with a passion much like my mother's. I was thinking... the dress is coming this way, Gigi and Rose are going to see it. Maybe I get out ahead of their confrontation – I put the dress on a mannequin in the window with a sign referencing the movie and Norma Monroe and at the same time I send out a press release locally and share it on social media. It might draw in brides-to-be. What do you say?'

Mallory had gone very quiet.

'Mallory...'

'You want to put the dress in the window,' Mallory said at last. 'This is going to explode in our faces, isn't it? I mean, I knew that when I took the dress, it's just that with every minute that passes this gets so much worse.'

'I won't do it if you don't agree.'

Mallory didn't hesitate for long. 'Do it, I agree.'

'It's for their own good,' said Penny firmly, more to convince herself really. 'Maybe it'll be like a storm when they realise what we've done... you know, when you have a balmy summer day which is hot and suffocating, then along comes the thunder, lightning strikes, heavy rain – and then once it's passed the air is cleared.'

'I'm not sure it'll go quite like that, but I admire the optimism.'

'Is Jilly excited about coming here?'

'I wouldn't say she's excited,' said Mallory, 'but she is happy we're coming to see you.'

'I'm looking forward to seeing her too.' Penny loved Jilly, she was a gorgeous girl, polite, friendly, much like her mother. 'And try not to stress about her, you're a good mum and she'll get there.' Mallory had messaged Penny the day Jilly got caught vaping and usually she would be dishing out more of a punishment for something so serious and yet there'd been no talk of grounding, curfews or cancelling an upcoming camping trip Jilly had planned with a friend. This time it seemed as though Mallory was choosing to let it go. Perhaps it was for the best.

From what Penny remembered about being thirteen, she'd made mistakes and sometimes moving on was the best way forwards.

'I wish I could control it,' said Mallory. 'I'm worried. If she's like this at thirteen, unfocused and not working to the best of her ability, what's going to happen when she gets to the more important academic years?'

'Have you thought about a tutor to address the slipping grades?'

'I have, but no luck finding one. And that's before I even tell her that's what I'm considering – she'll hate me for it, I'm sure.'

'She won't hate you,' said Penny. 'She loves you. Hang in there, I've heard daughters come back once they're through these teenage years... and the young adult stage. I did. Now, get yourself down here safely, I can't wait.'

As she went downstairs to suggest her mother go up to the flat for a cuppa and a couple of biscuits, she hoped Mallory wasn't fretting too much about Jilly, but more than that, she hoped she would be a support for her friend when she arrived. Mallory seemed so overwhelmed by everything lately but then again she was so lovely, stealing the dress must be tugging at her conscience. But sleeping in the day? That was unusual, even when she had erratic shifts. The woman usually had enough energy for the both of them and Penny was even more sure now that there must be something Mallory wasn't telling her. But she hadn't prodded for information; she hadn't done that in the Cotswolds, or since, because she knew it was no use asking Mallory what it was until they were face to face. Penny had been in enough meetings with jumped-up CEOs to read their body language, expressions and their tells, and she'd be watching Mallory closely when she got here.

Then she'd be able to work out what was really going on with her cousin.

Because the more they talked, the more bringing the wedding dress out of hiding and down to Saxby Green with the claim that it might help to reunite their mothers was beginning to feel like a convenient excuse for the real reason Mallory was coming.

10

ROSE

Ever since Gigi had met that man, Hector, in Waterloo, she hadn't stopped talking about him. Rose had gone back to London with Gigi in her quest to find him again. Gigi was convinced it would happen but it hadn't the first time – he was nowhere to be seen. Today they were trying again and Rose hoped that when Gigi didn't see him again then she'd lose this ridiculous infatuation with a stranger who could be anyone, who could have a past or present that Gigi should have no part of. All Rose wanted was her sister back, the sister who didn't have all those stars in her eyes.

Rose left Gigi at Waterloo while she went to the haberdashery to pick up the extra materials they needed for their competition piece. After an hour sourcing the fabric and accessories, she walked back to the station convinced she'd find her sister sitting there, forlorn, ready to move on from thinking about the man she'd met on the platform that day. But as she got closer to Waterloo there they were. Gigi and Hector. They were sitting on a bench to the side of the station, talking as though they'd known each other for years.

Rose waved over to Gigi to let her sister know she was back. Gigi knew what time they were scheduled to depart and Rose decided she would only interrupt the pair if it looked like her sister was so caught up with this man that they would miss their train. And that couldn't happen or their mother would start to worry.

When it was finally time to go they boarded the train and Rose undid her coat. The days were getting cooler but the heating inside the carriage was a bit much until autumn really hit.

Gigi waved dreamily out of the window to Hector as the train pulled away from the platform, as if they were two lovers separated rather than two strangers who had spent far less than twenty-four hours together.

Once they'd left Waterloo behind, Rose turned to her sister. 'You need to be careful, Gigi.'

'Careful?'

'With that man.'

'That man has a name.'

'I know he does, but—'

'I'm not scared of Hector. Why should I be?'

'I'm worried about you, Gigi.'

'Don't be.' She slipped her arm through Rose's. 'He's lovely, he was so pleased to see me again. He wants to make a picnic on Saturday and we'll eat it in a park near the station.'

'Gigi—'

'I like him so much, he's so kind. And, he said if you're worried then you can come too.'

'He said that?'

Gigi nodded. 'I told you he was kind.'

Rose folded the top of her bag over so the materials she'd bought didn't attract any dirt or dust. 'If Mum knew what you were doing...' She hated to think what their mother would say if she knew that this was what they were up to when she thought they were shopping for material.

'Mum doesn't like anyone who is different.'

'Exactly, she'll make your life tough if she finds out.'

Gigi leaned her head on Rose's shoulder. 'So don't tell her. Please.'

Rose let her head fall against her sister's. 'I won't. But be careful.'

'So will you go back to London this Saturday with me?'

'Mum will get suspicious if we go too often.'

'Not if we both go and if we come back with materials.'

'We don't need many more,' said Rose. 'But I'm sure we'll sort something.'

'Thank you, you're the best sister ever.'

'I know.' Rose laughed. 'And so are you.'

* * *

Rose went with Gigi to London that Saturday and followed Gigi and Hector to the park. While they spent time together, Rose read the dressmaking book she'd found at the library and stowed in her bag and then they hurried to the haberdashery and bought the cheapest fabric they could and stuffed it in a bag to take home with them in case coming home empty-handed raised suspicions.

Rose and Gigi juggled secretarial college with part-time work, dressmaking and their jaunts into London every week or so. If their parents suspected they were up to no good, they never said, and luckily both girls had enough savings for train fares and what they wanted to do with regards to the dress. Rose got some extra hours working at the flower shop again which paid better than the newsagent, and Gigi added babysitting duties to her shifts at the newsagent. She regularly looked after Sarah-Jayne, an eight-year-old with attitude who lived opposite, whose parents dedicated every Thursday evening to date night, probably in an attempt to get away from the girl who really did need to learn some manners.

It took months to make a wedding dress from scratch and with their hard work and dedication they were almost there. The sisters had practised their design with cheaper material already, not making the full dress but parts of it. Rose had read that experts in bridalwear often made a prototype, or toile, which sounded really posh, and involved making a template of the actual gown created to the bride-to-be's measurements. They used the mannequin for some of it, but put the gown on Gigi to get it exactly right. For two novices, their talent had brought them a long way and Rose was sure they had a real chance in the competition. They could do this!

Life was busy with all they had going on and Gigi was forever talking about Hector; Rose was forever waiting for her sister to realise there was no future in it. Rose had no problem with the colour of Hector's skin but their mother did, plenty of people in the village did. It wasn't like London where there were so many different people it felt like a whole new world, and Rose was worried her sister was going to get really hurt.

'His family came over from Jamaica,' Gigi told her one evening at almost midnight, two weeks before the competition closed. The dress was finished but Gigi was wearing it so Rose could ensure it didn't need any final adjustments.

'Whose?' Rose's focus was the dress they'd worked on tirelessly. Her sister had told her yesterday that even though she hadn't had much time with Hector, it was like they were destined to be together. Rose had been sure it would fizzle away to nothing, but Gigi was as infatuated now as she had been the first day she'd set eyes on him.

'Rose, are you even listening?'

'Of course.' Actually she was doing her best not to. She took the pin she'd put between her teeth and set it down on the side. The dress was perfect, no adjustments necessary.

Rose helped Gigi out of the dress and hung it up.

'Do you like him?' Gigi asked.

Rose turned from looking at their dress on the mannequin. 'Hector? From what I know of him...' Which wasn't much and the same could be said of Gigi's knowledge about the man. 'He seems nice.'

'I love him, Rose.'

Rose grabbed hold of her sister's hands in hers. 'I want you to be happy, but do you really think—'

'Don't spoil it by telling me I'm being silly.'

'I don't think you're being silly at all.' But was she really in love? Did she know this man well enough to be able to say that?

Rose wondered whether Hector was pushing Gigi more than he should. He was a couple of years older than her. Perhaps she should've paid better attention to him when they went to London, tried to get to know him some more to see whether he felt the same way as her sister did. Was Hector really the kind man that Gigi kept saying he was? Or were his acts of kindness just that? Acts.

'I promise you he's lovely. I wish I could bring him here to the village.'

'Gigi, you can't, you know Mum will go spare.'

'He has black skin,' said Gigi desperately. 'Is that so terrible? I don't think it is. I hate that it makes people react to him differently. It makes people look at me differently too.'

'What do you mean?'

'Some men yelled at us the other day when we were sitting together. You were at the haberdashery.'

'Why didn't you tell me?'

Gigi shrugged. 'I knew you'd worry.'

'What did you do?' This was what she was afraid of; this man was putting her sister in harm's way whether he intended to or not.

'Hector told me not to say anything or look their way. We left the area and didn't look back.'

'That was sensible.'

Gigi didn't say anything else other than goodnight and after she left Rose's bedroom Rose sat on her bed and stared at the beautiful dress they'd made together.

The dress had taken the sisters five months to make.

And their family, one day to break.

11

PENNY

Penny was upstairs in the flat working on the accounts while it was business as usual for Rose and Michelle in the shop. She had at least made her mother a cooked breakfast today, after checking Michelle could open up and give Rose half an hour more than she usually had. Penny suspected Michelle would offer Rose a lot more breaks than Rose could ever want. The issue was persuading her mother to take them.

She finished updating a spreadsheet. Her mother still did manual bookkeeping and although what Penny had scraped together was somewhat comprehensive, she had had to hunt down the paperwork which was dispersed in drawers dotted around the area out the back of the shop and up here in the flat.

From all the information Penny had gathered, she could see that the shop was certainly doing well enough. Running a business was tough but Rose Gold Bridal had survived during and following the pandemic – it helped that there weren't any direct competitors within a twenty-mile radius, but those years while the world adapted to its new normal had definitely taken their toll with a reduction of turnover. She'd noted it going through the books but hopefully a potential buyer would make an allowance for that and once the business was online they would be in a good position to start putting out the feelers for someone to take over if her mother was still on board with the idea of finally taking a step back.

She closed down the laptop once she was finished and made herself a coffee.

Penny remembered some of the conversations between her parents over the years when it came to this, their home. They'd talked about getting a garden for the kids to play in but her dad had insisted there was no point and that the flat would do. He'd said that once the shop was paid off then maybe they could revisit the idea. They never had. Mind you, Penny had never felt like they were missing out – their dad, still in his shirt and tie from work, had taken Penny and Stephen outside and down to the riverbanks to play whenever they requested it, and he'd told them that that was their playground. Neither of them had objected to it.

The flat above Rose Gold Bridal had three bedrooms, a kitchen, lounge and a bathroom. The shop had plenty of space for dressmaking so that had never fully migrated upstairs although sometimes Rose had worked up here, especially when Penny and Stephen were little.

When Penny was a pre-teen, some of the girls at school thought it must be ridiculously magical to live above a wedding dress emporium – their words rather than a descriptor for the boutique size it really was – but Penny's feet had never floated that far off the ground.

Despite Penny's relatively stable and happy childhood, by the time she finished school she couldn't wait to leave the village. She dreamt of greater excitement, discovery, working in

The Best Days of Our Lives

skyscraper buildings that people gushed about over dinner, places that were way out of reach for Saxby Green. And yet, when she hadn't known which way to turn when it came to Carlos and she'd begun to question the demands and stresses of her work life, the small village in the Surrey countryside had been the place she'd wanted to be.

Since completion of her further education, Penny hadn't stopped on what felt like a never-ending travelator – like those you got at airports but instead of taking her to the gate it had taken her to promotions, projects, meetings, corporate life. She felt as though she'd never been able to step off the travelator and for years she hadn't minded. Perhaps it was something about turning fifty that had made her finally feel the urge to leave the airport.

Mallory thought her airport analogy was hysterical; Carlos thought she was being dramatic and a little bit mad. Carlos thought she was going to return to London and pick up where she left off, once she was happy Rose was okay, but the truth was, it had only been a few days after arriving that Penny had realised she didn't necessarily want to leave. It wasn't that all of a sudden she'd found skills as a seamstress she never realised she had – but the total change was what she found herself drawn to. And as the days went on, the more she couldn't see herself going back to the way it was.

She'd just rinsed out her empty coffee mug when her phone chimed with a text message from Stephen. He was worried Rose was overdoing it too. He asked whether Penny thought he should come over before the planned visit at Easter. Stephen might live thousands of miles away in America but when the shit hit the fan, he'd be here despite the distance. Rose had been unwell three years ago; it was a bout of food poisoning but she was so miserable that Stephen had been on a flight within twenty-four hours, at her side in less than forty-eight.

Penny texted back that she had this. She told him she was making their mother take it a little bit easier and getting the business side more organised. She didn't mention the somewhat deranged idea of using a dress to try to reunite two estranged sisters. If she said that he might well be hopping on the next flight.

Penny went downstairs to join Rose's loyal assistant who was out the back of the shop beyond the beautifully appointed fitting room, gingerly putting a plastic container onto a wide wooden shelf that sat above the big table fabrics were laid out on, cut, and pieced together.

'Is that shelf still iffy?' The shelf had been there ever since Penny could remember. In fact, the shop itself and the area out the back hadn't changed much at all over the years. The little washroom by the rear door had been refitted once but other than that it was as though time had stood still. The table was the one that had originally been placed along the wall, the cupboards were the same, a desk, a stack of drawers. The machines were new, Rose updating those as and when needed, to keep up with the latest trends and requirements for bridalwear.

Michelle took the plastic container off again. 'It is. And until it's fixed maybe we shouldn't risk putting anything on it.' She proceeded to remove the other containers. 'If the shelf falls, never mind hurting one of us or damaging the machine below it, we'll have a sea of sequins, beads, buttons and crystals everywhere. Imagine sorting through those.'

Penny liked Michelle. She was bubbly, the sort of person who did well in a shop like this, someone who customers related to. Rose was the same. What Penny's mother lacked in business organisation she made up for with her passion for dressmaking and seeing that brides and bridal parties got everything they ever wished for.

'There's a local guy, Joel,' said Michelle as she stacked the last of the containers in the corner of the room past the desk. 'He usually does odd jobs around here if we need it.'

Penny was looking at the shelf. 'I ought to be able to fix it myself but I don't have a screwdriver and I *know* Mum doesn't have a toolbox upstairs.'

'I suggested she get one once but she told me she liked to keep local businesses going with her contribution – then she told me she didn't want to risk damaging her hands when they were needed for intricate work.'

'I suppose she had a point.' Penny remembered a couple of years ago when her mother had scalded herself with boiling water draining the pasta for dinner one night. She'd had to have a sterile dressing to cover it and trying to work on dresses had been a struggle. 'Do you have this local guy's number?'

'Should be on a card in the junk drawer.'

It took some rifling through the largest drawer filled with all sorts before Penny found a small business card with a little illustration – a cartoon character with a hard hat, giving the thumbs up with one hand, a hammer in the other.

'Cute,' she said, before dialling the number on the card.

She got voice mail.

'Thanks for this morning by the way,' Penny said to Michelle after she'd left a short message for the handyman.

'This morning?'

'For letting me keep my mother upstairs for longer. I swear she sometimes skips breakfast to get more hours down here in the shop.' She'd mentioned to Michelle when Rose wasn't listening that she was here to try to get some order to the business records, as well as to make sure her mother didn't overdo things.

'She's so dedicated,' said Michelle. 'But I will do my best to enforce breaks. If she'll let me – I mean she's my boss, not the other way round.'

'She loves you, I think you could get away with it.'

Michelle laughed and got back to what she was doing.

While Michelle worked on the dress out back, Penny lingered at the arch that separated the front of the shop from the back. She watched her mother who had just welcomed a couple of women – one of them, clearly the bride-to-be, was radiant. This was the first wedding gown shop she'd been in, she said, and Rose talked her through the different styles using the big book she'd put together and kept on the front counter.

'Mum, why don't you take a break?' Penny suggested when the women sat on the comfy wide armchairs in the shop so they could chat and Rose gave them some space. Her mother always stressed the importance of not being too overly attentive until the customer was ready. *Don't get too in their face straight away,* Rose had said the first time Penny had helped her one particularly busy summer.

'Are you sure?' Rose usually resisted the suggestion of a break, especially given she'd started work later than usual.

'Yes, off you go. I've got Michelle out back and you upstairs if I need you.'

Rose looked back at the customers, heads bent, nattering away. 'You'll know when to jump in,' she said. 'And if they want me again, come and get me. Although I think this group might take a while before they want any help.'

She was right, their heads were bent, the chatter incessant. Penny would far rather be going through more paperwork and chasing up the website creator than watching overly excited women and trying to suss out their little clues that they may be ready for some help but she'd do it for her mother.

Another lady came in on her own and said she was happy to browse in a way that suggested if she wasn't left to her own devices she'd probably walk out.

The group of women left and said they'd be back in an hour. They asked where the bakery was and Penny sent them off in that direction.

Penny cleaned the glass – so many mirrors obviously, and all of them seemed to cling onto every morsel of dust that might be floating through the air. Dirt and wedding dresses did not mix.

When the new filing cabinet arrived, Michelle took over on the shop floor while Penny had the guy bring it on a trolley out to the back. She signed the delivery note and yanked off the wrapping the cabinet had come in before slotting it with a bit of a shove next to the desk.

The night before last night Penny had had to ask Rose where her tax returns were. She could only find last year's.

'Those should be in the bottom kitchen drawer, the one under the bench that is hidden by the stools,' her mother had said as if it was perfectly normal.

'Of course, why didn't I think to look in the *kitchen* for business records?'

Penny had gone straight online after that and ordered this filing cabinet. She patted the top of it. No more being disorganised now. No more filing things in kitchen drawers and cupboards, or under the bed, or in the ottoman storage she hadn't even known existed until Rose revealed that was where she'd put the ownership papers for the shop, for safekeeping. Penny had retrieved them and told Rose they wouldn't be going astray again, they'd be under lock and key in a filing cabinet and soon all the paperwork would be kept together in one place.

Michelle was still with the customers so Penny ran the vacuum around out back. It didn't take long because neither the shop nor the out-the-back part of the premises were enormous. Rose had always told Penny that when she started up the business she hadn't wanted to take on the world, she'd just wanted to have a little slice of it for herself.

In Penny's eyes her mother had so many opportunities with Rose Gold Bridal. At one point when Penny had mentioned global reach, admittedly with the dreams of someone who wouldn't have to find the finance, Rose had quickly shut the idea down. Rose Gold Bridal in Saxby Green was enough for her – always had been, always would be. She'd told her daughter that she would just have to find alternative ways to channel her irrepressible business drive.

When Michelle, who was good with excited brides-to-be, came out back and hung a wedding dress in the fitting room ready for their customer to try on, Penny headed upstairs to check on Rose.

'How is my business going?' Rose asked the moment Penny stepped into the lounge where she was flipping through a sewing magazine. Her mother always had plenty of those in the rack, some dated back years as she'd kept those that she wanted to read again and again.

'Terrible.' But she smiled. 'I'm kidding. The only bad thing is that your shelf out back is dodgy.' Penny filled a glass with water and drank it in thirsty gulps.

'We should really get that sorted.' Rose put her magazine away, preparing to return downstairs.

'I left a message with a local handyman, Joel McNamara.'

Rose stopped in her tracks. She turned and smiled. 'Is he stopping by today?'

'Doesn't seem like it, he hasn't called me back.'

And yet Rose was still smiling. What was she up to?

'Don't worry,' said Rose, taking a biscuit from the tin and offering one to Penny. 'I'm sure he'll call.'

'Well, is he any good?' Penny asked as she took a biscuit and put the tin back on the side.

'Oh yes.' Rose beamed as she headed for the door. 'He's exceptional.'

Yep, she was definitely up to something.

12

MALLORY

Bumping into Skye that day in the high street had been fortuitous and Mallory was confident the house and the dog were in capable hands so she could focus on what came next.

She was eating her breakfast when Penny's text came through with a GIF of a woman leaping in the air with excitement. Mallory managed to smile despite the impending sense of dread at what her mother was going to say when she realised the dress had not only gone but *where* it had gone, not to mention having to line up all the people she loved the most in the world and deliver devastating news.

Mallory finished her food, took her medication and then went upstairs for her shower. She washed her hair gently with the mild shampoo the hospital had recommended for the wound at the back of her head. She hadn't been able to wash it for a while after the biopsy but she'd been so tired and emotional she'd barely cared whether she could get in the shower, let alone anything else.

Before Skye arrived at the house today and they left for Saxby Green, Mallory had a few chores for Jilly to do. She couldn't let her sleep in today. Lately she overthought everything – doing chores wasn't Jilly pulling her weight but rather it was teaching Jilly independence for when her mother had gone. Yesterday Jilly had made the dinner and rather than seeing it as a teenager wanting to be in charge of the kitchen and letting herself have some time out from cooking, Mallory had started putting together a list of dishes she wanted to teach Jilly to make before she wasn't able to. As a family they'd eaten much like most of her friends but sometimes her dad liked to make recipes he remembered from his own childhood like the curry shrimp with tomato and bell peppers, the brown stew chicken with its garlic and spices, the Jamaican fruit cake his mother had made for him. Mallory would love to pass on at least a part of their Jamaican heritage to her daughter before it was too late.

'Jilly, are you up yet?' She rapped on her daughter's bedroom door twice. Jilly had never been a morning person – getting her up on school days was sometimes near impossible. Mallory would have to go into her room to the alarm clock buzzing, shake her feet until she got a response. How she could sleep through the din was anyone's guess but burying herself under the duvet must have helped.

After the vaping incident at school, Mallory had thought about being strict with Jilly, making her get up early every day, but she hadn't had the heart or the energy to fight. Perhaps Jilly was simply being a normal teenager and her behaviour with the vaping and the lack of dedication to her schoolwork was nothing too out of the ordinary – all Mallory knew was that there was no scan that could diagnose the things Jilly was doing and prevent them from happening again.

'We're not going for ages,' Jilly groaned when she met Mallory at her bedroom door.

Mallory pulled her daughter in for a hug. She was warm, her hair all over the place and she smelt faintly of the sweet perfume all the girls her age seemed to wear. 'It's still time to get moving.' Mallory forced a smile to exude a jollity she definitely didn't feel. 'I need you to do a few things for me downstairs. I need you to empty the dishwasher and fold up the clothes from the dryer – I had to shove them in there so they would be dry in time to pack. There are two pairs of your jeans. We need to make sure the house is in a fit state to leave for Skye.'

She frowned at her mother's lengthy recall of what she had to do. 'Can I at least have a shower and get dressed first?'

'Of course you can, but make it quick.'

Downstairs, while she waited for Jilly to organise herself, Mallory finished boxing up the dried goods she'd bought to take with them so they at least had some basics.

Jilly came into the kitchen and picked up the cup of tea Mallory had made for her and left by the kettle in her favourite mug. She got on with doing the dishwasher and Mallory finished writing her lengthy instructions for taking care of the garden. It was all straightforward – if there was no rain for the day, please use the hose on the lawn and the pots. The lawn would need mowing once a week and the mower was in the shed – the key to which was in the drawer next to the dishwasher. Mallory had already put together a similar A4 single-sided instruction sheet for Cedella's routine and care and another one for the house itself and where to find bits and bobs, where the fuse box was located, and a handful of numbers in case of emergency.

'How are we getting to Saxby Green if you're banned from driving?' Jilly asked.

Mallory ignored the tiny little smirk she knew her daughter

was fighting to keep under control. 'I've ordered a taxi. I'm sure I told you.'

'I don't remember you saying. Isn't it a bit expensive to go all that way in a taxi?'

'Well, until you can drive, that's what we'll have to do.'

Her mouth fell open. 'You're banned for four years?'

'Well, no... but... anyway, did you remember to get all your school books together?'

Jilly froze, aghast. 'You're making me take school work over summer?'

Ah, maybe she'd forgotten to mention that too.

'I won't make you do school work the whole time,' said Mallory, 'but I think it would be a good idea to make sure you're ready for September. And you might be wanting something to do, it's a quiet village.'

'I'll get to see Penny, I can go for walks, and remember I've got the camping trip.'

'I haven't forgotten, it's in my diary.' At least she wasn't forgetting everything. Yet.

Jilly had been asked by a friend and her family to go on a camping trip with them and it worked out well because it was during the four weeks that Mallory had allocated for Saxby Green. It meant that Mallory and Penny had time to make their mothers see sense, had time with each other and together with Jilly, and then with Jilly away from the village for a while Mallory would tell Penny and Gigi the whole truth so they could be ready to support her daughter.

'Take the books anyway,' said Mallory before looking at her watch. She was expecting Skye to arrive at her house at any moment. Mallory hadn't told Jilly about Skye renting their spare room following the house sit but she suspected the news would pale into insignificance once Jilly knew the truth that her mum had been hiding.

Mallory hated lying to her daughter as well as everyone else. Gigi had never tolerated lying. She always said it was best to get everything out in the open and then there would be no misunderstandings. And so Mallory had tried to do that growing up – she hadn't lied, not unless you counted the things she hadn't told her mother by omission rather than outright fibs. Wasn't that what most of her so-called lies were now? Omissions? They were harmless things like not mentioning all her hospital appointments – her mum had never asked her about those, because she didn't know they'd taken place. Her mother didn't know she'd taken the dress because why on earth would she call from a cruise and ask such a random question. And she hadn't asked about Mallory's trip to Saxby Green because Gigi didn't know about that either yet.

Mallory cleared out the kitchen food cupboard while Jilly pressed on with her chores. She rescued a couple of potatoes from the very back that had already sprouted and a bulb of garlic which had begun to turn a peculiar colour and wouldn't be enticing for any house sitter. She put both into the food compost bin which reminded her to check the council's schedule and add a few notes to her instruction sheets about the bins – which went out on which day, and which week, and the name of the website if Skye wanted to double check.

She was almost organised.

Who said a brain tumour could stop her in her tracks?

Actually, every doctor she'd spoken to.

Twenty-four hours after she'd got her diagnosis she'd been eating her lunch under the watchful eye of Sasha who told her she had to eat and her thoughts had turned to Georgie, a four-year-old boy Mallory had cared for in the hospital over a two-year span. He'd been in for appointments, sometimes staying longer, and in the end he'd taken his final breath with his parents at his side before his cancer took him. During all that time Mallory had never once heard him moan, he'd carried on smiling, he'd often cheered other kids up rather than the other way round. Georgie hadn't even got the chance to turn five and have the dinosaur cake he'd sketched a picture of.

Mallory had told herself as she ate the food Sasha wasn't going to let her leave that if Georgie could keep his positivity knowing that he didn't have long left on this earth then so could she. She'd already had decades more than he had. She should feel grateful.

Except reminding herself of that on some days was hard.

When Skye arrived Cedella yapped excitedly at the door, barely backing off enough for Mallory to let the poor young woman in.

'I hope you're ready for her.' Mallory took the big cloth holdall from Skye's shoulder and noted the rucksack on her back and the carrier bag hooked over her arm. It looked like she'd brought everything.

And she looked much happier than the last time Mallory had seen her. She couldn't stop grinning at Cedella either as she delivered so much fuss Cedella might not want her to ever leave.

Mallory lowered her voice with Jilly in the kitchen. 'You left? You've brought all your things?'

Skye took a deep breath, put down the carrier bag and the rucksack and picked Cedella up into her arms. 'I left. I don't have many of my own things, these bags are it.'

Jilly appeared in the hallway.

'Skye, this is Jilly… Jilly, this is Skye.' Mallory made the introductions.

'Hey,' said Jilly. 'Mum, where's the bread?' Typical teenager, not much interest beyond their immediate requirements.

'It's on the table ready to be packed.'

'Can't see it.'

'Jilly... it's there. Look a little harder.'

Mallory wished she could freeze time. Jilly was in a pair of summer capri-style trousers exposing slender ankles, her T-shirt a crop top that fell off one shoulder. She wore no make-up, she looked so innocent.

'The butter is with the bread,' Mallory added before Jilly could ask the question. Fingers crossed it wouldn't have liquidised given the sun streaming in the kitchen window where she'd left it to soften on the windowsill. Mallory called after Jilly, 'The taxi comes in just over an hour. *Be ready.*'

Who was going to be the timekeeper when she no longer could be?

Cedella was wriggling now and Skye set her down.

Mallory took Skye's bags upstairs and showed her her bedroom.

'I don't know how to thank you,' said Skye. 'It's a lovely room, a lovely house. I've never lived anywhere like—'

Mallory stopped her. 'You can thank me by looking after Cedella and the house and garden. You're doing me a huge favour here, I mean it. I'll give you some time to unpack.'

Mallory went back to the kitchen where Jilly was making toast under the grill – huge slabs of bloomer loaf emerged golden brown and Jilly heaped on the butter. Then she put it back under briefly to melt it even more.

'What?' Jilly asked as she tucked into the toast and looked up to realise her mother was staring at her.

'Nothing.' She smiled. She loved watching these little habits, the mannerisms that made Jilly her very own person.

Skye came in to join them, her shyness not something Mallory had seen before now.

'Skye, please sit down, do you want anything to eat?' Mallory offered.

'I'm good, thanks. Are these the instructions for the house?' She'd spotted the papers Mallory had put together.

'There are a lot,' said Jilly between mouthfuls. 'Be warned. You might be busy.'

'I don't mind,' said Skye.

'She's very fussy,' Jilly remarked, mouth full of toast.

Mallory started to go through things with Skye and when Jilly had finished her breakfast she washed up her plate.

'Don't forget to pack your school books,' Mallory reminded her before she headed upstairs again.

Skye looked up, her finger marking the part she'd reached on the instructions about Cedella. 'School work over the summer?' she asked when it was just the two of them.

Mallory waited until she heard the familiar sound of Jilly's bedroom door closing upstairs. It wasn't a big house, it was easy enough to keep tabs on its occupants.

'Unfortunately she's not putting in the effort at school; she's been suspended and I'm afraid if I don't do something soon then...' She gulped back tears. Skye would never understand that her timescales had been condensed. She didn't have forever to parent; she didn't know how long she had. 'Sorry, we barely know each other. And here I am relaying all my problems.'

'For what it's worth I would've loved to have someone like you watching over me at Jilly's age.'

Mallory felt comforted somewhat by the remark. She was doing the right thing. It was difficult to know whether you were half the time.

She made them both a cup of tea and Skye accepted the offer of a chocolate digestive. Mallory was glad to sit down. She'd been overdoing it trying to get everything ready and if she could she'd go to bed, but she'd settle for a doze on the journey when Jilly would more than likely put her ear buds in.

Sitting at the table, they smiled at one another when they heard thudding about upstairs.

'As long as she hasn't jumped out the window, whatever else she's doing, I'm sure it'll be fine,' said Mallory.

'Has the school set her extra work for the summer?'

'Not much. But I need to push her a bit if I can.' Although she wasn't sure she was the right person to teach her daughter. And with everything Mallory had coming up, she might not be in a fit state for the job for much longer.

'There's always me.' A memory came back to Mallory even before Skye reminded her. 'I've done a bit of tutoring.'

'For kids Jilly's age?'

'I did some tutoring the year before last for a teenager in my building who was struggling with English, then earlier this year I taught her younger brother – he was a handful – and I helped him with English and history. I never told Dean about it, I always did it early on a Saturday morning and dinner time on a Wednesday – he was always too hungover on a weekend to notice I was absent, and Wednesdays was his day for darts at the pub with his mates. I got paid in cash and stashed the money away for one day when I'd leave. If I ever got the guts.'

'And now you have,' Mallory assured her.

'I'd say I can get recommendations about my tutoring but I don't want to go near that flat.' She gulped. 'Never ever again.'

'And you don't have to. After the summer I might well take you up on the offer.' After the summer, when everything would be different. 'We'll try it then.'

They both smiled at each other when another thud came from overhead.

'Make yourself at home, Skye, I'd better go and check my daughter is getting ready so we won't keep the taxi driver waiting when he gets here.'

They were on the road an hour later after the taxi had been packed, the wedding dress in its cover lying on top of everything else, and both Mallory and Jilly waved to Skye standing in the doorway with Cedella in her arms.

This was it. No turning back now. It was time to gather everyone together. It was time for the truth to come out.

And the wedding dress mystery was only a very small part of that. Although it was a part that needed solving.

Two sisters had fallen out and their estrangement had gone on too long.

And Mallory couldn't bear the thought of any other parts of their family not being whole. What was coming was going to put a big enough dent in it as it was.

13

GIGI

Gigi was lucky, she didn't suffer from sea sickness, but she'd seen a few passengers enduring it especially on choppier days. If her Mallory was here she'd be fussing over them all, putting a reassuring hand on their shoulder, giving them tips on how to manage the cruise.

She left her cabin and wound her way through the ship's interior with its shining floors, gleaming banisters leading up to more levels of adventure. It was a different world, giving passengers the power to forget where they were or even the person they might have been when they first got on board.

But Gigi still knew who she was. She was a widow, she'd lost her true love. And she'd never felt so lonely in her life.

As she emerged out onto the deck she almost collided with two young women, perhaps in their early twenties. She was struck by how much they reminded her of herself and Rose; it was the way they linked arms, the way they whispered to each other, as if they didn't have a care in the world. It gave Gigi a jolt when she thought about all the train journeys she'd made with Rose, the sense of adventure, the promises they'd made, the future they'd envisaged. And none of it had happened. Losing Hector, her beloved husband of almost sixty years, had only brought the pain of losing Rose closer, reminded her of all those years they'd been estranged.

She stood out on deck and embraced the tang of the salty sea air, closing her eyes in an attempt to feel something other than the despair and loneliness she felt. She and Hector had booked this cruise together eighteen months ago before either of them had had any inkling that Hector would contract pneumonia and die after a short time in hospital. They'd been so excited by all their plans about what they'd do on the trip, how different it would be from any other boat experience either of them had ever had; they'd giggled as if they were still those two inexperienced, naïve young adults who'd got together against all the odds.

Gigi's once strawberry-blonde and now grey bobbed hair insisted on whipping across her face out on deck and she kept hooking it behind her ears. As well as being a red head, Gigi was pale, and Hector had loved her complexion. He'd described it as porcelain when she moaned that she felt pasty; he'd told her that it was beautiful when she longed for some colour. He was the opposite of course, with Jamaican heritage, and while he talked about her beauty she complimented him on his. He'd told her beautiful sounded strange when talking about a man but she'd vehemently disagreed. He was beautiful inside and out, never mind when people saw them in the street together and judged them just because he was born in one place and looked a certain way and she was born in another. They'd been judged for their partnership, but it was those differences Gigi felt had given them so much strength together. They'd had to fight to be accepted, it hadn't come easy, and it would never have happened had either of them doubted their unwavering love.

She looked out over the choppy white-crested seas barely visible now the sky was darkening and breathed in the fresh air that reminded her she was still alive. She gazed down at the depths of water churning beneath the big ship cutting through its surface.

When Mallory had told Gigi that she could no longer come on the cruise in Hector's place, Gigi's gut reaction had been panic. But she'd had to swish it away. She'd promised Hector she'd do this so she had no choice but to come alone. And she hadn't wanted Mallory to feel guilty; she had her own life to lead.

Thinking about her promise to Hector was the only thing that had stopped Gigi from locking herself in her cabin for the entire duration of this cruise. Gigi had spent most of the first day on board trying to avoid lengthy conversations with anyone. She'd hoped to remain relatively incognito for the entire duration, explore each port, take photographs she could show Mallory and Jilly to make out that she'd had a whale of a time, enjoy the sunshine and find ways of occupying herself until she could disembark when they arrived back in Southampton and say that she'd done it.

On the second day she'd decided she had to at least make an effort and she'd dug out her swimming costume, still lurking at the bottom of her suitcase, and gone to find the swimming pool. Ever since that day she'd been for a morning swim unless they were docking at a port early. She'd always loved swimming but hadn't been much at all after she'd left the village to be with Hector. Their lives had been busy doing other things she supposed and so she'd never got around to it.

One day as she climbed out of the pool her attention was

captured by the three women roughly her age – although she'd never been great at guessing ages – three women whose friendship seemed strong, solid. It wasn't that they were doing anything in particular or saying anything especially riveting, but what struck Gigi was how in synch they were with each other. There was laughter, chatter, one of them helped the other with her lace-ups when she struggled to bend down, one had a menu and had decided where they'd have their lunch, the third ran back and rescued the towel one of them had left behind. And then they were gone.

It looked like the sort of closeness Gigi had never found again since she'd left her sister, Rose, behind.

But she'd had Hector who as well as being handsome and kind, had become her very best friend. Her wonderful Hector, the love of her life. She missed him incredibly, wished they'd been able to see out their days together, but she was grateful for the times they'd had. He was a wonderful father, a doting pappy to Jilly.

She caught the faint whiff of pipe tobacco out on the deck now as she walked past a gentleman en route to the main dining room. She slowed her pace. The smell reminded her of her late father, the aroma that had lingered in their house, the scent he had on his woollen jumpers when he pulled you in for a hug. When she left Saxby Green she'd missed Rose incredibly, but it was her dad she'd missed the most. She'd just been glad to spend time with him before he passed away, Rose staying out of the picture if Gigi was in the village, their mother already gone by then.

She arrived at the dining room. Despite trying to keep herself to herself she'd somehow managed to bond with a few people on board and she waved over to the group with whom she'd eaten for the last four evenings in a row. It was as though the five of them felt that a bit of familiarity was just what they needed.

Gigi had at least been embracing the plethora of meal choices on the ship and already she sensed she'd miss having a choice of cuisines at her fingertips when she returned home. Sailing around the Mediterranean had been like walking the length of the high street and all the side streets in town in one go, perusing eateries, selecting what she fancied there and then. Hector would've appreciated it, that was for sure. And so did she – it was vastly different to her usual scraping together of whatever she could find to cook a meal for one, resorting to a ready meal or just having a cup-a-soup with a piece of bread and butter. Some days she got to eat with Mallory and Jilly, but her daughter and granddaughter had so much on – work, school, their lives – that she tried not to become a burden. She was more likely to tell them she was busy herself, talk up her trips to the cricket club to help set up for an event, tell them she'd been cooking the jerk chicken from Hector's sister's recipe. She loved it, that was no fib, the succulent chicken, the spicy seasoning, but she never bothered making it for one. What was the point?

Gigi missed so much about Hector. They'd always done a lot together – strolled down to the cricket ground, although her attention span was never as long as his, shopped, gone for dinner or to the movies, and they'd talked at home, not all the time, but some evenings they'd while away the hours when it would be easy to think two people at their age had nothing left to talk about. They had their time apart as well – he liked to play cricket as well as watch it, she enjoyed gardening but you couldn't get Hector within a hundred yards of a spade or a trowel. He'd mow the lawn and as long as that was neat, it was Gigi who saw to the flowers, brought the colour to the beds, although they both loved the finished product and would spend hours outside in the warmer months.

But it wasn't only those things she missed, it was the minutiae of daily life – her taking the dishes to the sink, Hector loading the dishwasher while she wiped down the table; his ability to make a good shopping list while she was the one who came up with what dinners they would have down the week; he took care of all the utility bills while Gigi sorted the window cleaner, the council tax and the TV licence. It was the small questions dotted throughout their day too, the sharing of a life depicted with phrases like *pass the salt, please; what time do you want dinner? We're almost out of cling film; when did you last go to the dentist?*

Everything was down to her now. There would be no little reminders from Hector, which even though she might not need, she liked. Her world was empty without him in it.

The first time she'd come back to the house after Hector died, the silence was what had hit her the most. Previously, being alone in the house had been a welcome gift at times, she'd enjoyed it. But since Hector had died those endless days at home had become stifling.

'Good evening, Gigi.' Theodore, in his early eighties just like her, offered Gigi a smile that Gigi was becoming familiar with when she joined the group in the dining room. 'You are looking as bright as that sky out there.'

'Why thank you,' she said.

Softly spoken Theodore was kind, and much like Hector, never short of a compliment to offer. He was also a good conversationalist and unlike sixty-three-year-old chiropractor, Peter, to her right, knew how to listen as well as talk. Across from her was Kerry, solo cruise-goer, forty-four years old and escaping after a nasty divorce – something she'd told them all about after one too many Pinot Grigios – and next to Kerry was Lola, Peter's long-suffering wife. Oh, he wasn't so bad, she told herself, he just talked too much and as a consequence Lola was in his shadow. Hector never would've done that to Gigi, he'd included her wherever they went and vice versa. But she couldn't judge, she didn't know these people, not really, they'd only had a few dinners together.

Gigi ordered a mocktail. She was quite taken by them – the different glassware, the elaborate decorations of a paper umbrella and pieces of colourful fruit. She hated to think how many she'd had on this cruise, but her liver was thankful they had zero alcohol in them. This time she went for one with spicy watermelon and mint.

'The right chair isn't only important for comfort,' Peter droned on to the entire table once he'd placed an order for a beer. 'It's important for...'

Gigi let his voice fade. She was good at blocking out what she didn't want to hear, a technique she seemed to get better at with age. She wondered whether that was what Lola had got used to doing too. Gigi wasn't sure whether the total number of words Lola had uttered during these mealtimes would even stretch to forming a handful of sentences.

On the first night of the cruise Gigi had briefly considered finding something to eat and taking it back to her cabin, but Hector's voice had been in her head. 'Girl, get out there, enjoy it!' And so she'd gone to the main dining room. It had been Lola who had looked up and smiled over at Gigi when Gigi was desperately looking around for a table she could sit at alone or at least the end of a table she could squeeze onto, have her meal and slope off before anyone realised she was even there. The woman had looked friendly enough and was only with a man, presumably her husband, so Gigi had gone over to ask whether it would be okay to join them at the same time as Kerry had come to sit down. 'We're going to start a table of misfits,' Kerry told Gigi with a laugh before announcing she was on her own as well and Peter and Lola had generously suggested she sit with them.

Theodore had stumbled on the group – quite literally – by chance. He'd come in to the dining room, and had been looking around and his foot caught the edge of Peter's chair, which almost sent him flying. Peter, who seemed to have assigned himself the role of host, invited Theodore to join them – the more the merrier, he declared – and at the end of the meal they'd all agreed to meet at the Thai place the next evening. And so it had continued, returning to the main dining room once again this evening.

'How has your day been?' Theodore asked Gigi now after they'd chosen their meals and placed their orders.

Today was classed as a *day at sea* – so, in between stops. The cruise would take in eight ports in all and they'd already visited Vigo for its authentic Spanish culture and Seville with its medieval streets, history and architecture. Next up had been Malaga and Gigi had disembarked a little bit more comfortable in her own company. She'd had dinner with other people, but so far they'd kept the stops as sacred for themselves, and although it was tough in some ways, Gigi felt a sense of accomplishment doing that part on her own too. She'd loved the beaches, the beautiful palm trees and the culture, but had almost lost track of the time in one port as she enjoyed a coffee in a pretty little square. She'd had to jog a little of the route back to the ship because she couldn't risk not being on time. The ship didn't wait for you, apparently! Something she'd thought surely must be a mistake when she first overheard it.

'I always thought a day at sea would be terribly tiresome,' she admitted to Theodore at dinner now.

'I'm finding they're the opposite,' he said.

'I agree. I went and read my book in the park – I can't quite believe there's a park on board a ship, it's bigger than the one near my house at home.' Her trio of brightly coloured fabric-covered wooden bangles, a gift from Hector, clunked together as she reached for her glass of water.

'I played a round of mini golf, then stood watching youngsters launching themselves down the water slide. I think I was that brave once upon a time.'

'I don't think I ever was,' said Gigi. 'My sister-in-law told me once she went on a water slide and lost her bikini top.'

His rumble of laughter sounded like pure mischief. His company was delightful.

Getting to know this group of people so gradually for the handful of evenings they'd had together reminded Gigi of the friends they'd made when she and Hector moved in to their cottage in Buckinghamshire. She and Hector would go on walks, follow familiar routes, and gradually started to say hello to people who were doing the same. Those hellos progressed, they included a smile, an exchange of interest in the weather and what it was up to on that particular day – *it's glorious; mind out for the mud; it's so cold; I wish spring would hurry up.* And then eventually they'd started to have lengthier chats and some of those people had become friends.

Unfortunately some of those friends had moved away, others had become ill, some had died, and Gigi didn't have many people around these days.

'You're lonely, Mum,' Mallory had told her six or so months ago.

Gigi had denied it at first but when Mallory pushed it some

more she'd snapped, 'I know I am, you don't need to point it out. I'm not senile, I can see what my life is now.'

Mallory had burst into tears at the fact that she'd upset her mum, they'd cried together in their grief for Hector who had been taken away from them, and Mallory had never mentioned her mother's loneliness again. But Gigi suspected her daughter still knew no matter the front Gigi tried to put up.

The group asked Gigi about Hector when Peter finally stopped talking long enough about himself to realise that there were other people with problems sitting at this table.

She smiled. 'He was a thousand things. But most of all, he was kind. He was black, that gave us plenty of challenges from the very beginning.' She looked up at them but nobody had much of a reaction, not even Peter. She supposed times had changed a lot. 'I miss him.'

Theodore nodded. A widower himself, he knew just what it was like.

As talk turned to Peter and his experience with a black friend at school and the prejudice he faced, Gigi zoned out a bit. Rather than listening to Peter she looked around the restaurant, at the groups of people, perhaps strangers becoming friends, others doing their best to avoid certain people. She'd done that a few times. On her list to avoid was the man in the white Speedos by one of the pools who seemed to want everyone to look at the one place you really didn't want your eyes to wander – she'd give him a wide berth if she saw him anywhere on board, or on dry land for that matter – and then there was the woman who'd tried to link her arm on day two and told Gigi that her mother was Gigi's age and that she really should have a chaperone on this trip. Gigi had nipped that one straight in the bud because that woman would've volunteered for the job if she wasn't careful. Gigi had seen her yesterday and ducked behind a potted plant near an ice-creamery, then shrunk behind a crowd to escape.

Hector would've loved this cruise and the many ports they docked at. He would've appreciated Marseille, the art gallery she'd visited. She wasn't sure he would've liked the bustling markets but he would've enjoyed the signature dish, bouillabaisse, that she'd eaten in a little café when she took shelter from the rain. Hector would've embraced the camaraderie on board too, meeting all these people sat at her table chatting away as they got to know each other more.

Holidays had been curtailed when they had Mallory and for a long time they were in England or Wales. It was only once Mallory was older that they had their first long-haul trip together to Jamaica to visit Hector's homeland, an experience that had felt to Gigi like she'd got to know her husband on an even deeper level.

Hector had come to England from Jamaica in 1950 when he was nine years old on a ship with his mother and father, his brother, Patrice, who was a baby and his sister, Athena, who was seven at the time. It was in the early 1960s when he and Gigi crossed paths for the very first time. He loved to tell her the story, as if she didn't already know, and she had never grown tired of hearing it from his lips.

'You were the girl with the boldest laugh I'd ever heard,' he'd say, 'and the bounciest strawberry-blonde curls I'd ever seen.'

Her recollection was stalled when Theodore asked her, 'How's the steak?'

'It's cooked perfectly,' she said. 'Yours?'

'Wonderful.'

'The fish is amazing,' said Kerry. 'Can't get this sort back home.'

The mention of fish led to Peter talking about himself but dressing it up as part of the conversation – the first spiel was about the Greek islands where he'd found the freshest red mullet he'd ever tasted, except of course he tagged on about his snorkelling, then it was onto talk of the freshest lobster he'd tasted in America, tagging on the road trip from Chicago to New York that he'd taken Lola on.

Gigi caught Theodore's eye while Peter was still talking about driving on the right and she had to stifle a laugh. It felt good to smile, to enjoy herself.

But soon enough she declared exhaustion and left the group behind. She headed back to her cabin, went inside and closed the door behind her.

She took off her big dangly earrings and set them on the table beside the bed four steps from which were the balcony doors. She removed her bangles and set them in her jewellery case, took off her sandals, and stretched out her feet to pull at her calves which ached terribly.

She slid open the balcony doors to listen to the sea and took a small bottle of rum from the mini bar – she didn't drink it, she didn't like the taste, but it was Hector's favourite. He'd enjoyed a Smith and Cross Jamaican rum – which this wasn't, but it was rum nonetheless – most evenings and the smell reminded her so much of him, his hearty laugh as she'd snuggled next to him, his ability to make her laugh and feel like the only girl in the world.

She went out onto the balcony, closed her eyes, put her nose to the bottle, inhaled the smell.

She looked up at the stars that had come out from their hiding place. The night sky reminded her of Hector. The pair of them had often stood outside and gazed at the sky above, the sky that encompassed every country in the world.

She let the wind blow her hair away from her sun-spotted, wrinkled skin that showed a life lived. 'I did it, Hector. I came. You got your wish.'

If she stayed in her cocoon with other people at dinner, walked alongside groups every time they docked, if she surrounded herself with company, it would be easy for Gigi to pretend that she was as happy as she seemed.

But it didn't matter how much there was to do on board, how many beautiful ports they stopped at, what opportunities there were for experiences or forging new friendships… she was still just alone as she had been when she boarded in Southampton.

14

ROSE

The problem with finding your damn glasses was that if you weren't wearing them you couldn't very well see where you'd left them, could you?

Rose found them not in their case but in the bathroom on the top of the laundry basket lid, asking to be jumbled up in amongst her washing, not that she'd attempt to put that on without the glasses being in place. She'd end up with pink knickers and grey bras if she did that and she never wore underwear that was less than perfect. It didn't matter how old she was. Since she'd first got measured for a bra when she was twelve she'd vowed she'd always have on good underwear. You never knew who might see it.

Having her glasses in place unfortunately meant she could see every wrinkle in minute detail when she looked in the mirror to floss her teeth. She still had a full set of her own – not bad for someone her age. Millie down the road, Millie who'd run the bakery for forty years before she retired at seventy-five, had dentures. Rose couldn't imagine it, taking out your teeth every night, having them look at you like those toy teeth you wound up which could chase you across the floor and nip at your ankles. Still, it could be worse. For all the extra years Rose had got compared to others, she was incredibly grateful. Growing old was a privilege.

Rose got the pan ready to make herself poached eggs. The shop had been her life for so long – changing her habits had taken a bit of persuasion but slowly she was getting used to this extra time Penny insisted she took in the morning and hadn't realised how good it would feel.

She thought back to the very early days, when it all began.

The first day Rose had secured these premises ready to launch her new business, she and her late ex-husband, Albert, had let themselves in to a building that could be politely described as *showing promise*. Once a bookmaker's that the village had been glad to see the back of, the place smelled stale; it had been closed up for a while. It was the local support that had buoyed her on with her decision even more. Hearing congratulations when she told people she'd bought the old bookmaker's to turn it into a wedding boutique, having people ask her how much longer until it was open, feeling the excitement buzz around the village. She'd gone on jaunts to visit other wedding shops to get the measure of what she would need and had sketched out a rough plan while Albert had found someone who could do the work. Within three months she'd opened the doors at Rose Gold Bridal for the very first time.

Way before Rose had got the shop she'd found one of those old-fashioned bells that sat above a door and gave a delightful tinkle at a jumble sale. She'd bought it and kept it, and every time she'd looked at it she'd been reminded of the dream she'd had for so many years. Albert had put the bell above the door once the shop was ready and it had stayed in situ ever since, giving a little tinkle every time she had a customer or when she sent a satisfied bride-to-be on their way.

Rose had a natural talent for dressmaking and she'd always loved experimenting with fabric, seeing what things worked, what didn't. When Gigi left the village, taking the dress they'd designed and worked on together, Rose had thrown herself into dressmaking even more, determined to prove that it was she who had the real ideas and the raw talent, she who had the drive. She swore that was part of what had spurred her on over the years to make Rose Gold Bridal a success. Before she'd even looked for premises, she'd put herself on a bridalwear course to better herself and had got to grips with technical skills, creating bridalwear first with prototype garments and then with the real fabric. She learned skirt patterns, bodice designs, different cuts – drop waist, A-line, ballgown, empire – she learned more about adding embellishments including crystals, beads, appliqués, lace, all of which took the gown from beautiful to spectacular.

She was immensely proud of every single bridal dress and accoutrement she'd ever made. And that included the dress that had started this all off.

Rose hummed as she took some bread from the bread bin and slotted it into the toaster. She'd already put the pan of water on to boil. These days there was nobody constantly at her side to moan at her for humming. Albert had been irritated by it almost as much as she'd hated him leaving the toilet seat up.

Rose had met Albert one rainy day when her umbrella blew inside out in the wind and nearly took her with it. All of a sudden there was a man coming to her rescue – Albert with his golf umbrella able to withstand a lot more than her flimsy effort could. He'd held it over her, walked her home, and asked her out there and then. Rose had liked him – he was funny, always had a joke if she got too serious, and he had a strong mind just like hers. She'd been level-headed during their courtship, the same when he suggested they got married, because despite her dressmaking and plans to one day open her own bridal shop, Rose's head had never been in the clouds. Especially over a man. Marrying Albert had been a good decision. He saw things the way she did, had a vision of what he wanted his future to be. She'd seen that as true love. She'd thought it was perhaps the best thing for someone like her, a slow burn that could turn into more. And it had for a while. They'd been a team, they'd become parents, but then they'd drifted. It hadn't been his fault or hers, it was one of those things, and he'd ended up looking elsewhere for companionship. Albert had left the marriage behind, gone off with someone else, but Rose still had her wonderful children and she had her shop, and it had felt like enough.

Albert had been a good partner for a while but Rose had soon realised that you couldn't make yourself fall in love with someone just because you wanted it to be so. They'd met and married quickly; she'd thought they were both happy, and they were in many ways. Rose had opened her little shop in Saxby Green with his help, both financially and physically getting it ready, and then Penny had come along quickly enough and then eventually, Stephen. Their lives were busy, who had time for passion and sex? They didn't. Rose thought it was normal. She had nothing to compare the relationship to and neither did he. They muddled along and somehow they worked, or at least that's what she thought until he admitted to an affair that he'd been carrying on for almost a year. Rose had felt oddly numb; she wondered whether she'd have a nervous breakdown when the news sunk in, but she carried on with her business, she carried on being a mother, she moved into the spare room.

Rose had never told Penny or Stephen about the affair and she wouldn't. She didn't want to be the one to tarnish their memories of their late father. He'd passed away almost twelve years ago now and they had a right to protect their memories of him. As far as they knew he'd met someone after he moved out of the flat.

Did she ever regret her marriage? No. She didn't know there could be anything else out there, and she had two wonderful children she actually liked and was proud of. That wasn't a given – Graeme from the greengrocer's detested his twin sons, said they were gold diggers and so he was leaving everything to the cats' home when he shuffled off his mortal coil.

Rose took out the box of eggs and selected two. As she returned the box to the pantry she looked across at the photographs lined up on the mantelpiece above the gas fire. The first was of Penny and Stephen. Stephen was ten years Penny's junior and contrary to the wild boy he'd been at school, he'd found a job and settled down quickly. The picture had been taken at Stephen's wedding and the pair of them were grinning from ear to ear. Rose could remember why, too – it was Stephen's mother-in-law's *jive*. At least that's what the woman had claimed her dancing was. Rose wasn't so sure. The next framed photograph along was of her grandson, Marcus, the light of Penny's life. He was a handsome young man and she couldn't wait to see him when he returned from his travels and hear all about the mischief he'd got up to. Next to Marcus's picture was a photograph of Stephen, his wife, Delta, and Rose's other grandchildren, Mimi and Asher. Rose wondered whether her late husband would have adored these kids as much as she did, whether he would've regretted leaving the family behind when he found someone else. She couldn't imagine being without any of them.

Rose felt lucky to have her family. And her Penny was here now helping even more than Rose had expected. She'd thought Penny might get bored sorting through her decidedly disorganised paperwork, in a small village compared to the excitement of London. But she wasn't. In fact, she seemed very at home and it had given Rose a bit of an idea. Penny was no good at dressmaking, but what she was good at was business.

What if Rose Gold Bridal was just what Penny needed in her life? Penny really had taken to the organising of this place since she'd arrived. And it was good to see her looking more relaxed than she had in years. Saxby Green suited her.

Thanks to Penny, Rose's paperwork was in good order and it felt like a step in the right direction. Rose's body had been protesting for a while at the long days and the focus and dexterity required for bridalwear. She was tired, both physically and mentally, and making those mistakes with bridal gowns had upset her more than anyone else would ever know. She was embarrassed, devastated that she might have ruined the big day for someone had Michelle not come to her rescue.

But it was more than that. The shop had also begun to feel like a beacon of the things that had gone wrong in her life. She had planned to start the shop with her sister, she'd planned to put the first dress they ever made together in the window on the first day they opened. But nothing had worked out the way she'd wanted it to. Gigi had betrayed her by taking the dress and leaving the family behind but Rose hadn't been an innocent party and for that she felt terrible. It left her with a sadness and an emptiness inside her that she had no idea how to fill.

Rose set the timer for her eggs once they were in the water. She'd get down to the shop soon, she wanted to, she'd see her daughter's relaxed smile, her wonderful assistant, people who were here for her, people who didn't know what she'd done to Gigi.

Rose buttered her toast. She smiled. She really liked Michelle. Over the years assistants had come and gone from the shop. Usually they were good enough, but Rose still did the bulk of the work, and then they went on their way – one had left to start a family, another moved up North for her husband's job, one had simply had enough of working with dresses. When Rose interviewed Michelle she saw something in her, a spark none of the other assistants or job candidates had had. Michelle exuded the same passion as Rose; her enthusiasm shone through not just in the words she said in her interview but the way her eyes took in the whole boutique, the opulence of the materials, the wonderment of where they were created and worked on out back. On interview day Rose had excused herself to use the bathroom and come out to find Michelle talking with a customer in Rose's absence. She was knee-deep in explaining dress shapes, she asked about the bride's upcoming big day and what she envisaged. To Michelle, much like Rose, the customer wasn't just a revenue source, they were a person, someone to invest time and energy in, and she did it effortlessly.

Yesterday when Penny went to the supermarket to do the weekly shop, Rose had talked with Michelle honestly as they stood in the shop front after their customer left.

'Michelle, do you remember what you told me in your interview?'

'It was a long time ago, Rose.'

'I know, but as well as you telling me you'd put yourself

through several training courses and worked for an alteration service, you told me that some day you wanted to have a bridal business of your own.'

'Oh, I remember that.' She grinned. 'I thought I'd blown it with you when you asked whether I had come to learn from you.'

'And I appreciated your honesty when you said that you had.'

'I didn't want to lie.'

'I know you didn't, but your honesty sealed the deal.'

'I'm really glad,' said Michelle. 'I love this place.'

On the day of Michelle's interview Rose had had no intention of giving up her shop but she'd grabbed the chance to have Michelle work for her. In Michelle, Rose recognised the same drive, the personality, the talent, the wherewithal since she finished a graduate job in finance to go into the field she always dreamt of.

And now she had an idea.

'Michelle, one day, probably soon, I'm going to have to admit that this place is too much for me.'

'Oh no, this shop—'

But Rose shook her head. 'This shop is my dream, but I'm getting old. What I'd love is for someone to take over the business and keep it the way it is, as a bridalwear shop. I can't control that but I wanted to give you first refusal.' Was she really saying the words? She was, and for once it didn't feel so scary. Here was Michelle, the perfect person, waiting in the wings without Rose even realising.

'Rose... I think I can handle the dressmaking side but since working for you I'm not sure I could manage the rest. I'm not sure I want to. I've loved working here, with you, I do something I love every day.'

'Is that a no?'

She grappled with her answer. 'It's not, but I'm not sure—'

'I have an idea.' Because she'd sensed Michelle felt this way. 'What about if you did the dressmaking and someone else took on the business side?'

'That would be ideal. But who?'

Rose grinned.

'Penny?' Michelle seemed excited, at least Rose hoped she was. 'Do you really think she'd be interested?'

'Before she came here I would've said no, but now...'

'That would be amazing. Penny is lovely, organised, clever, she knows business.'

'Don't give me an answer right now.'

But Michelle took Rose's hands in hers. 'Are you kidding! If Penny is on board then of course, I'd absolutely love to take on more responsibility here, perhaps joint with Penny.' Her words tripped over themselves as she tried to get them out. 'I don't know how it would work exactly.'

'We can iron out all the details once I talk to Penny. I'll let her have more time here first, I've only just thought of this.'

'When you are ready we will take the steps,' said Michelle.

'Yes, we will.' And admitting to Michelle that she needed to let go of her dream shop didn't actually feel half as bad as she'd always feared.

Michelle still had hold of Rose's hands and gave them a squeeze. 'I do have one condition.'

'What's that?'

'I want access to you to consult. I want you to come in here even when I've taken over, even if it's only half a day a week.'

'My dear, nothing would give me greater pleasure.'

Rose finished her eggs and went downstairs to the shop. She heard the bell sound its familiar tinkle as a customer came in and she was right on it. The customer said they were just passing and thought they would take a look.

Rose loved walk-ins, people who just happened to pass by and might, some day, be in the market for a dress and rather than think of them as time wasters, she treated them as well as anyone who had made an appointment or brought their entourage – mothers, friends, sisters – with them. Walk-ins often ended up returning and making a purchase. Walk-ins had a mystery – you never knew what they might result in: a woman not even engaged might choose her dream dress, coming back the second her partner popped the question; a newly engaged couple might stop by on the spur of the moment in the quaint English village which spoke of fairytales and be enraptured by it thinking that this would mean their wedding would be a dream.

After her customer went on their way, Rose went out back. She admired the gown Michelle had just pinned at the hem – an asymmetrical pleated satin gown with a bodice waistline and delicate buttons running all the way down the back.

Michelle saw her watching and beamed a smile her way and Penny looked up from the desk where she was on a call.

Her daughter and her wonderful assistant could make this work, she knew they could.

If Penny said yes.

15

PENNY

Penny finished her call as her mother appeared in the shop.

'Nice breakfast?' Penny asked her.

'I had two poached eggs on toast.'

'You're getting the hang of this being kind to yourself business.' Penny smiled, put a hand on Rose's arm. 'I like it, you look relaxed.'

'And so do you.'

'Actually I'm really enjoying being here.' But she had to tell her mother that Mallory was coming to the village, she couldn't put it off any longer.

She followed Rose out back when her mother offered to make the workers both a cup of tea.

'Mum, Mallory is coming for a visit soon,' Penny blurted out.

Her mother had always been polite if her path crossed with her niece, which it had when Gigi came back to care for their sick father. The sisters had shared the care but successfully avoided one another, at least to talk to. They'd both attended the funeral, but that was as far as it had gone.

Because of their feud the two sisters had never got to know their nieces which had always made the cousins sad but neither Rose nor Gigi had ever made a fuss at the cousins getting to know each other and Penny and Mallory were both grateful for that. Mallory had been there for Penny when Penny lost her dad, Penny had been there for Mallory when she'd lost hers too. It was a nasty business losing a parent, but each of them had held the other up even when they were miles away. It was never too late for a phone call, she was never too busy for her friend. Carlos had found it amusing that Mallory was the only reason she'd hit pause on what she was doing if she was busy. Usually she wouldn't stop for anything. She was, in fact, known at work for being ruthless. She'd heard murmurings of the word *bitch* a few times. Carlos had said to take it as a compliment – as only a man would say – although a couple of her colleagues had agreed with the underlying belief that it meant people would listen to her, they'd get things done rather than fart arse around. And she supposed that had been true.

She couldn't wait to see Mallory again. Maybe Mallory just needed some time out from her job, a change of scene and pace, and she'd be back to her normal self rather than sounding distracted like half the time she wasn't listening or thinking clearly. It seemed to be working for Penny after all.

'That'll be nice,' said Rose as the kettle came to the boil.

'She's staying in Saxby Green for four weeks; she's rented a little cottage.'

Rose hid her surprise well as she dropped tea bags into mugs. 'Why would she want to come here for such a long time? There isn't much to do.'

At least now Rose was aware that Mallory wasn't only coming for a couple of days like past visits. She wondered whether her mum would do her best to avoid her niece until she went on her way again. Probably.

But all bets would be off when the dress was found missing and it appeared in the window of Rose Gold Bridal.

Penny had woken up in the middle of the night last night, asking herself whether she and Mallory were making a huge mistake, but there was no going back now. Both of them wanted their mothers to at least acknowledge what had happened, maybe salvage something, and if nothing else perhaps find a sense of closure. The fact that neither of them talked about that time period in their lives if they could help it told Mallory and Penny that they were both still likely to be hurting a great deal. And they were family, surely they had to try, even if it was for the last time.

Penny put the invoice she'd just paid into the relevant section of the filing cabinet and when a gaggle of women came in to the shop Rose insisted she serve them.

'They're all yours,' said Penny.

Michelle came out back to carry on at the sewing machine. 'I'll leave Rose to it for now, stand back in the wings.'

Penny finished what she was doing and then went out into the shop. She loved to watch her mother, she always had, and watching her now as she interacted with these women Penny could see how hard it must be to let all of this go when age wasn't on your side. Her mother had a real knack at putting customers at ease and by the time the group left the shop the bride-to-be had already tried on three dresses and made an appointment to come back with her mother next week.

Penny checked over the dresses and got them back on the rack as Rose put the woman's name into the appointment's book. Penny approved of this one thing being manual. The book looked special – satin-covered and as thick as a photo album, it sat by the till for convenience.

'I'll make sure I'm in the shop to cover the appointment,' said Rose, 'I want to close the sale.'

Penny put an arm around her mother's shoulders. 'I wouldn't have it any other way.'

When the bell above the door tinkled again Penny looked up to see not a female, as most of their customers obviously were, but a tall, rather handsome dark-haired man with beautifully sun-kissed skin.

It happened sometimes that fiancés would come in to collect items for their partner – not usually the dress itself, but other pieces easily hidden in a bag – but as far as Penny could remember they didn't have anything due for collection out back. Unless Michelle knew different.

And right now, when he smiled at her, all Penny could think was, *lucky bride.*

'May I help you?' She stopped reacting like a teenager and addressed the man – the a-good-half-a-foot-taller-than-Carlos guy with the effortless smile. He looked vaguely familiar; perhaps she'd passed him in the street on one of her visits down this way previously.

His eyes danced. But before he uttered a reply he held open his arms and for a moment Penny's heart beat faster because it looked like he wanted her to step into his embrace.

But Rose was soon the one accepting the hug.

Her mother looked up at the man, still smiling. 'It's wonderful to see you. How's your sister?'

'She's very well, she says to pass on her regards.' He looked to Penny and explained, 'My sister got married at the weekend. She lives in Northumberland but was visiting the family in

Saxby Green and just happened to pop in here shortly after her engagement and found her dress.'

'That's... nice.' Penny had no idea why the man and her mother were so pally-pally but she'd leave them to it.

'Penny...' Rose didn't seem to want her to do that. 'You called him, about the shelf.'

'The shelf?'

He stepped forward, held out his hand to Penny. 'I'm Joel. The handyman.'

'Oh, right. Yes. Sorry. I did call you. About the shelf. I'm Penny.'

'I know who you are.' It felt like his gaze grazed over her in a more personal way than it should. 'You don't recognise me, do you?'

'You do look familiar.'

'This oughta be interesting,' Rose murmured at her shoulder, revelling in the scene playing out.

'I'm Joel. Joel McNamara.'

'I know. The handyman.' They'd already established that, hadn't they?

'You don't remember the name?'

She frowned. 'I'm sorry, should I?'

He stood a while longer. Rose still had that ridiculous look on her face and slowly somewhere from the vault of her memories Penny remembered a Joel. The only Joel she'd known, come to think of it. But that Joel had worn half-mast school trousers, an un-ironed and ill-fitting shirt, had zits on his chin and had been shy. That Joel was nothing like this one.

It couldn't be...

'Not the Joel who—'

'Yes, the one who asked you on a date,' he finished for her. 'More than once.'

'I didn't recognise you.'

'I like to think I've changed a bit.'

She laughed nervously. He sure had. He definitely wasn't her type back then, and he still wasn't, not really. She noticed oil – or dirt – on the side of his hand and hoped he didn't touch any of their materials out back. He wasn't wearing half-masts but instead a pair of shorts, which she had to confess looked good on him, and he had a glow, implying he'd been hard at it all day with physical labour.

Yep. Not her type at all.

'I apologise,' she said. 'How are you?'

'I'm very well, thank you. So are you back in the village for a while?'

'I'm here temporarily, helping Mum.'

Penny registered Rose standing stock still in the middle of the shop, looking at Penny, then at Joel, then back again. She was probably enjoying how tongue-tied Penny had been since Joel came through the door, not something Penny had been for a very long time. Tongue-tied and board rooms didn't exactly mix when clients needed every confidence in her.

Michelle stepped in. Evidently she knew him too because they started talking about her husband as she led him out back to see to the shelf. The reason he was here in the first place.

Penny looked at her mother. 'Do not say a word.'

'Wasn't going to.' Rose held up her hands in defence.

Her mother knew about Joel asking her out at the end of class one day and she knew about the other times he'd asked her out after that – once by knocking on the door to the shop and asking to see Penny, another at the bus stop when he hadn't realised her mother was right behind him.

And if Penny knew her mother, which she did, very well,

she'd be up to something if only in her head right now. But she could forget it. Penny wasn't interested in dating the handyman. Her only interest was in whatever he could do in the way of repairs to the shop.

16

MALLORY

Mallory woke up a bit disorientated in a different bedroom, although she'd chosen a nice cottage for their stay. Her bedroom upstairs was nice and bright already and the curtains allowed the daylight to creep in at the sides.

Mallory and Jilly had arrived at the holiday house in Saxby Green yesterday, retrieved the key from the key safe, and let themselves in to a pleasant cottage with a small kitchen that had doors opening out to a little courtyard garden. It was perfect. A base for the two of them, a chance to spend time together and to be in the village to do what she needed to do.

Shortly after they'd arrived the heavens had opened, delivering them a decent spring shower that brought the earthy smell of the outside in through the open back doors. They'd ordered Indian takeaway for dinner with extra poppadoms and mango chutney and Jilly, despite her teenage concern that this village might be boring, seemed to relax. They'd watched *You've Got Mail* together, Jilly's head on Mallory's lap while Mallory stroked her hair.

It had been perfect.

As soon as the movie had finished Mallory had gone to the bathroom – but not to use the toilet, to cry without her daughter seeing her. Because with every perfect moment came the cruel reminder that she might not have many of those left.

When she first knew what she was dealing with she'd barely been able to say the words *brain tumour* out loud, or *oligodendroglioma* which was a complicated word in itself, never mind that it was a grade 3, malignant cancer. Sometimes all Mallory felt was disbelief. She'd stand, look in the mirror and repeat all the words associated with her diagnosis until it became real. And then she'd wish she hadn't; she'd curl up in a ball and want it all to go away.

As far as Penny knew they weren't arriving until this afternoon. Mallory had wanted to have a buffer; she didn't want to have to race to the shop with the dress and discuss next steps in that regard, she needed time, just her and Jilly, and to find her feet and a sense of calm. It was important for her not only emotionally but physically. Her symptoms were under control, the anti-convulsants were doing what they should, but she was always waiting for something else to happen, for another sign that the tumour was the boss of her now and the clock was ticking. Headaches were ongoing it seemed, but she managed those with painkillers and resting when she could, and her occasional vision problems didn't seem to be getting any worse so that was something.

She couldn't wait to see Penny, but how was she supposed to tell her what was going on with her?

'Hi Penny, here's the dress, oh, and by the way I have an inoperable brain tumour so do you think you could look out for Jilly when I'm no longer around?'

Or...

'Hi Penny, you know how you said you'd do anything for

me? Well, could you become a mother to my daughter when I die?'

There was no perfect way of doing it. All Mallory knew was that it couldn't happen yet. She'd say hello to Penny, then get the wedding dress drama out of the way because it wouldn't be long before Gigi came storming down here when she found the note Mallory had left for her confessing what she'd done.

After that she'd tackle the worst thing she had to do.

When Penny's son, Marcus, was ten, Penny had finally got around to changing her will. She had a good job, savings, property and also an ex who seemed allergic to responsibility. She wanted to make sure that Russell couldn't get his hands on any of her financial assets, but more importantly she wanted to leave instructions about Marcus. Russell wasn't interested in his own child and so Penny had asked Mallory to be her son's guardian should anything happen to her before Marcus turned eighteen and was able to look after himself.

When Mallory had ended up estranged from Jilly's father in much the same way Penny's relationship had turned out — they joked that they might be cousins and friends but this was a step too far, they didn't have to do *everything* the same, like finding no-hopers to father their kids — Penny had made sure Mallory drew up a will.

'I don't have much to leave,' Mallory, still on maternity leave with Jilly, had told her cousin.

'You have a house with only a small mortgage left to pay, you own its contents, you told me you have an ISA, you have premium bonds.'

'I want it all to go to Jilly.'

'Of course you do, so that will go in the will. But you also need to leave instructions for what happens to your daughter should something happen to you.'

Mallory had seen a solicitor shortly after their chat, had a will drawn up, and included a clause for Penny to become Jilly's legal guardian should anything happen to Mallory before Jilly reached the age of eighteen.

Of course neither of them had thought something would happen to the other one, at least not until way into the future.

Obsessing with how to break the news to those she loved wasn't doing Mallory much good right now. She threw back the sheet, got up out of the bed, which was bigger than her one at home and very comfortable, went over to the window and opened it up to a fresh new day.

She closed her eyes and breathed in the warmth, the lingering hint that rain had come and gone, the light floral fragrance from the bushes and plants down below.

She quietly left her bedroom, opening the little window on the landing and gingerly went downstairs, one hand on the banister at all times. That was something she was having to get used to as well, being cautious and not rushing in case she became unsteady, in case the thing in her head decided to remind her that it had set up camp and wasn't going anywhere.

In the kitchen she filled the kettle and dropped a tea bag into one of the bright red mugs with white insides hanging on the mug tree. There was a cupboard filled with every type of glass you could imagine and next to that another with mugs that wouldn't look quite so good on display. She'd put her medication there at the back where it would be hidden. She wanted it down here rather than upstairs because it was easier to sneak taking it when she was near a tap, and besides, Jilly was sharing a bathroom with her so she couldn't put pills in there. Jilly also sometimes borrowed her things too – tweezers, a spritz of perfume, a T-shirt. She couldn't risk it. And there was no way the two of them would ever use that many mugs that the pills would be unveiled.

She looked out into the courtyard. There was a bistro table at the back, two chairs. It would be the perfect place to relax, enjoy a glass of wine. Not that she could. The anti-convulsant medication, not to mention the tumour, made that inadvisable. No wonder the champagne hadn't gone down very well during her weekend away with Penny in the Cotswolds – her body would've been protesting, the tumour making her tired, making her head hurt, probably begging her not to have any more alcohol.

But, when your life had an expiry date closer than you'd ever expected, was there much point playing by the rules?

Some would say not. But Mallory being Mallory knew she would. Taking the car that day had been totally out of character, she still couldn't quite believe she'd done it.

She went into the lounge and sat on the arm of one of the chairs. The cottage had low-down windows so there was a better view from this height. She could see to the start of the street with cherry blossom trees at its mouth. Those trees didn't blossom for long so she'd missed what she imagined was a beautiful sight until the pink petal carpet would've graced the road and then been blown away by the wind or washed away by the rain.

Mallory liked Saxby Green. She didn't know it intimately, but she knew enough. If you walked beyond the end of the street, roughly fifteen minutes on foot would bring the river into view and a couple of minutes added on to that would take you to the riverbank and a small grassy area that could access the path that ran alongside the water, away from passing traffic.

She picked up her phone when it pinged. Sasha. Checking up on her.

She wrote a reply to say that she was doing okay.

Sasha sent back a GIF with a teddy bear opening its big furry arms, offering a hug. Mallory smiled, put her phone down and carried on staring out of the window.

She wondered whether she'd see the cherry blossoms bloom next year. By then she'd have her support network in place at least. By next year she was really going to need it.

She jumped when Jilly laid a hand on her shoulder.

'Sorry love, I was in a daydream. You're up early.'

'The birds are too noisy here.'

Mallory laughed. 'How terrible, should I complain to the landlord?'

'I need ear plugs,' Jilly grumbled.

Mallory followed her daughter out and into the kitchen where she made her a cup of tea. 'I'm going to go for a walk when I'm dressed.'

'No point in walking without Cedella. I miss her.'

'She's in good hands. Skye loves her and the feeling is mutual.'

'Can I FaceTime her later?' Jilly asked.

'The dog?'

'No! Well... yeah. I'll FaceTime Skye so I can see Cedella. She'll be missing me.'

'Of course you can.'

Jilly took her tea and disappeared off up the stairs, no doubt to tuck herself beneath the duvet for a while longer despite the noise from the birds.

* * *

Mallory ventured out less than an hour later with the birds trilling their songs – no ear plugs required – and the sun warm on her back. She wasn't surprised her mother had loved living here when she was younger. It was a beautiful village – not too small but not too big either. The air felt fresher, the open spaces wider, and a feeling of ease settled upon her the second she saw the river.

She had the dress in its cover over her arms and it was rather cumbersome but she didn't care. She still wanted to go down to the river, watch its current take the water whichever way it chose, the water having no choice but to go with the flow.

It was incredibly peaceful. A heron stood tall and patiently on the riverbank on the opposite side where there was no path, so still that Mallory had to watch it for some time before she was sure it was the real thing. When it moved its head, just an inch, as if aware of her presence and curious to know what she was doing here in its territory, she had her answer.

There weren't any swans today – Mallory would be fine if they were in the water, she'd leave if they weren't. Maybe they'd swum further today, perhaps they'd come back later and visit. She took a seat at the picnic table on the grassy area and watched a young boy racing along on a multi-coloured scooter, one leg striking the ground over and over, the other on the platform. A woman pushing a buggy followed after him, instructing the little boy now and again to not swerve towards the water's edge.

She sat for almost twenty minutes by the river before it was time to finally make her way back up the bank to the main street. She hoped she wouldn't see Aunt Rose when she went into the shop but at least the dress was covered up so if they did cross paths Rose would have no idea that it was *the* dress. And it wasn't like Rose was going to stop and chat to her and ask what she had in her arms, was it?

Mallory's nerves became heightened as she crossed over to the side of the road where the shop was. One foot in front of the other, it had been her mantra ever since her diagnosis and it was no different now.

When she was parallel to the bakery she stopped to peer in the window. Her stomach growled at the thought of one of those eye-wateringly delicious looking doughnuts – jam, her favourite – and she almost laughed. She'd already trailed the wedding dress in dust, causing a need to dry clean which led to the dress going missing and creating an extra drama to throw into the mix, she didn't need to bring jam into the equation.

A man passing the opposite way smiled at her and for a moment she thought she might recognise him – good looking, tall, dressed in jeans and a pale grey T-shirt – and as they drew side by side, he asked how she was.

Deep grey eyes fixed on her.

He seemed so familiar.

'You don't recognise me, do you?' He ran a strong hand across his jaw.

She was about to say that no, she didn't, when it all came rushing back to her.

This was the problem with looking different – with her dark skin it was more difficult to blend into the background, be mistaken for someone who looked similar but wasn't her.

They *had* met before and given the circumstances of their previous encounter Mallory wasn't surprised he hadn't forgotten her.

Because he was the man who had seen her emerge from the river, naked.

Will McGregor.

A couple of summers ago Mallory and Penny had come to Saxby Green for a long weekend. Mallory had left Jilly with her grandparents and she and Penny had rented a flat a short walk from town.

That summer the temperatures had climbed uncomfortably to the thirties every day with little respite at night. They'd slept with the windows open, cursed the mosquitos, and on the final night they finished their takeaway pizza and drank ice cold beers.

The heat got to Mallory more than it did Penny and Mallory couldn't stand it any longer. 'Ugh…' She moved from her seated position on the sofa to the cool floor tiles, arms and legs spread out like a star fish. 'It's so bloody hot!'

Penny hurled a cushion at her friend's head. 'We'll all be moaning it's too cold soon so make the most of it.'

'I can't sleep, it's worse in here than last night.' She pinged the pale pink mosquito repellent band around her wrist – Penny had one in red; they'd found them at the chemist today. So far so good; she hadn't added to the two little bites on her ankles.

'I'll get the fan from my bedroom,' said Penny.

Mallory closed her eyes. Perhaps if she relaxed, she'd cool down a bit.

She jumped at the icy feeling against her arm and opened her eyes to see Penny's hand holding two beer bottles by their necks.

'Get up,' said Penny, who didn't have the fan. 'I've got a much better idea.' She was slipping on her flip-flops as she spoke. 'We'll take these beers outside and enjoy them down by the river.'

'The mosquitos will love us down there.'

'We've got our bands. We'll be giving them a proper test run.'

Outside, beyond the confines of the flat, there was a nice

breeze but it was still warm. They walked along the riverbank, the water calmly passing them by. They'd be able to walk for miles along here – not many people did, most stayed in the part nearest to the village, but tonight they kept on going with the sun gradually dropping in the sky.

They found a section of riverbank and sat themselves down, clasping their half-drunk beers.

'We're so classy.' Mallory laughed. 'My mother would not approve.'

'Neither would mine. Drinking in the street would be very frowned upon.'

They lay back on the riverbank, feet crossed at the ankles and Mallory groaned when Penny suggested they get going; they were both out of beer now.

'Back to the sweat box.' Penny put out a hand and hauled Mallory to her feet. 'We didn't time our weekend away very well with the heat, did we?'

'Hey, we did well to get time off, the both of us, and be here at all.'

'Good point.'

But Mallory stopped walking. 'Or maybe we timed it just right.'

'What are you talking about?'

'Well, the water looks really enticing given how warm it still is this evening.'

Penny laughed. 'Come on, you, there's no way I'm jumping in there; this T-shirt is new. And besides, you can't just get in the river wherever you feel like it. Mum taught me and Stephen that over the years – or rather, she told us the rules and made us promise to stick by them. You need to go from an access point to stay safe.'

'Okay, so where is the access point?'

Penny grinned and gestured for Mallory to turn around. 'We need to go back the way we just came from. There's an access point not too far away, I went a few times when I was little. We really should ask the owners' permission though.'

'It's a bit late to knock on someone's door.'

'True.'

And when they reached the spot Mallory whispered, 'Come on, let's live a little, we'll have a dip, nobody will be any the wiser. And it's after nine, nobody wants a knock on their door this late, they won't even know, we're miles from the house... well, a hundred metres, give or take, judging by the length of their garden, but far enough.'

'I guess...'

'Come on, Penn.' Mallory whipped off her T-shirt and unzipped her floaty cotton skirt which pooled at her feet.

'You're going in in your bra and knickers?' Penny was aghast. 'Your *Victoria's Secret* lingerie?'

Mallory had been walking tentatively along the wooden jetty, the access point for swimmers who had permission, or a boat maybe owned by the family. 'You're right, they'll get ruined.'

'Exactly.'

But if Penny thought she'd won the argument and Mallory had seen sense about going in the river she was kidding herself.

Mallory walked back over to where she'd left her clothes, and with a smile, she unhooked her bra, took it off, and the knickers went the same way.

Penny was laughing, covering her eyes, looking around them. 'You did not just do that!'

'I did.' And then she walked the length of the jetty and jumped into the water.

'Two beers and you're a nightmare!' Penny laughed into the night.

Mallory gasped. The water was freezing! But in no time at all she called out to Penny, 'It's so nice in here! Come on!'

Penny grunted in frustration, then kicked off her flip-flops and undressed down to her bra and knickers. 'I'm wearing M&S, they'll be fine.' She couldn't stop laughing as she jumped into the river.

The water was heavenly. Mallory swam on her front, a little bit down from the jetty, turned in the water, looking up at the sky, its burnt orange colour growing more powerful as the sun went down. 'It's so beautiful here.'

'Now I'm in,' said Penny, 'I have to agree with you. And this is way nicer than our stifling flat.'

They were laughing away when Penny froze. 'Did you hear something?'

'All I can hear is a mosquito, buzzing loud. These bands... maybe they don't work in the water.' But no sooner had she finished her sentence than she realised it wasn't a mosquito she could hear at all but the sound of a motorboat in the distance and it was fast approaching.

'Over there in the reeds,' Penny suggested.

'Our clothes are at the end of the jetty. And I'm not going into those reeds. God knows what's in there.'

The motorboat engine grew louder. They could see its lights and it was almost with them now.

'Shit,' said Penny. 'This will be the owners and we're here without permission.'

Treading water, Mallory suggested they pretend they didn't know the rules. 'Say we're out of towners, villagers, whatever.'

'I grew up here, remember.'

And now it was too late to do anything other than face the

music because the boat had pulled up next to the jetty and the man on board had pulled the vessel in and secured it.

He'd seen them but didn't say a word to the two heads bobbing in the water. Maybe he wouldn't.

Mallory was starting to feel pretty cold and right now she was beginning to regret doing this.

The man spoke in a calm voice as he finished securing the other end of his boat. 'You two are trespassing.'

Penny called out their apologies. 'We're sorry, we didn't realise. We're not from around here.' She pulled a face at Mallory as she went with the original suggestion she'd dismissed.

But the plan didn't work.

The man called over, 'You're Rose's daughter, you grew up here.'

'Shit,' Penny muttered.

The man, who they could see in the lights from the boat, was tall, good looking, with dark hair sticking out from beneath a baseball cap. 'If you want to use the access point, it's strictly with the owners' permission. Did you go to the house first?' he asked.

'It's my fault,' said Mallory. 'I'm not from around here and I was in the water before Penny could tell me that was what we had to do. My apologies, it won't happen again.'

'Time to move on,' he said, arms folded, standing in position at the end of the jetty like a security guard.

'Sure, will do,' said Mallory as Penny offered her profuse apologies again.

Penny whispered to Mallory, 'I'll get out first, I'm in undies, I'll get rid of him and then you can get out.'

'Come on, you two, I don't want to be a killjoy but this is my parents' property and they have been known to get scared when they see someone hanging around at the foot of the garden, which this technically is.' The man gestured behind them to the land that extended beyond the property to this open jetty and area along the riverbank. 'I'd hate to see them put in a call with the police.'

Penny swam over and took the steps up and the man had the good grace to avert his eyes.

But he didn't move away. He was waiting for Mallory, who by now couldn't feel her toes.

Penny was doing her best to distract the man now she had her T-shirt on but it wasn't working.

Oh to hell with it, thought Mallory. She had no intention of risking hypothermia. She'd have to get out. And it was only a body she was about to reveal – she'd seen enough bodies in her job and much closer up than this man was going to see hers.

She climbed out of the water.

The man's eyes widened before he quickly turned away, almost losing his footing on the jetty. 'You're naked!'

'Yes, I didn't come prepared,' said Mallory as though this were a normal conversation with a stranger she'd just met. The fact that he was so good looking somehow made it ten times worse despite her confidence.

She walked up the jetty as if she was passing him by on the street. He was looking away, out to the water.

Mallory grabbed her clothes. Putting them on when she wasn't dry wasn't the easiest, especially when it required rushing.

'I'm going to stay here, looking at the river for five more minutes,' said the man, 'that should give you enough time to dress and move along.'

'Thank you,' said Penny.

'Good to meet you!' Mallory called back with a giggle as she ran with Penny, shoes in her left hand, empty beer bottles clinking against each other in her right, along the riverbank, away from trouble.

In the street in Saxby Green now, Mallory was face to face with the man from that night.

'I do recognise you,' she said. He didn't look much different to the way he had at the jetty that day – perhaps a few greys in what she'd remembered as dark hair, the same athletic physique, the same deep voice and eyes she'd seen him attempt to shield with a hand before he turned away when she'd emerged from the water with no clothes on.

His mouth twitched slightly. 'The last time we met you looked… a little different.'

'Yes, yes I did.' She smiled back. 'And my apologies once again for trespassing that evening. It was wrong of us. And totally my idea, not Penny's.'

'It was really hot,' he said. 'That night, I mean. Not you… not that you aren't hot…' He shook his head. 'I'll just shut up now, shall I?'

She grinned. He was entertaining and it made her feel good despite the sea of worry she'd been engulfed in lately.

After a pause he asked, 'Are you in Saxby Green for long?'

'Four weeks.'

'No heatwaves forecast yet.' Much like that night a couple of summers ago, he didn't seem ready to move along.

'That's good to know,' said Mallory.

'Well, if the weather heats up and you do have a desire to wild water swim, knock on the door to the main house.'

'Thank you. And I promise I won't be skinny dipping again.'

She was pretty sure she heard him say 'that's a shame' as she walked off, and at least he'd been a good distraction. She was still smiling as she pushed open the door to Rose Gold Bridal.

Penny came hurtling towards her.

'You're here!' She wrapped her in a tight hug.

'Hey, watch the garment,' said Mallory, laughing. 'And the head.'

'Oh, I forgot. The accident you had when you were on your course.' She did her best to look at the back of Mallory's head to see what the damage was. 'Did you sue whoever was running it?'

'Don't be ridiculous.'

'You're too kind,' Penny scolded. 'I can't see it anyway.'

'Luckily I had enough hair to cover it up.'

Mallory was cautious that Rose could be out back but Penny leapt in to tell her that Rose was at the bank so wouldn't be back for a while.

'Who was that you were talking to just now?' Penny asked. She never missed a thing.

'You saw me?'

'Yes, and you looked… engaged.'

'That was the man who caught us, or me, skinny dipping.'

'No!' She tried to spot him in the street but he'd turned a corner on the other side and was gone from sight. 'That was Will McGregor? I haven't seen him since that night.'

Mallory just laughed as she followed Penny inside and they took the access door at the back up to the flat to stash the dress in Penny's wardrobe.

Will. Will McGregor. He was handsome, seemed kind, and he would have no idea how much he'd brightened her day. It had felt like the sun coming out after months of grey skies.

She wondered then whether she'd see him again.

She really hoped she would.

17

PENNY

Penny sprinkled the tops of the homemade pizzas with cheese once Jilly had finished her part, which was arranging the pepperoni. When Mallory had brought the dress in to the shop today it had been wonderful to see her but they hadn't had long to talk because Michelle had needed Penny's help and so Mallory had invited Penny over to the cottage this evening. Mallory had looked so tired when Penny arrived that Penny had sent her for a long luxurious soak in the tub while she took charge of dinner with Jilly. She was doing her best not to worry about her friend but the exhaustion was unusual. Something was going on but she wouldn't push. Mallory would tell her when she was ready.

Since their first encounter in Saxby Green all those years ago, Penny and Mallory had gradually got to know each other as friends as well as cousins by calling each other on the phone and meeting up whenever Mallory came to the village. In later years they'd got together in London, which was often the most convenient place for the both of them. Penny had supported Mallory during her nursing studies by taking her out clubbing when the stress got too much and she looked like she was going into meltdown. Mallory supported Penny when Penny was going through a rigorous interview process for her first job. She'd come into London that day to meet her beforehand, and rushed into a nearby department store for a fresh pair of tights when Penny laddered hers half an hour before she was due at one of the towering buildings in the financial district.

When Mallory fell pregnant to a man Penny hoped she wasn't going to stay with long term, Penny had been there for her from the day she'd peed on the stick. Mallory had taken the test thinking this was a nightmare, this wasn't what she wanted, and she hadn't been able to even look at the result. So Penny had done it.

Penny had started to smile before holding out the stick in front of her with its two pink, very solid, lines.

Mallory looked up at her and then the test, her mouth agape.

'How do you feel?' Penny asked.

Her eyes pricked with tears. 'I think I might actually be happy.'

There'd been tears, of fear, of joy, because Mallory had always wanted to be a mum.

But when Penny pushed her to make a decision about contacting the father and telling him, Mallory wouldn't answer her. She needed to do it in her own time. Penny tried to counsel her as the days went on and a tiny bump on Mallory's frame was beginning to give the game away but still, Mallory had to get there on her own. She did eventually but that day had really taught Penny something about her cousin. When a situation or a decision was monumental, Mallory needed time and space to think it through on her terms not anyone else's, at least not at the start.

With the pizzas in the oven, Jilly took charge of setting the table. They were talking about Marcus's travelling and Jilly was enthralled.

'I can't imagine going off on my own to see the world.' Jilly distributed place mats from the pile in the centre of the table followed by the cutlery. 'I bet it's exciting and scary at the same time.'

'The excitement will win when you're older,' said Penny as she wiped down the chopping board.

Jilly took three wine glasses from the cupboard on the wall. 'I can't wait to be old enough for wine.' She caught Penny looking. 'Chill, I'm pouring lemonade into mine.'

'Glad to hear it, you're way too young. I'm not sure Mallory will be drinking though. I offered her a glass to take into the bathroom but she wasn't interested.' She wondered whether Jilly would give anything away. 'Is everything all right with your mum?'

Jilly shrugged. 'As far as I know. She went on a course recently; she's been tired since then.'

Penny nodded. Maybe the course hadn't helped, but it was more than that, she was sure of it. 'The time off here should do her good.'

'She works a lot.'

Penny was tempted to probe more but she didn't want Jilly to worry unnecessarily so she changed tack. 'What do you think of Saxby Green?' She took the bottle of lemonade from the fridge over to the table. 'Cool enough for a thirteen-year-old?'

Jilly scrunched up her nose. 'It's a bit boring.'

'Well yes, there's a reason Marcus isn't doing part of his travelling here. And I grew up in the village, remember. I used to go into London a lot, for a bit of life.'

'But now you've moved back?'

'Yes and no. Yes, for a while. But I'm not sure how long I'll be here yet.'

'You've been to loads of places with your job – a quiet village must be a lot different.'

'Sometimes you need a change. I do, anyway. Especially now I'm old.' She made a face as though she was shrivelling up before Jilly's very eyes.

Jilly giggled.

The older she got, the more Penny appreciated the village for what it was every time she came here. It wasn't buzzing, it didn't have a load of shops or nightlife, but she didn't really yearn for those things these days. The river was a drawcard and already she was thinking about her visits come autumn – walks by the water, the leaves on the path crunching beneath her feet, the temperature pleasant enough but the cosy season upon them. And thinking that she might have gone back to London by then was oddly disconcerting.

When Mallory emerged from the bathroom at the top of the stairs Penny called out to her, 'I was starting to think we'd have to send in a rescue party.'

'I'll get myself dressed.' And off she went.

When Mallory finally came downstairs to join them she wrapped her arms around Jilly. 'The pizzas smell really good.'

'Jilly has done a great job,' said Penny. 'I've never made dough from scratch. Did you teach her how to do that?'

'I sure did.'

'Mum seems to think I can't cook,' said Jilly.

Mallory still had her arms around her daughter. 'I don't think that at all.'

'Mum, in the last month you've had me making casseroles, a roast dinner, Pappy's Jamaican corn soup, and pizza.'

Penny pulled the pizza wheel from the drawer. 'That's a good thing, Jilly. My mum had me and my brother cooking from an early age. You're never too young in my book.'

As she'd anticipated, Mallory didn't want wine but Penny had a small glass with her dinner. The pizzas were delicious. Jilly had brushed the base with roasted garlic oil and it made all the difference.

'Let me clear up,' said Penny once the food was devoured. 'You two sit and talk.'

As she took everything over to the sink and made a start loading the dishwasher, Penny listened to Mallory and Jilly chat about Cedella, their house sitter, Jilly's upcoming camping trip with a friend, and her school work. It reminded Penny of when Marcus was that age. He'd been into football, hockey, both playing and watching, but he'd still been the kind of boy who could spend an evening with his mum and talk about all sorts. It was something she'd missed since he left home, something she cherished when he visited her.

'Penny, can we do anything at all?' Mallory called over eventually.

'Nope, all done.' Penny draped the rinsed-out dishcloth over the tap to dry. She went to re-join the others. 'So, Jilly, can you tell me *anything* about your mum's love life?'

'Penny!' Mallory shot her a look but her daughter obliged and answered the query.

'There was a guy at work,' said Jilly. 'I think he was a surgeon.'

'He was,' Mallory confirmed.

Jilly wasn't finished. 'He came round to pick her up a couple of times. He had a fancy car, they went to a posh restaurant.'

Mallory rolled her eyes. 'All the important things in life.

Jilly, why don't you ask Penny about her love life, that's way more interesting than mine.'

'Oh yes please.' Jilly's eyes danced.

'I think the local handyman might be interested in our Penny,' Mallory teased.

'Stop it!' Penny was laughing but she'd be lying if she said she hadn't thought of Joel more than once since they'd crossed paths again.

'Are you still dating that good-looking man you work with sometimes?' Jilly asked.

Penny smiled. 'Carlos. And I don't always work with him. We're contracted out by the same company so sometimes we're on the same project, other times we're not.'

'Is it serious?' Jilly wanted to know.

'No, we're just going with the flow right now.' Thank goodness Carlos wasn't here to witness her saying that, as his idea of what their relationship was had started to veer in the opposite direction to hers. This morning he'd called her and asked whether he could come visit again. He didn't usually ask, he hadn't last time. Part of what she'd really liked about him all along was his decisiveness but now everything was changing. She felt as if their relationship had been exposed for what it might well really be – a fling that had gone on a bit too long. She enjoyed her time with him, she'd probably still want it if he hadn't asked her to make more of a commitment and if she was still in London. Or perhaps she wouldn't. Perhaps she was changing and maybe there was nothing wrong with that.

When Jilly's friend called her, Jilly grabbed a choc ice from the freezer and took her phone upstairs to her bedroom for privacy.

'Is that the friend she's going camping with soon?' Penny asked Mallory.

'It is. They know each other from gymnastics, no vapes involved.'

'Well, thank goodness for that. She's a great kid, you know.'

'She really is.'

'She knows her way around the kitchen too.'

'My dad taught me to cook. He would've liked to teach her I expect, we just never got around to it.'

Penny unscrewed the bottle of red wine and poured some more into her glass but Mallory shook her head at the offer again. 'I wish you could relax a bit more while you're here, Mallory.'

'I'm okay.'

Penny hesitated. 'You seem so tense.'

Mallory opened her mouth, closed it and then came out with, 'It's worrying me to think what Mum is going to say when she finds out about the dress.'

Penny sat back against the sofa. 'We're in for it, aren't we?'

'I'll say.'

Thinking about the shop and the dress brought Mallory's earlier encounter in the street with a face from the past to mind. 'So,' she said and began to grin. 'Will McGregor.'

'What about him?'

'You've seen him again, and I bet he looked at you the same way he did that night at the river.'

'I highly doubt it.' A smile played on her lips. 'I was wearing clothes this time.'

Penny began to laugh and soon Mallory joined in. 'He's a catch, you know. He's still single apparently. Who knows, you could repeat that night and wild swimming could lead to wild sex.'

'You have quite the imagination, Penn.'

'I wonder if he thinks of you naked. He'd have to, wouldn't he?'

'Ew.' Jilly had come down the stairs without them realising. But all she wanted was a charger. 'We've got so much to plan for the camping trip,' she added excitedly as she disappeared back the way she'd come to continue her call.

'Tent, tick,' said Penny, 'sleeping bag, airbed. What else is there?'

'Knowing those two, a lot.'

Penny made Mallory a cup of lemon tea, keen to get back to the topic of Will. 'I don't know much about the McGregors apart from they own a furniture business – Will has been a part of it for years according to Mum who often gets a nice discount when she wants furniture for the flat.' She passed the mug to Mallory. 'Careful, blow on it first, no milk, remember.'

She sat down again and picked up her glass of wine. 'I wonder if you'll see him again.'

'Will?'

'Maybe he'll ask you out.'

'I'm only here for a month.'

'Plenty of time.'

'Penny...'

'All right. I'll leave it... for now.' She tapped her fingers against her glass. 'Have you heard anything from Gigi yet?'

The warm smile Mallory had been unable to hold back when they talked about Will disappeared altogether. 'She's home today. I'm expecting an angry message any time now.'

'You think she'll come straight down here.'

'I know she will. And I also know she'll unleash a fury that would make the worst storm seem like a passing shower.'

They talked some more about the social media post, the history of the dress.

'It was the talk of the village for a while by the sounds of it.' Penny had her iPad on her lap to show Mallory the other information she'd found online when she looked earlier. There were a few write-ups about the movie, the actress, the photographs of the filming that took place in the village. 'After reading all of this,' she said, 'I think that utilising the dress's history to draw in customers could really work for the business and take it up a notch ready for sale.'

'If my mother doesn't claw your eyes out before you do it.'

'And if my mother doesn't murder me when she finds out. I think we get it in the window before either of our mothers know. It's risky but once it's on display looking beautiful, not to mention a little harder to snatch away in a rage, then we get them both to the shop and make them talk.'

'We must have lost our marbles doing this.'

Penny nudged Mallory. 'Hey, if this was me and you and we'd fallen out, wouldn't you want someone to try to help us find a way back to each other? No matter what it took?'

'I really would.' She frowned. 'How are you going to get word out about the dress when it's in the window; how will customers know about it?'

Penny told her her idea to run an article in the local press about the dress, naming the movie and the actress, including a few photographs of the filming if she could source some from a photo library.

'Brides-to-be should love the history behind the wedding gown and the filming in the village.' Mallory hesitated. 'What will you do if any of them want to try on the dress? Will you allow it? Will Michelle?'

Penny's lips twisted. 'I hadn't thought of that.'

'It was the dress my mum married my dad in. It's special to Gigi and to Rose. Me too.'

Penny leaned back against the sofa; the iPad slipped onto the cushion beside her. 'This seemed a great idea at the time. But what if...'

'What if we've made the biggest mistake ever?' Mallory finished up her tea. 'Then both of us will just have to face the consequences.'

'It's so sad – they're sisters. I don't want us to ever fall out like that.'

'We won't.'

'Even if I meddle and try to get you a date with Will McGregor?'

Mallory's eyes twinkled when she smiled. 'Even then.'

18

ROSE

'I wanted to win, but coming in as the runner up...' Rose looked at the wedding dress they'd poured their hearts and souls into. Gigi had worn it for the photos to enter the competition, she'd worn it in front of the judges, but now it was back on Helpful Harriet, the mannequin, where its life had begun.

'I no longer have to worry about weight fluctuations.' Gigi nudged her sister from her position next to Rose on the bed, legs outstretched, backs against the headboard. 'I'm going to have so many mince pies this Christmas.'

'You've got to get through the enormous chocolate cake after dinner first.' Their parents had both been so over the moon at their success that they'd walked into the village and brought home a big celebratory cake from the bakery.

What might have seemed an out-of-reach idea to even enter the competition had turned out to be the best thing the sisters had ever done – to Rose, it felt like they were already on the path to having their own shop some day.

'What would we call it?' Rose asked Gigi.

'What would we call what?'

'Our shop of course.'

'I've no idea.'

Rose turned onto her side, her head propped on one elbow. 'You still want to have a shop, right?'

'Sure.'

'A bridalwear shop. We're clearly good at making wedding dresses.'

'You did most of it,' said Gigi with a disinterest Rose picked up on. Maybe she'd get more excited as time went on.

'You did a lot too,' said Rose. 'We'll have to save, we'll need capital.'

'A lot of capital. A bit more than we make with our part-time jobs.'

Rose had a sinking feeling that her sister might not want this as much as she did. Or maybe it was because it seemed so impossible right now what with the money they'd need behind them. Perhaps that was it. Gigi had doubted they'd be able to pull off a dress and have any chance in the competition and look what had happened! Maybe Gigi just needed to go with the flow, believe in herself, and they'd succeed, she just knew they would.

But the thought still niggled her. What if Gigi *didn't* want this? What if Gigi *never* wanted to start a business? Could Rose do it alone? Would she?

She'd have to. Now she'd got the seed of the idea in her head, there was little else she saw herself doing for the rest of her life.

* * *

Rose waited on the platform at Saxby Green station. She could barely stand still, not just because of the plummeting winter temperature but because she had news and she couldn't wait to tell her sister.

A week after coming runners up in the local competition and receiving the cash prize they'd split between them, Gigi had gone into London again to meet Hector, this time under the guise of the girls making another dress. Rose was Gigi's alibi once again but rather than walking the streets of London to go to the haberdashery, Rose had stayed in the village. Gigi had promised to bring back something from a haberdashery to maintain their cover and Rose had gone to the café past the station – their parents never went there so she knew she would be safe and she could meet Gigi's train to carry on the pretence that they'd been together all this time.

'You look happier than I am,' said Gigi when she got off the train and came over to Rose who was waving madly. 'I got some offcuts really cheap.' She gestured to the bag she was carrying.

'Great.' Rose slipped her arm through Gigi's as they walked out through the front entrance. 'I have some news.' And for once they were going to focus on that first rather than Hector.

'What is it? You're almost busting!'

Rose giggled. 'I went to the café today. I sat with a cup of tea perusing a bridalwear magazine.'

'You're not asking me to make another one, are you? Not yet – let's finish secretarial college first, get a qualification.' It was a conversation they'd had a couple of times – Rose eager to move forwards, Gigi putting on the brakes with her sensible approach.

'Just listen, would you.'

And as they walked Rose told her sister what had happened to her that day.

She'd been sitting in the café and while most conversations were white noise, one had stood out. There was a table crammed with customers, none of whom looked like locals and Rose couldn't help overhearing what they were talking about, largely because of the swear words that flew into conversation as if that might be the way these people talked all the time.

'I soon worked out that they were a film crew,' said Rose, 'and they had problems with the costume department. A lot of costumes were ruined in the recent storms, most had been replaced easily, but they still needed a wedding dress for their starring actress. The man was quite awful, talking about how Saxby Green was the arse end of nowhere – his words not mine – but I put aside any offence and kept listening. They sounded totally desperate to find another wedding dress. So, emboldened, I interrupted them. We've always been taught not to do that, haven't we?' she said to Gigi. 'But I did it anyway. I asked them what size the bride was, told them I had a dress available for hire.'

'What do you mean you have a dress for hire?'

Rose rolled her eyes. 'Our dress. Our competition dress. It's just hanging there and I thought it would be perfect.'

Rose was a bit put out that Gigi wasn't more excited; she was ruining this story by a lack of enthusiasm, although Rose hadn't got to the best part yet.

Rose ploughed on. She put on a gruff voice which at least made Gigi laugh when she impersonated the man. 'He said, "Look love, this is a private conversation, so if you don't mind." And then he shooed me away but the woman with him was far nicer, she asked if I could really help. I held my nerve, described the dress and as I had a piece of paper with your measurements tucked into my magazine – I wanted to use them to help me visualise what we could make next – she looked at those and that was when she said she was *very* interested. Gigi, I talked to her like hiring dresses was something I did all the time!'

'What happened next?'

'I big-noted the dress of course, told them it was one of a kind, that it had been admired by many people already and was runner up in a recent competition. They got the actress to provide her measurements and an hour later they were at the house. Mum and Dad were out and so I sneaked in to get the dress to show them. They admitted to me on the spot that they'd fully expected it to be no good given the particulars they had for era and style. But when they saw it and the fact the actress's measurements were almost the same, apart from their actress being an inch shorter than you, they offered a price that made my eyes water. They wanted to buy it—'

'No! They can't buy it! It's *our* dress.'

They crossed to the other side of the street. 'Don't worry, I said it was only available for hire. I made it look like I'd walk away but then they offered a fee for hire instead.' And she was still giddy thinking about it.

Gigi's eyes widened when Rose revealed what they'd offered. 'Half of that is yours, Gigi. I'm so excited! Our dress, the dress we worked so hard on will be in a movie.' Her face might begin to hurt soon she was smiling so much. 'The dress will be worn by *the* Norma Monroe.'

Gigi gasped. 'You never told me that!'

'I saved that bit for last. I didn't know when I was negotiating the use of the dress and the price, but now I know I'm even more excited! We can go and watch the film being made too, we're welcome on set as long as we don't get in the way.'

'I don't believe it.'

'Believe it, it's real.' Rose twirled on the spot and apologised to the man walking behind who hadn't expected the stationary person to start doing any sort of dance. 'I've said we'll take the dress over to the van that will be parked by the church tomorrow at 10 a.m.'

'And they'll look after it?'

'Of course they will.'

'It's a lot of money,' said Gigi, who was smiling by now.

'They're filming in Saxby Green for the next few days. It's unreal.'

Gigi grinned. 'Our dress and our little village, famous. I'll have to tell Hector all about it, he's heard about this place, the river, its beauty.'

'You will.' And because Rose was so happy right now she didn't even mind hearing about Hector all the way home.

* * *

Unfortunately, the day after Rose had given her sister the amazing news, Gigi had come down with terrible flu and she'd missed out on all of it – taking the dress to the crew, watching *the* Norma Monroe wearing it at the entrance to the church. Rose had shivered her way through the day, there was so much waiting around, she only got brief glimpses of the dress as the actress emerged into the daylight. Special lights and heaters allowed them to film the scene which, in Rose's opinion, would've been a lot nicer in the summer. She'd even got to meet the actress and she was still telling everyone she bumped into that Norma Monroe had thanked her and Gigi for letting them use the dress in the movie. Rose couldn't wait to see it when it came out, it all felt like a dream.

Gigi was still unwell over a week later. She'd missed meeting Hector when she promised she would, and their mother had told her that she shouldn't leave the house until she was completely better. Rose had escaped the dreadful bug and had kept her distance from Gigi but told her about her idea to try hiring the wedding dress out again. They might not get quite as much as they'd earned from the filmmakers but all of it would help go towards their savings. She wasn't daft, she knew they'd need a lot more than a small pot of savings to start a shop, but every little bit helped and showing their work around could be part of what built up their reputation.

Rose made her way home from secretarial college – Gigi hadn't been since she'd got sick but Rose was bringing her the homework exercises so she didn't get behind. Really Rose was only doing the course to appease her mother who said they both needed a skill – clearly their dress being used in a movie didn't count – and she was still thinking about the jobs it might lead to in the short-term that would help her long-term goal as she turned onto the high street and made her way past the riverbank that led down to the water. It was only 4 p.m. but already dark and when a man approached her she gasped.

She knew right away who it was. Black men didn't frequent Saxby Green, and Hector most certainly never had. 'What are you doing here?'

Unsure of himself, he kept a few steps back from her. 'I didn't mean to startle you.' He was polite, softly spoken, he looked kind just like Gigi said he was. 'I came here looking for Gigi. She didn't meet me when she said she would. I went to the house.'

Rose's heart sank. 'You shouldn't have done that. Our parents... our mother...'

'Your mother sent me away. But I need to know that Gigi is okay.'

'She's fine.' Rose wasn't sure how much she wanted to tell him.

'I walked up and down the street here, along by the river, I thought I might bump into her.'

Rose said quickly, 'She's at home.'

A man walking by looked over as if Rose was doing something wrong and she shifted uncomfortably. Was this what it was like for Hector all the time, because of the colour of his skin? Was this what it would be like for Gigi if she kept seeing this man?

From the battered old brown cloth bag on his shoulder Hector took out an envelope with Gigi's name scribbled on the front. 'Would you give this to her?'

'What is it?'

'I wrote her a letter. I was waiting until it was dark to go back to your house and post it through the door.'

'Don't go to the house again,' she urged. 'My mum will open the letter if she sees it.'

'Gigi told me I should never go there,' he admitted. 'But I had to try. Would you give her the letter?'

Rose couldn't bring herself to tell him that the only reason Gigi hadn't met him was because she was unwell and hadn't left the house. This man seemed kind, gentle, but their mother would never give Gigi her blessing and where did that leave them all? Would Gigi be ousted from the family? No more summers together, no Christmases or birthdays, no giggling in each other's bedrooms and certainly no making wedding gowns together. This relationship might be what Gigi wanted right now but didn't she realise it could very well blow her world apart?

He was still holding out the letter. 'Please.'

She took it but only a second before a voice hollered over to them.

Rose's heart beat faster. 'You have to go,' she told Hector. 'Go now, please!'

Her mother was marching towards them, straw basket resting over one arm.

Hector took off so fast he'd win a hundred-metre sprint hands down and Rose quickly shoved the letter into her pocket.

'What were you doing talking to that man?' Her mother's greying hair was pinned in its usual low bun, and she ushered Rose on her way, back in the direction of home. 'Do you know him? He was at the house looking for your sister. Who is he?'

'I've no idea.'

'What did he want with you then?'

She thought quickly, she had to. 'He was lost, he asked where the station was.'

'Of course he's lost, he's not from around here.' The pinched look on her mother's face was enough to tell Rose what that really meant. *Not from around here* didn't mean Saxby Green, it meant England. A black man didn't belong, not in her mother's opinion.

And her mother went on about it all the way home, she went on about it to their dad when they came in through the door, and no doubt she'd dine out on this story for weeks, warning everyone that a black man was hanging around the village talking to young women.

Before Rose went upstairs to check on her sister her mother called her back.

'You are not to mention that man to Gigi,' her mother said in a way that brooked no argument. 'Do you hear me, Rose? I don't want him mentioned ever again in this house. He won't come back if he knows what's good for him. I told him as much.'

Rose's feet heavily trod their way upstairs. She pushed open Gigi's door but Gigi was sleeping soundly. She really had suffered with this bout of flu; she'd never seen her sister sleep so much.

Perhaps it was better that Gigi didn't know Hector had come to the house. Rose didn't like to imagine the almighty row that might happen if she found out.

But what was she supposed to do now? She couldn't leave the letter for her sister when she woke up; there was no way she wanted to risk anyone else finding it first.

She went into her bedroom and pushed the envelope into her desk drawer. She didn't look at it, she wouldn't, it was private.

But during the night when Rose couldn't sleep because of the nightmare about her mother and father throwing Gigi out of the house for falling for a black man, and then the constant thought of her mother's reaction to Hector being in the village, she climbed out of bed and took the letter from the drawer. Using her torch, she tore open the envelope and before she could change her mind she began to read.

The writing wasn't very legible – Hector didn't have the neat handwriting the sisters had had drummed into them at school. It wasn't a very long letter either, but what it said had Rose sinking down onto her bed and curling up into a ball.

Hector wrote that he had come to the village to find Gigi because he was worried. He wanted Gigi to go to London. He said he wanted them to be together, that it didn't matter what her family thought, it was her feelings that were the most important. He said that he'd waited for her to come to London on the day they arranged but every day that she didn't show, he lost a bit more hope. Her visits had got so regular that he wasn't used to her absence for such a long stretch of time. He began to fear she'd changed her mind about him and so he gave her a day and time to meet him and said that if she didn't come then he would respect her decision, but he would never stop loving her.

Part of Rose's heart broke for Hector, the handsome man who had fallen for her sister. She slumped down on the edge of her bed. The thing was, it *did* matter what their family thought. Family was important, it was their anchor, so was Saxby Green. Rose didn't want to see Gigi throw any of it away for a man who was so different that they were going to face dreadful challenges along the way. Gigi had already told her they'd been yelled at, that people looked at them differently, that she knew they were judged. Rose couldn't bear the thought of her sister living that way, that the life she chose might slowly bash away at the lovely young woman she was.

Gigi could meet someone else – someone suitable who was welcomed into the family with open arms. Rose felt sure of it.

And so she pushed the letter to the very back of her desk drawer. She considered throwing it away but what if she changed her mind and wanted to pass it to her sister?

No, she'd keep it and each day until the day Hector had requested they meet Rose would think about it, decide whether or not she'd made the right decision for her sister and for her family.

19

GIGI

Gigi had seen beautiful beaches, towns and cities bathed in sunshine, enjoyed local cuisines never having to lift a finger to prepare her own food, but there was nothing quite like the green green grass of home and she'd felt her heart settle as the ship docked back at Southampton. She met the car service she'd pre-booked, chatted with the driver until they reached the main road, and then let herself drift into her own thoughts.

She'd done it. She'd been on the cruise just like Hector had wanted.

'You must think I'm a terrible passenger,' she said to the driver when they pulled up outside her house. 'I'm afraid I'm a bit tired after the cruise.'

He chuckled. 'Not at all. Some like a natter, some like silence. I'm fine with either, keeps my day interesting.'

He helped her with her luggage – one suitcase and a holdall – and she waved him goodbye before closing the door behind her.

It hit her all over again. The silence. The loneliness. She

should've talked to the driver more, made the most of the company while she could.

She left the bags where they were, went into the kitchen and flicked on the kettle. Time to get back to normal. Time to keep moving forwards the best she could. It was something she'd done on the cruise without thinking, she'd allowed herself those moments of happiness without really having to try. Here at home she felt as if she was going to have to summon the effort all over again. She had been invited to a social at the cricket club. Maybe she should go after all, although without Hector she hadn't braved one yet. She was surprised she was still on the organiser's list.

Gigi and Mallory had watched Hector play cricket when Mallory was little. Mallory loved to set up their stripey deck chairs and watch her dad, although her attention span was limited and so they usually ended up getting ice-creams and having a walk before waving over to her dad to say they were off. He knew what they were both like, he didn't mind, he was happy.

Gigi took out a mug for her tea and found some peppermint tea bags – she didn't have any milk for the regular Earl Grey she favoured. She couldn't wait to see Mallory and Jilly again, tell them all about the cruise. Maybe they could come for dinner this evening – they could get fish and chips, Jilly always loved the fish and chip shop around the corner. Jilly would insist on getting the enormous pickled onions and Mallory would always turn her nose up at the slippery brown things.

Gigi sat at the kitchen table to drink her tea. It was where she and Hector had spent so many hours. Sometimes they'd forget they had the lounge and they'd stay here talking long after dinner was over. She liked this spot, sunny right up until midday and cool in the afternoons as the sun moved round. Come winter, the Aga warmed it thoroughly and turned it into the second cosiest room after the lounge with the open fire.

She looked at the photograph of Hector on the windowsill.

Her late husband smiled back at her from the print taken during a cricket match. He was wearing his cricket whites and joy exuded from him, his whole personality shone in the picture. Hector had loved the camaraderie at the local cricket club. It was where she'd had the wake for him following the funeral because it was one of the places he was at his happiest.

The first time he came home after a day at the club he'd told her, in his deep mellifluous tone, 'I feel so welcome there.' She'd told him, 'Of course you're welcome.' And then she'd kissed him on the lips, laid her head against his chest as they stood in the back garden beneath the sunshine.

It brought her to tears sometimes to think of how much prejudice and judgement he'd come up against in his life, not to mention the objections they'd both faced over the years – a white girl with a black man in a relationship in the 1960s and the early 1970s had turned heads more than it would today. They'd started their first days living together in London where there was still racial tension, but it was nothing like what it would've been had they tried to stay in Saxby Green.

Gigi finished her tea and left her cup in the sink. She supposed she should unpack.

She went back to the hallway but her eyes fell on an out-of-place envelope propped in front of the carriage clock on her mantelpiece in the lounge as she passed by.

Puzzled, she went to see what it was. The room was still cool, it would warm up later on, and she picked up the envelope with Mallory's handwriting on the front.

Why hadn't her daughter just sent a text? Mallory hadn't

notified her of any emergencies, so there wouldn't have been the need to come here, not even for the garden because Gigi's neighbour, Beryl, had been taking care of that, accessing it via the side gate with the key Gigi had given her.

She tore at the edges of the envelope, took out the folded piece of paper and opened it up. But her pleasure at a mysterious note from her daughter soon faded when she read the contents.

Mallory had gone to Saxby Green.

And she'd taken Gigi's treasured wedding dress with her.

I know this is a shock, Mallory had written, *but you and Rose need to sort this out once and for all.*

Gigi wasn't sure whether to scream or cry.

What right did anyone have to interfere? What right did Mallory have to take her dress and worse, take it to Saxby Green?

Her eyes filled with tears. She thought she'd be glad to be home but she almost wished she was back in her little cabin at sea, rather than here where her world was being smashed apart even more than it already had been.

She couldn't push out the images of Saxby Green that played in her mind like a show reel. She'd never been able to forget the place. She'd tried to at first, when she'd left to be with Hector. She'd done her best to close off that chapter of her life. She'd been back when her mother died, just for the funeral, given they weren't particularly close or even on proper speaking terms and given her death was sudden. Gigi had been back much more for her dad when he got sick. She'd spent a lot of time with him; Mallory had been content amusing herself a lot of the time because she'd made a friend. And with everything going on with her dad, Gigi hadn't had time to worry about who that friend was.

Gigi had kept the full history about her and Hector and by extension, Rose, from Mallory. Their daughter might have picked up bits here and there from hushed conversations, but she'd never been told all of it. One day Gigi had come home from her job at a haberdashery where she worked three days a week, doing secretarial work on the other two, and found Mallory crying in her bedroom. She'd pulled her into her arms and asked whatever was the matter. Apparently the girls at school had been making fun of her dark skin and the fact her father was black and her mother white. Conversation had turned to what it was like in Gigi's own teenage years and early adulthood. She'd explained how she and Hector had faced a lot of opposition, but she hadn't elaborated. And then she'd told their daughter the story of how she and Hector met one day on a platform at Waterloo. Mallory loved the story almost as much as Gigi and Hector did.

Over the years Gigi had been tempted to lay out the complete truth about everything that had happened when she lived in Saxby Green, but how could she when some of it didn't paint her in a very good light?

Sometimes Gigi had thought – hoped – the friendship between cousins Mallory and Penny would fizzle out and it would be another step removed from her estranged sister, Rose. After all, Penny seemed so different to Mallory. Mallory had a softness, a homeliness and a compassion to her, whereas from what Gigi knew of her niece, Penny seemed completely career focused, strived for success and never wavered off course. Like mother, like daughter, Gigi supposed.

Gigi left the note on the table and climbed the stairs wearily.

Mallory had taken the dress – it felt unreal.

She got the pole from the airing cupboard and hooked it

into the brass loop to push the loft hatch open. She had to see it for herself – she had to see the loft and know that the dress had really gone.

She pulled down the ladder and cautiously climbed up. If Mallory could see her now she'd have words. *Get down from there! Whatever are you doing?* Well, it was her fault she was even doing this in the first place.

She reached the top, looked down to the far end, past the Christmas decorations, the boxes of photo albums and another of jigsaw puzzles, and she felt her body sag.

The lid was off the big, square box with a gold trim, the box that would protect the dress, wouldn't allow it to be ruined from sunlight or artificial light or anything else that may attack the materials and cause them to break down over time.

Even without climbing all the way in to the loft space Gigi could tell that her beautiful wedding gown really had gone.

She carefully climbed back down the ladder and went downstairs. She found her phone and was about to send Mallory a furious text asking what on earth she was playing at when she thought better of it.

She threw down her phone, glad it had a case or the screen might well have smashed to smithereens as it hit the coffee table.

Had Penny instigated this? Had Mallory's cousin persuaded Mallory to get the dress, meaning that Rose had got to Penny and told her side of the story first?

She paced in the lounge, thinking, deciding what to do.

But it didn't take long to work it out.

She had to book a train ticket, go down to the village and get back what was hers.

If Rose had played any part in this little stunt, she'd be

absolutely furious. What had happened between them was history, as was their family and their sibling relationship.

She wouldn't be apologising, not ever.

* * *

The next day Gigi was on her way to Saxby Green, not a place she'd ever thought she'd return to. She was still angry but overnight that anger had simmered into more of an upset, a tug at her emotions at everything that had happened since she was a young woman.

Being on a train was a source of comfort for Gigi. Given the way she and Hector had met, she felt a closeness to him whenever she was on board. Hector had started out working for London Transport as a cleaner – that was what he was doing the day he'd seen her on the platform at Waterloo. He'd become a ticket clerk for a while, then a porter. None of his work was well paid but between them they had enough. And they had each other, more importantly.

Gigi and Hector had loved to go off for the day on the train whenever finances and jobs permitted. They'd disappear to little villages they'd never heard of with tiny stations that wouldn't see anywhere near the footfall of the big city. They'd seen such beauty on those days, parts of the English countryside that were so pretty all they needed to do was stop and embrace it all while eating the sandwiches they'd made and taken with them.

Those jaunts had never taken them back to Saxby Green. But now she was heading there, to the village with its delightful river and compact high street, and a woman she really didn't want to face.

All she wanted was her dress.

She went over and over it in her head as the countryside rushed past the window. Mallory had no idea what she was messing with. She loved her daughter but she wasn't quite sure how she was going to forgive her for this.

Gigi had booked her train ticket online – she was good at doing things online since Mallory had taught her – and she'd also rented a room above the pub in Saxby Green. She'd booked for a week but messaged the owner to ask whether she'd be able to adjust her stay as needed. He'd been most accommodating and Gigi knew as soon as she had that dress, she'd be leaving Saxby Green behind again. The pub was conveniently at the far edge of the village, nowhere near the bridal shop, and so she wouldn't have to worry about bumping into Rose. She no longer knew the landlord and landlady of the pub either – it had changed hands a couple of times since she'd lived in the village, and she knew very few people back there these days. She'd get herself settled and then show up at Mallory's Airbnb – her daughter had forwarded her the address and phone number there in case of emergency.

The train pulled out of the station they'd stopped at, gathering speed, taking them onto the next. One of the most beautiful trips she and Hector had been on once he retired was to Yorkshire where they'd joined a steam railway tour. It was like stepping back in time, the sounds of whistling and hissing as the engine got ready to move, the smell of coal, steam and great machinery as it took them off to see the beauty of this county neither of them had visited before. Gigi had joked on that trip that not many people retired and then spent their free time on what was a big reminder of their workplace. But Hector said the railways had given him work, allowed him to make a living, and trains had led him to the girl he fell in love with from the moment he saw her.

The thinking behind the cruise had been that they should both try something different before they got too old to do so. Trains were a comfort to Hector, that was how he saw them, but the cruise would take them to worlds they knew were out there but had never had the chance to see together. It stung that he'd never got to fulfil the dream and for a while Gigi hadn't wanted to leave the house, let alone go on a cruise on her own.

As the train trundled towards Saxby Green, some passengers began fidgeting – yanking out suitcases and holdalls from the overhead racks even though they weren't at the station yet, zipping up bags, putting away books and tablets.

Coming home yesterday had been a shock, the emptiness and the quiet confronting, and in a way this trip felt better than those walls surrounding her and making her feel like she could barely breathe without Hector. But seeing Rose again? She couldn't contemplate it – Rose might well be holding the dress right now thinking she'd won.

Gigi gazed out of the window of the train as it slowed even more. The train carriage became busy with people engaging in a contest to get off the train first. It wouldn't make much difference, she wanted to tell them. Relax, enjoy the end of the journey, that's what Hector always had them do. And he was right. He always thanked any staff who passed them by when they disembarked from one of their journeys, tipped his flat cap, gave them one of his beaming smiles.

Gigi waited for the rush to pass and at last it was clear enough for her to go to the luggage rack by the doors and retrieve her case, the last one remaining.

She stepped down onto the platform. It didn't matter how beautiful it was here. This visit had one purpose and one purpose only.

To get her dress back.

20

MALLORY

Mallory went to the shop as soon as the coast was clear. While Rose was at a doctor's appointment followed by a trip to the shops, her absence gave Mallory and Penny a chance to get the dress onto the mannequin out the back of Rose Gold Bridal. Penny took an impressive picture of the gown, the lighting just right so that the sequins delivered a sparkle, and she emailed the local press with the information they had.

'No turning back now,' said Penny.

'No turning back,' Mallory repeated, hugging her cousin. They were in this together.

Mallory and Penny had agreed to put the dress in the window once they knew both women would see it around the same time. They wanted maximum impact, for the sisters to see their past through the dress they'd made together and hopefully take a step towards talking to each other at least. It might not end up mending their relationship but it was worth a try.

They removed the dress from the mannequin carefully and while Penny went upstairs to the flat to hide it in her bedroom again, Mallory went off to use the bathroom. She wanted to take some painkillers without facing a barrage of questions and close her eyes for a few minutes.

It was almost time for the next part of Mallory's plan because knowing Gigi she'd be on her way down here right now. At any minute she might march into the shop or find Mallory at her Airbnb and all hell would let loose. It was daunting, overwhelming, and yet Mallory was glad her mum was coming because she had to get on with it. She had to see whether this would get the two sisters talking so that her mother had family and support in her life to cope with the bombshell Mallory was about to drop.

Four weeks didn't feel anywhere near long enough for what she needed to do, but it would have to be, because after that things were going to change even more when treatment started. This couldn't be her secret for much longer.

In the bathroom, Mallory took her painkillers. She stretched her neck side to side. She ached, her head hurt, she felt nauseous. But for now she had to pretend none of that was happening. Apart from needing loved ones to confide in, she was also beginning to realise why you needed a good support system around you. It was hard to pretend you weren't having symptoms, that fatigue didn't creep up on her, that sometimes she felt a little like she could pass out and had to sit and wait for the feeling to go.

She thought of Jilly, which always helped, and she even smiled as she finished up in the bathroom because this morning Jilly had voluntarily got some school books out and, as it transpired, she was going to do a Zoom call with Skye. Mallory had told her that Skye had experience tutoring and her daughter seemed on board with the idea even without Mallory suggesting it.

By the time she made her way from the bathroom, Michelle was at one of the sewing machines out back and Penny was in the shop.

Mallory went to join her cousin but stopped when she saw Penny talking to a man who was asking about a shelf.

Mallory sat on the stool behind the till – it was safer for her to sit down for the time being.

She watched Penny with the man. Mallory had met Carlos once or twice, he was good looking, worldly and confident, just Penny's type. This man wasn't and yet…

As soon as the guy left Mallory asked Penny who he was.

'That was the handyman – Joel. Turns out I knew him at school. He asked me out a couple of times. I didn't recognise him at all when he came to fix up a shelf for us.'

'So he came in again to ask about his shelf?' She raised an eyebrow.

'Okay, that's enough.' But Penny couldn't stop smiling. 'I know what you're thinking.'

'Didn't say a thing.'

'You didn't have to. You know, he's actually good friends with Will McGregor.'

'That's nice.' Mallory narrowed her eyes. 'Don't tell me you mentioned my name.'

'Not directly, but I did confirm that Will is still single.'

'You're interfering.'

'And you weren't just now, talking about Joel?'

Busted. 'You got me there.' She stood up carefully. 'I'll get going, I need some lunch and knowing Jilly, she'll be eating rubbish if I don't get back to the cottage soon.'

Penny adjusted a satin wedding shoe on the display in the centre of the shop next to all kinds of other accessories – a bag, pearls, a tiara and a beautifully bound guest book for a wedding reception. She regarded her friend who hadn't moved from the spot. 'You sure you're okay? You look a little peaky.'

'Thanks.'

'You know I meant it in the best possible way. Treat yourself to a power nap after some lunch, yeah?'

'You know, I might just do that.' She hugged Penny goodbye and got out of the shop before the tears welling in her eyes spilled over.

Just a while longer to pretend everything was normal, to hold it together until she didn't have to any more. She hadn't realised quite how hard this would be, not telling the truth, making excuses all the time. With her own fear building in her mind, it was becoming harder with every passing day.

Mallory closed the door to the bridal boutique behind her. She'd never had a wedding. She wished she had – even if the marriage hadn't lasted, she wouldn't have minded the experience. Or was it better to have not gone down that road in the first place?

She made her way to the bakery to pick up some bagels for lunch. She'd love to take a nap as Penny suggested but with Jilly it wasn't always possible. If she did it too much her daughter would ask questions and she wasn't ready for that yet.

As she waited in line for the bagels she wondered what excuse she could make to justify a sleep during the day – she could pretend she'd been for a power walk along the river rather than hanging out at the shop with Penny, or, she could say she hadn't slept last night. She might have to do one of those two things because as much as Mallory was trying to carry on as normal she knew she had to listen to her body rather than fight it. She was good at doling out advice at hospital – rest as much as you need, get plenty of fluids, listen to your body – and making sure patients followed her instructions. But now it was time to be the boss of herself even though she might not always want to do what she was told.

She stepped out of the bakery, the warmth of the bagels and the scent of fresh dough drifting from the paper bag so tempting that she took one out and bit into it.

It made her feel better. She bit off another piece, then another. She leaned against a wall, eyes closed.

She only realised she must have made some questionable groans of pleasure at the taste when she heard a voice say her name.

She opened her eyes, wiped a finger at the edges of her mouth, because there was Will McGregor opening up the back of a truck.

'Hey,' she called out, a little embarrassed to be caught stuffing her face.

'They're good, aren't they?'

She held the remains of the bagel aloft. 'The best,' she said, unable to look away when he took the end of what emerged from the truck gradually to identify itself as a wardrobe. Will's strong, tanned forearms looked as if they had no problem with the weight; he could even walk backwards with control with that in his arms.

And now she was staring at him as he went about his work day with the family furniture business.

She turned round to walk away before she embarrassed herself further but the next thing she knew the world started spinning.

She fell to the ground.

She heard footsteps.

He was coming for her.

The two arms had her sitting up on the pavement, but when she focused, it wasn't Will McGregor.

Her voice cracked, the tears came. 'Mum?'

Gigi flapped. She might well be angry but her daughter crying brought out her doting side, her motherly side she was so good at. 'What happened? You fell over just like that. Are you all right?'

Mallory leaned into her mother's arms. She couldn't let go, she didn't want to, not ever.

Here was another one of her ducks in the village and getting in a row. And all she wanted to do was fall against her and weep. She wanted to cling onto her mother the way she'd apparently done the first time Gigi had dropped her off at nursery, she wanted to stay with her and for her mum to make everything better the way she'd done with a scraped knee when she was little.

She bit back the tears and let Gigi help her up and over to a nearby bench. There was no sign of Will, he must have disappeared inside the building with the wardrobe before she fell.

Gigi took a tissue from her pocket and dabbed at what she said was a bit of blood on Mallory's forehead. She dabbed once more and then took the tissue away. 'Just a graze. How did you manage to fall? It's not a side effect from your head injury, is it?'

'I don't think so.' She hated that her mother was worrying about her injury which had been yet another lie she'd texted Gigi about in an ever-increasing web of them. 'I'm just clumsy, I guess.' Although she had a sneaky suspicion it was a symptom of her tumour.

'Clumsy, yes.' Gigi's sympathy dissipated. 'Now, tell me, how would you feel if you came home from a holiday only to find someone had stolen something very precious to you? And not only that, they'd taken it to the one place and the one person they never wanted it to go to?'

Her voice wobbled. 'Mum, I—'

'What were you thinking? Where's my dress?'

But the questions stopped when Mallory put a hand to her head. She was still a little dizzy, she felt sick too.

'What is it? Do we need to take you to the hospital?'

'I just need to get back to my accommodation, lie down.'

'All right.' Gigi stood, put out her arm for her daughter to link it. 'But then we talk.'

Mallory held onto her mother's arm all the way back to the cottage and wished she could stay that way, close without having to talk, rather than face what was coming and the inevitable fallout.

* * *

Back at the cottage Mallory put her feet up on the sofa at Gigi's insistence while Jilly made mugs of tea for them.

Thank goodness for Jilly. She diluted Gigi's fury a little, because Gigi doted on her granddaughter and the confrontation was put aside temporarily.

The pair talked all about Gigi's cruise. Jilly wanted to know all the details – everything from the sort of cabin Gigi had stayed in to the people on board, the entertainment, the crew and the food.

'The food sounds amazing,' Jilly gushed as Gigi finished describing some of the restaurants on board the ship and some of the meals she'd enjoyed. Jilly turned to Mallory who had sat up to drink her tea and already felt better. 'Imagine, Mum. Eating what you want every day, whenever you feel like it. They even have drinks packages – I could literally walk around with an empty cup and get a fizzy drink whenever I felt like it.' She put a hand to the side of her mouth even though she made no effort to lower her voice when she told her gran, 'Mum makes me drink water and she has boring food in the cupboards, says it's healthy. She won't even let me have chocolatey cereal any more.'

'Good for her. You know your pappy always hated the stuff. Full of sugar, little nutrition. It was oats every morning for him. He'd make us both porridge – wonderful in the winter especially. He said it set him up for the day.'

'He made it for me too,' said Jilly. 'He'd put an extra blob of jam on top for me and I'd try to make it last right until the last mouthful of porridge.'

'Dad would've been so proud of you for going on the cruise, Mum,' said Mallory.

'I'm proud of myself.' But the look she shot her daughter suggested she might well be wondering whether Mallory had lied and cancelled her part in the cruise only so she could steal the dress.

Mallory noticed her phone on the side table flash up with Penny's name again. It had already done that a couple of times and she'd put it on silent so she could speak to Gigi. There was a chance Penny would've seen her with Gigi when they walked past on the opposite side of the road after her fall.

Mallory registered that her mother only had her handbag. 'Where's your luggage?' She'd been so preoccupied with holding it together, walking home holding Gigi's arm and trying to pretend that she really was fine, that she hadn't registered her mum was here without many belongings at all. 'Have you come all this way just for a day?'

'I'm staying at the pub.'

'No, stay here,' said Mallory. 'There's an extra room.' She felt terrible that her mother hadn't even thought it an option.

'Yes, Gran, stay here,' Jilly pleaded. 'I'll be off soon on a camping trip so Mum will be on her own.'

'I've paid for the room already. I wasn't sure how much space you had here.' She gave a weak smile at Mallory but pulled Jilly in for a hug.

As Gigi asked Jilly to tell her all about her upcoming camping trip, Mallory let the sounds of their voices seep into her soul and she closed her eyes.

But as soon as Jilly went off to use the bathroom, Gigi jostled her. Had she been dozing?

'The dress, Mallory,' Gigi prompted. 'Where is it?'

'Mum…'

'Where is it?'

'At the dry cleaner's.' Mallory was getting way too used to fibs, this one rolled right out; she had to buy them some time until they knew both women would see the dress at the same time or thereabouts. 'I trailed it in a bit of dust. But it's fine, I promise.'

Gigi put her head in her hands. 'Oh Mallory. Why did you take it?'

'I can explain. I promise I will, soon. The dress is safe. Have some time with Jilly, she's missed you, she misses Pappy.'

'Don't try to push this aside by distracting me.'

'I won't, I promise. I'll get a call about the dress soon to say it's ready and you can have it back.'

'Does Rose know about this?'

'She doesn't know anything.'

'Does Penny?'

'Yes.' Mallory went over to sit next to her mother. 'We want you two to talk. You promised Dad when he died that you would go on a cruise. But he made me promise him something too.' She squeezed Gigi's hand. 'He made me promise that I would try to get you and Rose together again.'

Gigi's eyes glistened with tears. 'That man always did have a good sense of humour.' She sniffed. 'This is all a lot to deal with.'

'I know, but trust me for now.'

'I'm not sure I can.'

It almost broke Mallory's heart to hear those words but at least mentioning her dad's dying wish seemed to have made Gigi somewhat calmer.

And talking to Jilly again when she came out of the bathroom had the same effect.

These two at least had each other. And that felt good.

No matter what came next.

21

PENNY

Penny had been in the shop all afternoon waiting for a response and was relieved to finally get Mallory's reply to her text message. She was still alive after facing Gigi's wrath and she'd bought some time for them by saying the dress was at the dry cleaner's.

When Penny had seen Gigi with Mallory earlier, walking arm in arm on the opposite side of the street, she'd wondered whether Mallory had collected Gigi from the station. But that had started off another train of thought – why didn't Mallory have her car with her? When they were eating pizzas the other night Jilly had made a remark about the house sitter and it being lucky she was watching over Cedella, the garden, her mum's new car. Penny had thought it odd but Mallory had swiftly moved on to some story about the last time they tried to take Cedella away from the house and the dog had gone a little crazy making for the opposite of a relaxing time away.

Penny had forgotten all about it since then. Perhaps it was Mallory doing her bit for the environment, or maybe coming on the train made her feel closer to her dad. She'd always said trains did that given the line of work Hector had been in.

'You okay?' Michelle came out into the shop to check the record book by the till. 'You're frowning.'

'Sorry, just thinking, that's all. I couldn't remember what time Susie Pittway said she was coming for her fitting today,' Penny lied. She was sure it was 5 p.m., she'd put it in the book herself.

'Five,' said Michelle.

Penny checked the book even though she didn't need to. 'Yes, and the entry is in my writing so I should know.'

'You sure you're okay?'

'Yes. You know, a lot to get my head around here.'

'You're doing a great job, it's lovely to have you looking out for the place.'

Although Penny was mainly here to do the business side of things, she helped out in the shop too. It made things easier for Michelle, it meant Rose didn't feel obliged to be here every day for a full day, and actually she was quite enjoying the change of scene. Okay, so she couldn't talk materials and styles as well as Michelle or Rose, she didn't love gushing about dresses, but she was a woman, she still had opinions, she knew what suited someone and what didn't.

Penny took down a box of buttons from the shelf Joel had fixed. There was no sign of it wobbling now, he'd done a perfect job.

Joel McNamara. From school. Who would've thought she'd ever see him again?

While Michelle got to work on the sewing machine out back Penny picked up the glass cleaner and a cloth from the very end of the shelf. It was on their list of jobs – clean the glass in the shop space multiple times a day, fingerprints and smudges were not welcome in a bridal boutique where they were aiming for perfection or as close to it as they could get anyway.

She started with the inside of the front door of Rose Gold Bridal. She moved on to one of the many mirrors next, the one positioned so potential brides or members of a bridal party could hover a tiara over their head, or a veil, or see what a little satin clutch would look like on their person.

The bell tinkled and this time it announced Jilly's arrival.

The teenager didn't seem too comfortable. 'Is it all right that I came here?'

'What's happened?' Penny put down the glass cleaner and the cloth.

'Oh, what? No, nothing has happened. I just wanted to get outside, leave Mum and my gran chatting, get some fresh air. I miss Cedella. It's harder to go for a walk when you don't have a reason.'

Penny put an arm around Jilly shoulders. 'You're always welcome to pop in.' She felt a shot of relief that Gigi had obviously held back a lot of her anger while she waited for the dress to come back from the fictitious dry cleaner's. Mallory had thought fast on her feet for that one.

Jilly was looking around, almost enchanted.

'Don't tell me you're going to be my youngest bride ever.' Penny feigned shock.

'I've never even had a boyfriend. I don't think I'll be getting married for a while.'

'Well that's a relief. Come on, can I get you a drink? We have some fizzy out back – I bought some so I don't have to drink tea all day. And I won't tell your mum, I know she doesn't like you to have too much.'

'I'm not allowed any,' said Jilly, clearly eager for a cold fizzy drink.

Penny grabbed one for herself as well and they stood at the till, away from the dresses, to drink them. Penny would put hers beneath the desk should a customer come in.

'Are you looking forward to your camping trip?' she asked Jilly.

'I can't wait.'

'I'll bet. Fingers crossed for some good weather for you.'

Jilly smiled. 'I hope so too.'

'Your mum says you've been doing a bit of catching up with school work and talking to Skye.'

'She's nice. She's quite young; I think she remembers what it's like to be at school. It helps.'

'And your mother and I don't because we're old hags?'

Jilly started to laugh. 'Your words, not mine.'

'Seriously though, is it really tough at school?' She'd already finished her drink so she picked up the cleaner and the cloth to do the next mirror. It might make this sound less like an inquisition if she was working at the same time.

'Did Mum tell you I got suspended?'

Penny looked around, one hand pressing the cloth to the mirror. 'She did.'

'It was stupid, the vaping. I don't even know why I did it.'

As she chatted she carried on polishing the glass to a high sheen. 'When I was at school the people who usually got into trouble were either struggling with the work or they just weren't interested in being there.'

'You want to know which of those is me, right?' Jilly asked after a while.

Penny finished up with the mirror and put the cloth beneath the till with the cleaner. 'Yeah.'

'I'm struggling with the work.'

'In what way? Is it too hard?'

'Some of it is,' Jilly admitted. 'The teachers are pushing maths and sciences.'

'You'll need maths and English for any job, so those are the two to make sure you focus on.'

'My friend's sister had to re-sit her maths GCSE alongside her A levels. I don't want to do that.'

'Then you need to keep up with the work, put the effort in. Once you get that GCSE you don't have to look at a maths book ever again if you don't want to.' Penny waited before she asked, 'Is that all that's bothering you?'

'It's Mum too. I worry about her. I think she's lonely.'

Penny put her arm around Jilly's shoulders again. 'She's always busy; she's made a good home for you both.'

'I know that but I wish... I wish she could meet someone like my pappy, someone kind, someone who's there for her. She's always there for everyone else.'

'Oh, Jilly, I want that for her too, and maybe she will one day. Unless you think fifty is too old for all that.'

Jilly started to laugh. 'Fifty isn't old.' But the laughter faded. 'I worry that I'll move out some day and she won't have anyone.'

'Hey, she'll always have you no matter where you are. And she'll always have me.' Penny smiled. 'You know, if your mum knew you put this much thought into her happiness she'd be really proud. But it's not a kid's job to worry, it's the other way round, and your mum would be the first to tell you that.'

'What about you? Did you never want to get married again?' She looked around the dress shop as if she thought perhaps it should be in Penny's genetic make-up.

'Being single isn't so bad. I have my job, I have a good life, I've got Marcus even though he doesn't live with me any more.'

Penny took the discarded cans of drink and put them in the bin. Back with Jilly in the shop she got away from the subject of her love life. 'So if you don't like maths or science – and by the way, thirteen is a bit too young to not keep your options open – then what do you like at school?'

She twirled her long, dark hair around her fingers, a habit Penny remembered her doing ever since she was a little girl. With dark skin, although not quite as dark as her mother's, she wasn't the image of Mallory but a unique version, a blend of both parents' lineage.

'I enjoy food technology, drama, I like textiles.'

'I bet you got the love of textiles from Gigi.'

'I suppose I must have done.' Sheepishly she added, 'I always thought she made her wedding dress but I know your mum played a very big part in it.' She looked all around them at the many gowns hanging waiting for a bride to step right into them. 'It makes sense now I've seen this shop. It's amazing.'

'Thank you, and I agree. It does seem that Gigi and Rose both made the dress.'

'You and Mum are trying to mend things between them, aren't you?'

'We're giving it our best shot.'

'Gran never talks about her sister and she never did anything like opening a shop like your mum. She was a secretary for a while and worked in a haberdashery for a bit. She used to mend Pappy's clothes.'

'Well, I don't think you should give up on what you enjoy,' said Penny, returning to the subject of what was bothering Jilly. 'Maths and English might be important but so is doing what you love.'

'My teachers are already talking about doing more academic subjects so I can go to university. I'm not even sure if university is what I want. It's expensive.'

'You're only thirteen, plenty of time to make decisions in that regard. You have to follow your own path at the end of the day – mine was university and business, your mum's was nursing. Can you imagine either of us doing what the other is doing?'

'You'd make a terrible nurse.'

'Hey!' But she laughed and conceded, 'Actually you're right – I'm okay with blood, needles' – she rocked her hand side to side in an I'm-not-too-bad-with-them motion – 'but faeces and puke, no chance. And your mum would find a boardroom entirely dull whereas I've loved it over the years.'

When the phone rang Penny excused herself to answer a call to a lady due in at the weekend to try on her dress who also wanted to alter the veil she'd gone for. Penny made the relevant notes in the appointment book and by the time she returned the phone to its cradle she realised Jilly had gone out back.

Penny went to join them. 'Is she bothering you, Michelle?'

'Not at all. In fact, I've just finished the sleeve I was working on so happy to talk fabrics and anything else.'

Penny was about to say that that wasn't necessary but Jilly had already launched in with another question.

Penny took a call from the local journalist she'd contacted with her press release and she felt her insides flutter when they told her they were leaping on the story and running it in tomorrow's press!

Penny fired off a text to Mallory to let her know.

Jilly came through from the back. 'Time for me to go.' She hugged Penny goodbye before shrugging on the little rucksack she'd brought with her.

'Have a wonderful time on your camping trip.'

'I will. I'm getting the train on my own too.'

'You're ready for it and you're very sensible, your mum knows that.'

Penny watched her go. She was a great kid, a real credit to Mallory and if she lived closer Penny suspected she'd see a lot more of Jilly. She always remembered Jilly's birthday, every Christmas, she talked to Jilly when she and Mallory came to visit or she went to see Mallory at her house, she'd taken Jilly on shopping days to give Mallory a break, seen her school concerts and looked after her when she was unwell and Mallory had to work. She hadn't always been available but she'd stepped in when she could and she'd been more than happy to.

Mallory's reply came through on Penny's phone congratulating Penny on getting the press coverage. And with a few texts back and forth they agreed that with Jilly off on her trip tomorrow and with Rose out until around the same time as Jilly's train was due to depart from Saxby Green, Penny would get the dress back onto the mannequin and put it in the window.

Gigi and Rose would see the dress around the same time.

And they'd all have to see what happened from there.

22

GIGI

Gigi was finally feeling better after what felt like a ridiculous amount of time in bed feeling completely away with the fairies. She wasn't sure she'd ever had flu so bad and she couldn't wait to go into London at the weekend. She'd missed the time and day she and Hector were supposed to meet up. She hated imagining him waiting for her at the station, looking up and down the platform expecting her to appear and when she didn't how upset and confused he'd be. But she'd been so unwell she never would've been able to get the train. He'd probably come back to the station every day he wasn't working just to see whether she was there and the thought of how much he cared made her smile and feel a tingle all over. She really was in love. For the first time in her life she knew what love felt like.

She opened up the door to her sister's bedroom just to sneak a look at the wedding dress now covered in plastic to protect it. Rose always gushed about her dream of having a bridalwear shop whenever they looked at the dress, but Gigi didn't. When she'd been the model for the dress, when she'd worn it to the competition, her hair beautifully styled and make-up applied, all she'd been able to think was that she was going to marry Hector one day. And she wanted to marry him in this dress. It was perfect. Buying the material for it had led her to him in the first place, it was a sign that fate had been at play that day.

When Rose told her a film company wanted to borrow the dress Gigi's heart had constricted. It wasn't right to have someone else wearing it. But, the money was good and while Rose would squirrel away her half to put towards a bridalwear business some day, Gigi had already decided her share would be saved for her life with Hector. They were so in love, her sister had no idea how serious they were. She never wanted to listen when Gigi talked about him. To Rose, Hector was a problem for the family that she was waiting to disappear.

Just two days of secretarial college to get through until she'd go into London. She'd have to ask Rose for a favour again, get her to be her alibi, but one day she'd be brave enough to ask Hector to come here. She'd tell her family and if they couldn't accept him? She'd face the consequences.

It sounded so cavalier but that was love all over, wasn't it? When it was true love and totally worth it you took a chance, you did the unthinkable.

Rose had already left the house that day but Gigi had been to see the doctor, to make sure she was recovering well. She was, but her mother had insisted on the appointment.

'Make sure you get to college quickly,' her mother told her before she left the house to go to the shops. Gigi's father was at work; he'd kissed her goodbye this morning and brought her a hot mug of tea before she'd climbed out of bed. He'd told her to warm up first, it was a cold day and he didn't want her to get sick again.

Gigi couldn't find her red woollen scarf no matter how

much she turned her drawers upside down and so she went into Rose's room to see whether she had it. Rose had borrowed her red bobble hat last week when she couldn't find her own, so it wouldn't be a surprise.

Gigi pulled open the bottom drawer where Rose usually kept her winter hats, gloves and scarves but it wasn't there. She opened up the drawer above and the one above that but no sign of it.

She'd only just closed the top drawer but pulled it open again because she'd seen an envelope with her name on it.

Puzzled, she opened the flap and took out a piece of paper.

And as soon as she began to read, a sense of betrayal hit her hard.

The letter was from Hector. He'd come here, he'd been in her village. He was worried about her, he loved her, but he respected whatever she decided. He'd given her a day and a time to meet him in London and said if she didn't show then he'd know Gigi didn't want to be with him any more. He thought her lack of visits to the big city was because she no longer loved him.

Gigi caught her breath. The day he'd suggested was today. She looked at the time. The time he'd written was in less than three hours.

Rose had hidden this from her. How could she?

Gigi burst into tears, great wracking sobs she could do without another person in the house.

She had to see Hector, she had to go to him.

If Rose had hidden this letter, what hope did they have? If her sister couldn't accept him, her mother definitely wouldn't.

And Gigi was in love. This was the man she was going to marry no matter what anyone else thought. They'd talked about sharing their lives, where they might live, the family they might have. By hiding this letter Rose was no different to their mother – she'd pretended to want what was best for Gigi, but she clearly didn't if she could do this.

She rushed into her bedroom and on her knees pulled out the small battered suitcase from beneath her bed. She threw it open and dumped most of her clothes inside messily, there was no time to fold them properly. She added her wash bag, a few personal items. She emptied her savings out of her moneybox and put all of the money into a purse she'd keep in her shoulder bag.

She pulled on her coat and with one last look at her bedroom she turned her back.

She was walking past Rose's bedroom when she stopped. The dress was right there, hanging on the front of the wardrobe, the dress they'd both made and the dress she'd imagined marrying Hector in some day.

She set down her suitcase and took out her purse from her bag. She found an amount she thought would suffice and left it on top of Rose's chest of drawers. She pulled a shorthand pad from Rose's desk drawer and on it she scribbled a note to say that the amount of money should cover her share of the materials for the dress. She wrote a second note to her parents, a longer one telling them that she'd met someone and she was leaving. Her heart pounded double time, tears trickled down her cheeks at the thought of her dad's face when he realised she'd gone. She'd be back some day but not for a while. For now, she had to do what was right for her.

She had to start her own life.

Her dreams weren't Rose's dreams – her sister longed to have a bridalwear boutique and run a successful business. Gigi just wanted to be with the man she loved and make a home and a family with him.

No matter what.

She left the house that day, along with the wedding dress and tears streaking down her face all the way to the station. She waited at Waterloo for over an hour until the time Hector had said he'd be there and when she saw him coming towards the station she ran to him. She fell into his arms and she knew from that moment on there was no going back.

Saxby Green was the past. Hector was her future.

23

MALLORY

'Oh Mallory, whatever is wrong with you?' Gigi frowned at Mallory who was crying as she folded up the last of Jilly's T-shirts she'd be taking on her camping trip. Gigi hadn't unleashed any more anger about the dress. Mallory knew she'd held it in for her granddaughter's sake but it was definitely brewing. 'You went away with a friend at her age, it's an adventure. Don't let her see your worry.'

If only her mother knew why this was so hard. Mallory had been tempted to ask Jilly not to go on the trip. She wanted to spend every moment with her daughter for as long as she could. But she couldn't do that to Jilly. Jilly had to be allowed to grow up like any other teenager in as many ways as possible and if Mallory didn't let her she'd be failing at the one job she'd always wanted to get right no matter what.

She pulled herself together. It reminded her of the times at work when a patient's prognosis was so dire that she'd had to force her emotions back as she explained it to them. And now she knew what it was like to be on the receiving end. She'd seen the regret in her doctor's eyes when he'd told her her diagnosis; she knew he would've wished that he could take some of the pain away. Working in the medical field brought so much reward but at other times it was beyond devastating.

After her fall the other day, Mallory had made an appointment to see her specialist. It wasn't that long until her next one, but she knew she had to get herself checked over again before then. The fall had been on her mind ever since it happened. She always told patients not to worry until they knew what they were dealing with, but already she was wondering whether the tumour had grown a ridiculous amount before she'd even had the chance to tackle it with chemo and radiotherapy.

The questions she asked herself continuously were exhausting in themselves and almost too much to bear on some days.

'What's this?' Gigi had picked up the project Mallory was working on and had left out on the sideboard. Mallory had worked on it last night when Jilly was watching a movie on her iPad in her bedroom and she'd forgotten to put it away.

Ever since her diagnosis Mallory had needed some way to make sense of what was happening. She knew she had to cherish her time, however long she had, whether it was ten weeks, ten months, ten years at the best end of the scale. She'd logged on to support groups, and participated in a couple of online sessions with people going through the same thing. She'd gathered information – cases similar to hers, outcomes good and bad, prognoses, treatments, side effects. As she'd looked into what she was facing, the usual points had come up repeatedly, that this was an important time for the whole family, for your loved ones, that they would have to come to terms with this too. She'd started to think a lot about when Jilly was a baby, the sleepless nights, the exhausted haze she'd been in, the way friends had told her to make the most of it, that the time would go too fast.

That was what was happening now, wasn't it? Time was going too fast.

When Jilly was a baby Mallory's dad had taken so many photographs – a lot of which Mallory had protested about because she thought she wasn't presentable enough for a camera – but when he gifted her a small album of Jilly's first year, she realised how special it was to have those memories. For a man who'd worked on the railways he had a way with the camera that captured not perfection but realism. He did it with Gigi too, took pictures of her when she wasn't aware, thus capturing her beauty, not in the way she looked into the lens and posed or smiled, but in the way she truly was.

Mallory had thought of that album a week after her diagnosis and she'd gone into town, chosen a beautiful suede-covered photo album, one of those with free pages so you could stick a picture in but put words alongside too. She'd started with a selection of pictures over the years of some of the best times with Jilly – the first time she rode a merry-go-round at the funfair and was bawling her eyes out on horseback and Mallory had had to beg the operator to stop the ride to get her off – she'd added that in her notes – the sandcastle they'd built on Bournemouth beach with turrets and a drawbridge of sorts that they'd watched over until the tide came in enough to fill the moat and then take the whole thing away. There were the photos of Jilly's birthdays over the years and always memories attached – the blue train cake for her seventh that her friend's dog had demolished before her friends even finished singing 'Happy Birthday', the photograph of her with the bike Pappy got her when she turned nine, the trip to a waffle house when

Jilly turned double figures and she'd chosen anything she liked from the menu.

Mallory had added to those pictures she already had. She'd got a couple of great shots without Penny or Jilly knowing the other night. She'd been waiting for the bath to fill and as the pair of them made the pizzas, unaware she had come out, she'd taken a picture of them that was so natural it had made her cry when she sank down into the bubbles looking at it. Penny, as if she'd been on the same wavelength, had taken one of her with Jilly at the girls' night and both of them were laughing at something Mallory couldn't quite remember. What her friend had captured was magical, the way Mallory wanted her daughter to remember their time together.

Saxby Green had a pharmacy where they printed photos and so Mallory had wasted no time getting copies of the pictures on her phone and putting them inside the album along with a small explanation. She'd keep doing this album, keep making memories for as long as she could.

Mallory came up with an explanation for Gigi, or at least an explanation for now. 'You know what we're like nowadays, all our photos are on our phones, we don't print them any more. I thought Jilly might like it if I did it the old-fashioned way. She might not, I suppose.'

'It's like the one your dad gave you.'

'I know, and I also know how much I've always treasured it.' She'd give that to Jilly too, because it was their memory, their first year together.

'When will you give it to her?'

'I'm not sure, I've got a lot of pages to fill yet.' She put the album out of sight when Jilly came trotting downstairs.

'Have you got enough money?' Mallory asked her daughter as she picked up the pile of clothes that Mallory had folded.

'I've got my card and some cash, not that anyone takes it these days.'

'They will if your card won't work.'

Jilly zipped up her enormous rucksack.

'And Laura's parents are meeting you at the station the other end?'

'Yes,' said Jilly.

'And you have your phone charger. There'll be places to charge it up?'

'Yes and yes.'

'You'll have a wonderful time.' Mallory hugged her tightly. She knew she'd have to make the hug very short on the platform at the station because otherwise she might just fall apart. Jilly was growing up so fast and Mallory only had a finite amount of time to witness it. What a privilege it was to assume you'd see your child finish school, to witness all the milestones in between, to see them fall in love, see them going out into the world. It all felt like an out-of-reach dream right now and she knew the chances were she wouldn't get to see Jilly do so many things. She was unlikely to see her daughter meet the man of her dreams, get married, have a baby of her own.

Mallory gulped back her emotions and went to get the little plastic box she'd put together with a sandwich inside for the journey along with a packet of crisps and a can of Coke.

Jilly smiled when she saw the drink. 'I'm going on holiday, Mum, I'm not going away for ever.'

'It's your first time, I won't be so bad if you do it again.'

Gigi tried to heave Jilly's bag out of the way of the cloakroom door so she could use the toilet before they set off to the station. 'It's so heavy. Won't you struggle to carry it?'

'Once it's on and the straps are done up it takes away some of the weight.' Jilly put it on to demonstrate.

Gigi smiled and when she emerged from the cloakroom Mallory and Jilly were ready to go.

'At least it's not too far a walk to the station,' said Gigi, picking up her own bag.

'Good job it's a nice day.' Mallory deflected the threat that her mother was about to mention the absence of her car by ushering them out of the door.

* * *

On the way back from the station, Gigi didn't say a word. She was under the impression they were heading towards the dry cleaning shop past the main shops on the high street, on the opposite side of the road to Rose Gold Bridal.

Mallory wasn't sure how much further she wanted to walk or more accurately, how much further she would be able to walk before she was too tired. She wasn't sleeping very well at night, she was worrying about the progression of the tumour after she'd fallen over, she was panicking about her mother seeing the dress. She'd been thinking about Will McGregor too and Penny's insane idea that they were going to start something.

And as if her thoughts conjured him up, all of a sudden here he was in front of them.

Could he tell she was thinking about him? She doubted it but she still had to gather herself.

'Mallory, it's good to see you,' he said.

'Good to see you too.' At least her voice didn't wobble, she sounded relatively together.

He looked even more handsome than the last time she'd seen him. The jeans and a sweatshirt with the sleeves rolled up strong forearms to his elbows, suited him.

She remembered her manners. 'Will, this is my mum, Gigi.'

He held out his hand for Gigi to shake and properly introduced himself. 'Will McGregor, good to meet you, Gigi.' But his eyes were soon firmly on Mallory again. 'Are you enjoying your visit to the village?'

'I am, thank you.'

Gigi frowned. 'Did you say your surname was McGregor?'

'I did.'

Gigi smiled. 'I remember your grandparents, they were always very nice to me.'

'I'm glad to hear that.' He looked at Mallory once more. 'I'd better get on, I've got furniture to deliver. But enjoy your stay in Saxby Green, both of you.'

As they walked on, Mallory asked about his grandparents.

'They saw me with your dad once,' said Gigi. 'It was one of the few times Hector came here. They treated us just like any other couple, said hello, smiled, told us it was a beautiful day. It wasn't much, but I always remembered them for that because nobody else was quite as kind.'

'They sound lovely.'

Gigi wasn't about to disappear on a memory. 'How do you know Will? You've only been here in the village for five minutes.'

'I met him once before.' The words were out before she could think of what else to say.

'When?'

'A while ago, Mum. It isn't important.'

'Judging by the way you got all nervous and your voice took on that shake you get when you're out of your depth, I'd say it's very important.'

They stepped out of the way of the postman opening up the post box to gather up the letters inside.

'He likes you,' Gigi pushed on.

'Mum, you have spent all of a minute, maybe ninety seconds, in his company, how can you possibly know that?'

'The way he was looking at you, not too dissimilar to the way your dad looked at me when we first met, when we were teetering on the brink of starting something.'

Mallory wished that was even a possibility, but with her situation, it wasn't.

'You're reading way too much into it, Mum.'

'So how did you meet? I won't stop asking until you tell me.'

Mallory knew she meant it too. And it was preferable to the tension between them as they kept walking. Soon she'd be veering across to the other side and the dress would be there, front and centre, in the window of Rose's shop.

And so she told her the story.

It went down well and Gigi couldn't stop laughing. 'You got out of the water naked! I don't believe it.'

'I was a bit rebellious.'

'I'll say!'

Hearing her mother laugh, seeing the way her face lit up, Mallory hated herself that little bit more. She almost began to cry, her emotions ready to spill out. And soon, they would – they had to with the truth.

'Cross over here, Mum,' said Mallory, her heart thumping in her chest.

'Here? But the dry cleaner's is around the corner.'

Mallory took her mother's arm, guided her across the road, and then they were there. Outside Rose Gold Bridal.

And the truth was out.

The dress was in the window and her mother froze on the spot.

24

ROSE

Rose spent the morning visiting Millie who had once run the bakery in Saxby Green. In the same way as Rose had been doing for the last few years, Millie had held on to her business for as long as she could. In the end she'd passed it down to her son and she loved the fact that it was in the family, that she could still talk about the business side, and see it thriving.

Rose had taken some iced buns to Millie's and they enjoyed them over a mug of tea. Millie had had a hip replacement and was laid up in bed. Rose had visited her knowing she was likely going crazy being stuck in the one place. Rose hadn't been bedridden since she'd been pregnant with Stephen – what felt like aeons ago – and diagnosed with an incompetent cervix. The doctor had put her on bed rest for the last three months of her pregnancy.

Rose and Millie ended up discussing Rose's shop and Rose admitted that she was almost ready to retire. She also confided that she'd never thought she'd be able to keep the shop in the family, but over the last few days she'd begun to wonder whether actually, she would. Penny was a businesswoman, a successful one at that, but the more Rose saw her daughter in Rose Gold Bridal, the way she and Michelle kept the place going while Rose had some time out, gave her hope. It was early days of course, Penny might very well get bored considering she was used to multi-million-pound contracts for big companies rather than a little backwater shop. But perhaps this might be a change she would consider.

Over their tea and buns Millie had also talked about her late brother who had run the bakery alongside Millie until he died suddenly at the age of sixty-two. It had made Rose wonder what it might have been like if Gigi had stuck around. Would they have opened the shop together? Or was Gigi never really interested enough to take the risk?

Gigi had left a note for their parents when she walked out and a much shorter scribbled note for Rose along with the money to cover half the cost of the dress. Rose had been so upset. Her sister had chosen a man over her entire family. They'd been close, Rose and Gigi, and she had never understood how anyone could do anything so utterly devastating. And to take the dress was a low act. To make matters worse, Rose found out by way of a letter to their dad that less than a year later Gigi had married Hector in the dress they'd made together, the dress they'd spent hours on, the dress that was special to both of them, not just Gigi.

When their mother found out Gigi had married a black man she'd cried. Their dad had tried to tell her it was best they gave their blessing but their mother had said 'never' and refused to talk about it.

Gigi had come back a few times to the village, on short visits, but Rose hadn't wanted to see her.

Not after what she'd done.

Rose had made mistakes herself, they both had, but Gigi's actions had split their family apart.

Rose walked from Millie's back along the high street and stopped at the bakery once more. She'd take some Danish pastries for Michelle and Penny, her workers. And rather than wanting to race back and take charge in the shop she quite pictured herself putting her feet up with yet another cup of tea to enjoy another sweet treat.

She waved to Joel as she came out of the bakery and he drove past with the car window down.

Rose laughed to herself. Her imagination was running riot, thinking not only could Penny take on the business side of the shop, what if she and Joel got together! The way her daughter had reacted to Joel when he came into the boutique had caught Rose's attention like an addictive twist in a soap opera. Her daughter had turned the poor boy down all those times in high school but here he was, fully grown and a wonderful man who was kind, down to earth and still seemed as interested in Penny as he was back then.

Rose crossed over towards Rose Gold Bridal. Maybe if Penny stayed long enough in Saxby Green she'd give him a chance.

Since Mallory had arrived in the village Rose had tried to be cautious when she went to and from the shop because it would be far too awkward to bump into her. Mallory was her niece and yet, she didn't know her at all. Part of her wished she did, she and Penny were so close, but Gigi had ruined that for all of them and it was easier to keep her distance.

But she needn't have worried about seeing Mallory because what she saw in the window of her own shop as she reached the other side of the road was enough of a shock.

She stopped in her tracks.

Her mouth fell open.

'It can't be...' she said out loud.

What she was looking at wasn't the white high-necked design with lace across the front that had been on the mannequin the last time she was here.

Now, she was looking at a dress that melted her heart because of the memories it came with. The cream, ankle-length gown with sequins and hand sewn details was one of a kind, a thing of beauty.

She'd recognise it anywhere.

Because she'd designed and made it all those years ago in her teenage bedroom in her former family home in a street not too far from here.

And she'd made it with her sister.

25

PENNY

Penny finished in the bathroom out the back of the shop. Her heart was doing double time waiting for the inevitable showdown between Gigi and Rose and her and Mallory.

She checked her watch again. Any minute now and Mallory would be walking over with Gigi on their way back from the station. Any minute now and Rose would be back from her visit with Millie.

Any minute now and all hell would break loose.

The dress was in the window and there was no turning back.

The local press had jumped quickly onto the story of the dress and Penny had already shared the published piece on social media via the Facebook page and the Instagram account she'd set up for Rose Gold Bridal. She'd used hashtags with the name of the movie, the name of the actress, other hashtags for brides-to-be that she thought might garner attention.

It was funny. She didn't know brides or the wedding business, but being here had a certain magic to it. Her mother was lucky to have talent and business acumen. Penny had the latter but no talent for dressmaking. Michelle had been talking to her earlier about how she had once dreamed of her own shop but decided she didn't have the business knowledge to make it work and it had got Penny to thinking, what would it be like if she managed the shop and kept Michelle here to work her magic with the gowns? There would probably be too much work for just one person with the ability to know one end of a sewing machine from the other but perhaps they could take someone else on part time?

Michelle had helped her get the dress onto the mannequin and into the window and when Penny emerged into the shop Michelle turned to her. 'You said that it was a long story when I asked about the dress,' she said.

'You could say that.'

'And I assume this story involves Rose?'

'Of course it does.'

Michelle looked awkward. 'Then I think you should know, she's outside, and she doesn't look happy.'

Penny took a few steps closer to the front door of the shop and came face to face with her mother who was standing on the pavement not moving an inch.

'I'll take my lunch now,' said Michelle.

'Probably a good idea.' Penny had prepared for this, but seeing her mother's fury, she hadn't quite prepared for feeling so terrible. 'See you in—' But Penny didn't add 'in an hour' because in her peripheral vision on the opposite side to Rose she saw Mallory come into view and moments later, Gigi.

Michelle scarpered. Penny stood in the doorway, the other three women stood out on the street in close proximity to one another.

Gigi was the first to speak. 'You two girls had better have a damned good explanation for this.'

Rose's eyes flitted to her sister. She looked bewildered, as if a fondness had taken over her before her expression changed to a veil of fury coming down like blackout blinds closing out the light.

'You'd better all come inside,' said Penny.

She turned the sign on the door to closed and ushered them all out the back.

Penny hated the look of pain on her mother's face, hated that they'd done this to her. And to Gigi. But Gigi wouldn't have come to the village unless Mallory had taken the dress and Rose wouldn't be hanging around if they hadn't taken a drastic step. She'd be hiding if she knew her sister was anywhere in the vicinity.

Mallory looked just as gutted as Penny was. Penny could see she'd been crying.

Nobody accepted the offer of tea and so Mallory reiterated her father's dying wish that Gigi and Rose try to repair their relationship. Penny ran through the reasons for putting the dress in the window.

And then silence.

Penny couldn't stand it. She was first to speak up again. 'I know this was a drastic thing to do—'

'I'll say,' Rose interrupted with more than a bite in her tone.

'We wanted to take the risk,' said Penny. 'We thought it might be worth it. You were once so close. You're sisters. Family. It's not our right to know what happened between you but we're hoping you'll tell us and that you can find a way to at least speak to each other.' She looked across at Mallory. 'Mallory and I both know that if it was us, we'd be devastated to lose each other.' Penny's mouth felt dry. This was nosey, intrusive, and yet she had no regrets. Even if all that happened now was that Gigi and Rose had a row and went back to shutting each other out, at least they'd tried because from what Penny and Mallory had discussed over time, neither of their mothers had been at peace with the end of their relationship.

'It's nobody's business but ours,' said Rose, lips in a tight thin line, eyes trained on a row of white dresses at the side of the shop.

'Mum, you mean the world to me, Gigi means the world to Mallory. Both of us want our mothers to be happy.'

This time Gigi spoke. 'I don't appreciate the meddling. And it was wrong to take the dress.'

Mallory opened her mouth to speak but no words came out.

Penny took charge. 'It was wrong, but we were trying to do something right. We knew you'd never come here again, Gigi, not unless you had a big reason to. And Mum, you were never going to reach out to Gigi. Each of you thinks you were wronged by the other one. Mum, doesn't it mean something that Hector died and one of his dying wishes was for Gigi to come and find you?'

Rose looked up then, her eyes glassy with tears, her lips relaxed some more but still unable to speak.

'Dad really wanted that, Aunt Rose,' said Mallory. Rose seemed to let a little bit of her anger go at her niece using the identifier that linked them as family out loud. 'He never told me anything about why the two of you fell out, but that was what he wanted.' She looked at her own mother. 'He really did, Mum. And now you're here. You might leave soon, but I really hope you don't. I really hope you and Rose can both find some kind of peace because whatever went on has been eating you up for years.'

Gigi seemed about to protest but she said nothing.

Penny looked at Rose. She knew her mother. She was just

as hurt and that hurt had chipped away at her over time. Her way of coping had sounded much the same as Gigi's – to not talk about it. And if she thought she was completely in the right, Penny knew her mother would be yelling right now. Yet she wasn't, which suggested there was some remorse in there somewhere for her part in all of this.

Penny stood next to her mother. 'Mum, you never told me about the dress that started it all.'

'I didn't see the point. The dress was gone.' She didn't even look at Gigi.

'You were both so young when you made it, your dress was in a movie, hired and worn by a famous actress. Do you realise how incredibly proud I am of your talent?'

Rose's hand shook as she reached for her daughter's. She was usually so strong and in control but right now she was vulnerable.

'We came runner-up in a big competition too,' said Rose. 'We didn't win but we had talent.'

Gigi harrumphed. 'You were the whizz more than I was.'

It was a start; they weren't exactly talking but they'd made an exchange of sorts.

'You never made much over the years, Mum.' Mallory was at Gigi's side. She unscrewed the cap on a water bottle and took several noisy glugs. 'You never seemed interested.'

Gigi shrugged. 'I did the basics. I didn't have quite the same passion as I got older.'

'The dress was made to your measurements,' said Mallory.

'We had to pick one of us to be the model. A mannequin helps but one of us had to wear it for the competition.' Gigi looked briefly at Rose but when Rose met her gaze she looked away.

'So what happened after the dress was finished?' Penny probed.

'It's in the past,' Gigi insisted.

'I don't think it is,' said Mallory. 'You and Aunt Rose have a lot to sort out.'

They stood in yet another silence that seemed to stretch forever until Rose spoke.

'We could've made a lot of money from that dress if we'd hired it out after it was returned once the movie shooting was complete,' said Rose. 'If *she* hadn't taken it. And I was going to use it to launch the shop. The shop we were supposed to open together.'

'It was never my dream!' Gigi roared at her sister.

'But all those nights in my bedroom working on the dress – you worked as hard as I did. And you said you wanted to open the shop with me. Or at least you didn't say that that wasn't what you wanted.'

Gigi took a while to reply and when she did, her voice softened. 'I liked dressmaking, as a hobby. I was never as passionate about it as you were.'

Rose didn't reply to that, instead she said, 'You abandoned our family, Gigi. You abandoned me.'

Gigi's voice caught. 'I had no choice. And I tried to back come here, make amends, but you were never around. And Mum didn't make it easy or pleasant so Hector left visits to me after that. Mum only gave me the time of day because I had Mallory and she adored her as much as her other grandchildren.'

'She was never an easy woman.' Rose looked at Gigi, an understanding passing between them.

Gigi told her sister, 'Having a shop was never my dream. I should have been clear about that with myself and with you.'

'It might have been your dream if you hadn't gone all gooey eyed over a man.'

Mallory went on the defensive. 'That man was my father.'

'I'm sorry,' said Rose. 'I shouldn't have said that.'

Mallory smiled her thanks for the apology and then turned to Gigi. 'Why *did* you take the dress? When it belonged to both of you, why take it?'

'I left half the money,' said Gigi.

'That was hardly the point,' Rose countered.

'Every time I put the dress on I thought about marrying Hector,' Gigi admitted. 'I'd imagine our special day, and all the days after when we would start our lives together.' But her pleasant tone faded. 'And I took the dress because my so-called sister did her best to take away the person who meant the most to me, the man I'd fallen in love with.'

Penny looked at Rose. 'Mum...' Her mother had paled and she looked down at her shoes the way a guilty child might do when they knew they were in the wrong.

Rose looked her daughter right in the eye and Penny knew that Gigi was telling the truth.

'You found the letter,' said Rose, turning to her sister. 'I... I—'

'It doesn't matter now,' said Gigi. 'What's done is done. I'm just glad I realised or I might never have seen Hector again.'

'I thought you were about to make a terrible mistake.' Rose's voice had a hint of fear when she spoke. 'I thought of how much you loved your family, the village, and I didn't want you to ruin your life because I knew Mum would never forgive you if you went off with him. I worried he didn't have the right intentions, I—'

'It was my choice!' Gigi yelled. 'You're not God, you don't get to decide who should end up with whom.'

Things were unravelling again and Mallory looked like she'd rather be anywhere than here. She was quiet, probably regretting upsetting her mother so much despite their best intentions. Penny was feeling the same.

'I know it was your choice,' said Rose timidly. 'But I thought I was doing the right thing. I was trying to help keep you safe.'

All four of them stood out back and the only thing to interrupt them was Michelle returning from lunch. Penny rallied and went into the shop, turned the sign to 'Open', and Michelle, being a professional, didn't ask for any explanations.

Rose was the first to come through from the back, acknowledging Michelle but not saying goodbye to Penny before she left.

Gigi was next. Out she went. Away from the shop.

And then came Mallory. 'I should go after Mum.'

But Penny caught Mallory's arm. 'Maybe let her cool down first.' She nodded to Michelle that she'd watch the shop while Michelle carried on working out back.

The shop was noticeably quiet once the drama dissipated.

Penny and Mallory stood next to each other adjacent to the display table in the middle of the shop. They looked at the back of the dress on the mannequin, the dress that had caused trouble spanning six decades.

'Do you wish we hadn't done it?' Penny asked.

Mallory shook her head. 'I'm glad we did it. They were both upset, rather than absolutely furious. There's something still there between them, I'm sure there is.'

'How do you do that?'

'How do I do what?'

'See the good in a situation? All I see is two angry mothers, two silly daughters messing in their business, and a whole heap of shit to come our way.' She didn't get a reaction and when she looked at Mallory, Mallory had a hand on her head. 'Have you got a headache?'

'You could say that. But it's fine. It's tension. I'll have a walk around, cool off.'

'I can get you some painkillers?'

'I'm fine.' She managed a smile. 'Do you think my mum or yours will come in and take the dress?'

'Well, my mum lives upstairs so I'd say she's the more likely of the pair. But I don't think she'll do it.' After a beat she said, 'I hate that she tried to stop your parents from being together.'

'It sounds like she thought she was doing the right thing. It was a different time in the sixties. It makes me realise how lucky we are now not to face the same level of opposition.'

'It must have been very difficult. And now I guess we just have to brace ourselves for whatever round two brings us when your mother or my mother comes at us again.'

'I think I'll head home and have a rest first; I'm going to need some energy for that.'

'You go back to the cottage and try to relax.' Because she looked even more exhausted than Penny felt with all of this.

When the bell above the door tinkled shortly after Mallory left, Penny expected it to be their 3 p.m. appointment but instead it was Joel.

'I'm here to unblock those gutters outside, thought I'd tell you in case you hear me making a noise and wonder what it is,' he said with his trademark smile, the same smile Penny could remember from all those years ago.

Penny couldn't recall booking him in to do the guttering but before she could say that he said, 'I'll do it today. Rose told me it's been a while since they were last cleared.'

So her mother had sent him in. She almost laughed. Rose would've loved to have been here now, to see Penny's unease around a man who made her feel so much younger than fifty years old.

'Email me the invoice at the end,' she said, drinking him in. He wore a cotton shirt well, and dirty jeans, due to his trade, and he looked good. At least his presence helped to take her mind off everything else that was going on.

'Will do.' He paused but when neither of them said anything he hooked a thumb over his shoulder. 'I'll get on then.'

'Great.'

Imagine if her board meetings ran like this. They'd never get a thing done.

He left her to it, went outside and from where she was standing she could see him pulling the ladder from the roof of his truck ready to carry round to the side.

She turned her back. She wasn't about to be caught ogling.

She was about to get her mind back to business when the door opened again. She looked up and smiled, ready to see Joel but instead it was someone else.

Carlos leaned in the doorway, his hand still on the handle. 'There's my girl.'

He was here again, already? It felt like he'd only just left. Which he had really. She was used to seeing him a lot when she was in London but down here it felt more jarring, the surprise something she could've done without on today of all days.

She smiled despite everything she had whirling around in her head and went over to greet him with a hug. But she pulled away when he tried to kiss her. 'Not here,' she said. 'It's a professional business.'

'Sorry, I missed you, that's all.'

She led the way towards the back of the shop. 'What are you doing in Saxby Green again so soon?'

'Is that a problem?'

'No, not at all. Just a surprise.' One she wasn't all that impressed with. She needed space and if he kept turning up, she wasn't going to get it.

When Michelle came out to the shop front Penny had an excuse to step away from his side and she made the introductions even though they had met once before.

'I'll look after the shop if you want to go up to the flat,' said Michelle.

'That would be great. Just give me a yell when you need me.'

Up in the flat, Carlos dropped his holdall in the hallway and they went into the kitchen.

'Coffee?' Penny offered, taking two mugs from the cupboard because she already knew what his answer would be.

'Yes please.' He hugged her from behind making it difficult to move over to get a teaspoon from the drawer, the milk from the fridge. This was the total opposite of the space she needed.

'I've booked us in to the same hotel as before,' he said when he finally backed off to let her finish the coffees.

'It's going to be really difficult to get away just now. It's a crazy time – Gigi is here.'

'Wow, so the sisters have come face to face?'

'You could say that.'

'And was it high drama?'

Penny handed him his coffee. '*Very* high drama.'

'Did they thank you for meddling?'

'Not quite.' She held her mug of coffee and leant against the benchtop while she recapped about the dress going on the mannequin, both sisters seeing it at around the same time, the showdown earlier on, the local press running the article and the social media she hoped would help the shop.

'You sound as though you're taking the bridal business by storm. I knew you'd take charge, but you'll love being back at work when you can get your teeth into something a bit bigger.' He slurped his coffee. 'I know you well.'

She smiled. Did he really?

Did he really know her at all?

Because she'd only just started to get to know this new version of herself. And it was one that wasn't quite so hungry for the corporate game or the London life any more, it was one that was starting to appreciate a village away from it all and a business that she was beginning to fall for more than anything else.

26

MALLORY

'Mum, please talk to me.' Mallory was sitting in her mother's bedroom at the pub. At least Gigi hadn't turned her away when she came here, there was always that possibility.

'What were you both thinking?' Gigi stood, looking out of the window, across the beer garden and to the field beyond.

When Mallory said nothing she turned around. 'You think you can fix me and Rose just like that? Too much happened, too much you don't understand.'

Mallory sat down on the edge of the bed. 'So why don't you try explaining it to me? Forget for a moment that I stole the dress and brought it here *and* that it's currently in the window of your sister's bridalwear shop. Forget that and for now tell me what I don't know, tell me what happened.'

'It was all such a long time ago.' She'd gone back to looking out of the window. 'I never thought I'd see Rose again.'

Mallory waited a beat. 'How did it feel? Seeing her?'

'Strange. Sad.'

'Dad wanted you to see her again. He never told me anything about her or that time in your life, but he would've been worried about how you'd cope when he was gone. I suspect asking me to get you to talk to Rose was his way of helping even when he was no longer here.' Mallory gulped, the poignancy of her words almost getting the better of her.

'She betrayed me,' said Gigi.

'You don't mean—'

Gigi turned round. 'No, nothing like that. She wasn't interested in Hector.' She pulled on her lambswool cardigan. It was colder in here than the outside; this side of the pub wouldn't get the sun until much later. 'Hector came to the village to see me one day. I'd been unwell, I hadn't been to London, and he was worried.'

'That sounds like Dad.'

'He went to the house and my mother told him to go away, told him he wasn't welcome and never would be. It upsets me even now to think how much she despised him simply because of the colour of his skin. I never forgave her for that, you know. She only had me back in her life because of you, because she wanted to see her grandchild.'

'She still loved you.'

'In her own way.' She pulled her cardigan tighter. 'Hector wrote me a letter, he was going to drop it at the house, but he knew he'd have to wait until dark so my mother didn't see him and even then it would be a risk. He saw Rose by the river while he was waiting around for night to descend and he asked her to pass it to me instead. But she never did. I found it almost a week later in a drawer in her bedroom. Hector was worried that I had changed my mind about him. He gave me a day and time to meet him and said if I didn't go then he would respect my decision but he would never stop loving me.

'Everyone else was out of the house that day. And I knew

what I needed to do. So I packed my bags, left a note for my parents, took the dress and I went to meet your dad.'

'Oh Mum...'

'I came so close to never seeing him again. We might never have shared our lives if my mother and then Rose had had their way. And you would never have been born.' The thought seemed to soften her towards Mallory, despite what she and Penny had done.

'I went to London where Hector and his family lived. They took me in, they were very kind.'

'Did you miss your family?'

'Of course I did.' Dewy-eyed she added, 'I even missed Rose despite what she'd done. But I was safe, Hector's family were warm, welcoming, accepting. They were nothing like our mother was when it came to race and relationships. It broke my heart that I left my dad behind and I wrote to him a fortnight after I left. He wrote back to me, but I hate that I didn't see him as much as I should have because of your gran. I'd brought shame to them, she said.

'I took the dress out of anger, out of spite, but also because I'd always imagined wearing it to marry your father. I knew I'd never be able to afford to buy my own wedding dress either. We had a very hard start to our lives together, your dad and I.'

Gigi went to sit next to Mallory on the bed. 'London was easier than a small village like this though. We managed to rent a room in a house of multiple occupation when your dad's family returned to the Caribbean. They never really settled in London but Hector had, with me and with his work. I got a second job as a secretary to make ends meet. Hector continued to work on the railways, and we got married at a registry office without any of our loved ones there. When we came outside there was a group of men hurling abuse at us – they said the most ghastly things, but I held your dad's hand tight, I never wanted to let him go.'

'I can't imagine what it must have been like for you. Dad never told me much.'

'He didn't want his pain to become yours.'

'I understand that.' She'd do anything to protect Jilly. It wasn't always possible but you did it when you could. 'Did Rose ever try to get in touch with you over the years?'

'I think she was too angry that I'd left without saying goodbye and that I'd taken the dress we made together.'

'You must have been so upset with her for hiding the letter.'

'I was incredibly upset about that, but also I was so sad I'd lost my sister. In all the times I'd imagined marrying Hector, I'd always pictured Rose at my side. And then all of a sudden she wasn't.'

'It's why I wanted the two of you to come face to face again.'

Gigi sighed. 'You couldn't have thought of a less dramatic way?'

Mallory leaned her head on her mother's shoulder. 'Your dress has a history, it was famous for being worn in a movie.'

'None of that mattered to me. I just wanted to marry Hector.'

'Were you upset that your parents weren't there?'

'More so about Dad than Mum. He told me once, when Mum wasn't in the room, that he thought Hector was kind, a man of the deepest sincerity. He only met him a few times – the first not long after we got married and I came here to see them. Dad was disappointed he never got to give me away, he shook hands with Hector while Mum made tea, kept it civil, but she couldn't even look Hector in the eye.

'Me and Dad exchanged a lot of letters after I left. Mum never told him not to write to me, she never intercepted our correspondence. When you came along they both visited us in London. Mum congratulated us and she loved you at first sight.' A sad smile accompanied Gigi's recall of what went on all those years ago. 'But even if she'd warmed slightly to Hector, by then she'd already damaged what might have been. All she should have wanted was for her child to be happy, cared for, loved. And I was. She couldn't see that because of her own prejudices, but it was a different time, maybe I can't blame her entirely. She was a good mother in many ways.'

'I'm sorry it was so hard for you and Dad. I know how lucky I was at school. I had a few digs about my dad being black but it never really snowballed. I guess there were enough people who accepted it that what prejudice remained became watered down.'

'It was hard,' said Gigi. 'But we were still happy. Even happier when you came along and then Jilly filled our hearts even more.' She smiled. 'Have you heard from my beautiful granddaughter by the way?'

'I have. She's having a brilliant time camping.'

'She told me you've been getting her to do some school work before returning in September.'

'I had to, Mum. She's been falling behind a bit but now she seems to be making an effort. And I've lined up my house sitter, Skye, to tutor her come September, get her school work back up to scratch. It's a better option than me trying to teach her anything.'

'Children don't want to listen to their parents. I never did.'

'I hope Jilly listens to me a while longer. I want her to be happy, to have a good life.'

'And she will. She has you. You're a good mother.'

Should she tell her now? Should she tell her why she'd

come here, why the desperate need to put plans into place, to have Gigi settled and Jilly surrounded by her loved ones?

But when Gigi stood up again and went over to the kettle she'd missed her moment.

Gigi picked a tea bag from the selection. 'I think I need to be on my own for a bit now, Mallory. Today has been a lot to take in.'

Mallory shouldn't be surprised. She picked up her bag. 'I understand. Thank you for talking to me about it. You know where I am if you need me.'

She kissed her mother on the cheek but before she crossed the room Gigi's voice followed her. 'Penny seems rather lovely. I wish I'd been able to get to know her before.'

Mallory stopped, her hand on the door knob. 'She's not only my cousin, she's my best friend.'

Gigi turned and went over to the sink, filled the kettle at the tap.

And Mallory left her to it.

* * *

Mallory called Skye as she left the pub. She liked to check in, ask whether Cedella was behaving – she was – and see that the house was still okay, that the garden was surviving.

'Cedella is insisting on sleeping at the end of my bed.' Skye was cautious in her delivery.

'She's naughty. She knows she sleeps downstairs but I'm not surprised she's pushing it... it's totally up to you, if you're happy with her there then let her stay. Jilly does it sometimes.' She used to tell her daughter off but lately she hadn't had the heart to. Mind you, she suspected that in the long run she wasn't doing Jilly any favours by letting her have more of a free rein.

She didn't need to contact a parenting guru for advice on that one.

Skye chattered on. She told Mallory she'd got a job at the local pub for four nights a week starting in a fortnight and she envisioned being able to save money to take the course she so wanted to do and start a career in teaching.

'I'm really pleased for you,' Mallory said as she walked down towards the river. 'I'm glad things are working out. Are you still interested in renting my spare room?'

'If it's still on offer? Don't feel you have to. The pub has a room I can stay in.'

'You choose, Skye. If you'd rather stay there, I'm happy with that, but if you'd like to be at my home I'm equally happy to give that a go.'

'Maybe we do a trial run. You might find me annoying.'

Mallory laughed. 'You might find me unbearable. Or Jilly.'

Skye's own laughter faded. 'I couldn't have done any of this without your help. I just... well, I don't know how to possibly thank you.'

'I was helping out a friend.' Silence. 'Hello?' And then a sniffle. 'Skye?'

'Nobody has ever given me so much consideration. I don't know what to say.'

'Just say you'll still be happy to tutor Jilly for me, it's a real weight off my mind. And Jilly's. She won't want me attempting to tutor her. I'll pay a good rate, we'll organise the particulars when I'm back.'

After her call Mallory stood by the river, looking at the water, the contented little ripples as the current took it one way. She'd picked up a cinnamon bun from the bakery and sat down on the nearby bench to enjoy it. Walking the Thames Path when she was at home in Marlow was a wonderful escape, but this was different, this was far away from it all and something she really needed.

She turned when she heard her name and she watched Will McGregor coming towards her.

Oh, how she wished it were different. Before her diagnosis she would have been thrilled to have the attention, hopeful that something more might happen between them, but how could she possibly even think that way now?

'Nice?' He nodded towards her cinnamon bun, the bun she was now self-conscious about finishing in front of him. That was when you knew you were interested in a man – when eating in front of him was difficult to do.

'Very good. Highly recommend.'

'I seem to have a knack at spotting you after you've been to the bakery.'

'Yes, it would seem that way.'

He sat down on the opposite side of the picnic bench. 'So is it comfort food?'

'What makes you ask that?'

'You looked deep in thought. I said your name a few times and you didn't hear me.'

'Sorry, got a lot on my mind, that's all.'

'I'm a good listener if you need an ear. I saw you earlier. I walked past the bridal boutique and you and Penny were in there with Rose and Gigi. It looked serious.'

'Our mothers are not happy with us.'

When he smiled creases deepened on either side of his face near his temples. 'You're a bit old to be in trouble with your mother, aren't you?'

She nibbled another piece of cinnamon bun. 'Just a bit. But we did a bad thing.'

'I told you, I'm a good listener. And besides, I'm waiting for my dad to finish with the doc. He needs a lift home but he'll be an hour or so, so I'm just hanging around, lost.'

'You really want to hear it? I probably shouldn't tell you, it's their business, but I might explode if I have to keep another thing quiet.'

'Then go for it.'

And she did. She told him everything she knew about Rose, Gigi, Hector, the dress, the shop, the two sisters, the betrayals and the shattered dreams. She told him what she and Penny had done, about the dress in the window.

'You know I'd heard about a movie being filmed here,' he said, 'but I never heard about the wedding dress. Bit before my time.'

'Rose would've kept it all quiet once the dress was gone, I suspect.'

'Seems very sad that it came between them.'

She popped the rest of the cinnamon bun into her mouth. 'Me and Penny might well have been crazy to think bringing the dress here was a good idea, but it at least got Gigi and Rose in the same place. It's a start.'

'It sounds like you did it for the right reasons. You were thinking about your mothers. I get that. My parents are doing okay but Dad is really showing his age, he's slowed down a lot. I worry about what it will be like for Mum if he goes first, what it would be like for him if it was the other way round.'

'Losing Dad left a gaping hole for my mum. It's really hard losing a parent and seeing the one left behind suffering as they try to adjust to a life without them in it.'

'And it's hard for you too, I bet.'

'It has been, yes.' In more ways than he realised. She scrunched up the empty paper bag. 'I'd better get going.'

He checked his watch. 'I should go too. Time got away with me, I was enjoying talking to you.'

She felt herself warm to him even more. 'You were right, you know.'

'About what?'

'You're a good listener.'

They began walking up the grass bank, back to the main street.

'What are you doing tomorrow?' he asked before they reached the top.

'Tomorrow?'

'Would you like to have lunch or dinner with me?'

Oh, if only. 'I can't.'

'Breakfast then...' He came closer, his presence looming over her, not in a threatening way but in a way that made her want to yell the word, 'Yes!'

'You want a breakfast date?' She grinned. 'Sounds a little odd.'

'We'll have breakfast down on the riverbank at one of the barbecues, 9 a.m.?'

She should say no. She shouldn't get involved. She needed to keep her focus on the reason she'd come here.

She could feel the heat of his body so close to hers; it had a power that made her unable to think clearly.

'Yes.' The word was out. And when she looked up at him his face had broken into the brightest of smiles.

27

PENNY

It was already light outside, given it was the summer, but it was nowhere near opening time for the shop. Penny was down here early to take a delivery of fabric at 7.30 a.m. Yesterday she'd left Michelle in charge as closing time approached and with Rose still not talking to her she'd gone to the hotel to meet Carlos. She'd stayed with him until almost midnight when she came back here leaving him to get a good night's sleep before an early start to return to London in time for his meeting. He'd been unimpressed that she had so much on her mind when he thought he was going to get an evening of passion. But she hadn't had time to worry about his feelings when she was worrying about her mother and what on earth happened next.

Penny had woken up in a cold sweat in the middle of the night, having had a dream that someone had smashed the glass at the front of the shop, reached in and taken the mannequin along with the dress. She'd crept down here in the early hours to check everything was as it should be. It was, of course, and she couldn't help wondering how many nights that dream would be on replay.

Mallory had called her when she was at the hotel last night – another gripe for Carlos was that she'd taken the call – and shared the information she'd got from her own mum. It appeared both women had done things wrong, each was hurt, but Mallory and Penny still hoped they would find a way through this. Surely there was a chance?

Penny made herself a mug of tea out the back and took it into the shop. She sat on the stool near the till. This was one of the nicest times of the day and very different to starting a day in the corporate world. There she'd made herself a coffee but got straight on with what she was doing – scheduling a meeting, going through notes, working on a PowerPoint, studying the figures. There was no sitting back and just taking it all in like she was doing now.

After she finished her tea, Penny went upstairs to get ready for the day. Rose walked past her as she emerged from her bedroom but offered nothing other than the silent treatment for now. She had to talk to her eventually but there was no telling how long it would be before she did.

Back downstairs once again she'd only just turned the sign on the door to read 'Open' when the phone by the till rang. And any melancholy from the situation dissipated when the customer told her how they'd come to know about Rose Gold Bridal.

The woman on the other end of the line, the mother of the bride, told her, 'I'm from Wales and I remember that movie! The dress was so beautiful and I wished I'd been able to have one just like it.'

'Did you see the article in the press?'

'No, I saw it on Facebook. I was searching wedding dress shops and found it under a hashtag. I can't remember which one now. I'd have to look. Anyway, I told my daughter we should go and see the dress in the shop – she's seen the movie too – and that maybe we would find something equally as beautiful for her big day. We'll be in London to see a show and we thought we might make an appointment to come and see you.' She barely took a breath in her whole delivery.

Penny could see how Rose's passion had kept burning all these years if this woman was anything to go by. The enthusiasm, over-the-top explanations to a stranger, it was all part of it.

'Can she try on the actual dress?' the woman went on.

Penny wondered what size the daughter was. She imagined a *Cinderella* situation except with a dress rather than a shoe that didn't fit, women trying to squeeze into the dress just because they wanted it to be perfect for them.

Tactfully, and because the dress wasn't for sale or hire, she said, 'It's more of a display piece, but we have others with similarities, or, of course, we do make to order. Now when would you like to come in?'

She noted the appointment in the book and as soon as she'd done that she picked up her phone to text her mother. She wouldn't try telling her face to face, maybe she had a better chance of her mother reading a text from her hiding place in her bedroom upstairs. In her message she told Rose all about the call, how the customer had responded to her post on social media. The details didn't matter but she wanted to get Rose to at least start facing reality. The dress was here in her shop at long last, Gigi was finally back in the village. Perhaps it was time for the sisters to rake over the past and make some sense of it.

When the bell above the door tinkled, Penny looked up from the desk expecting to see Michelle but it wasn't Rose's talented assistant, it was Mallory.

Before Mallory could say a word Penny blurted out about the dress enquiry.

'Wow, that was fast.'

Penny had hold of her phone. 'I'm going to look on Instagram and Facebook, see how many likes we've had, how many shares we've got.'

'It's good news, Penn.'

'I hope so.' She frowned. 'What are you even doing here so early? Everything okay? Well, apart from the obvious.'

Mallory smiled and Penny noticed the carefully applied subtle make-up against her glowing dark skin, the look of someone who hadn't had the stress of the last twenty-four hours thrown at them, even though Penny knew different.

'What's going on with you? I thought you'd be as stressed as I am. Rose isn't even talking to me.'

'She'll come round.'

Penny observed her friend. 'And you cannot stop smiling.' She also had on a short, sexy dress that showed off beautifully slender legs.

'I have a date.' The words spilled out of her.

Penny gasped. 'With Will?'

'A breakfast date.' She beamed but her exuberance soon faded. 'I'm nervous. I shouldn't be doing this.'

'Yes, you should.'

'Can I have a drink of water? I didn't bring a bottle with me.'

'Come on out back.' She led the way, filled a glass of water at the tap in the tiny area for the purpose, well away from the machines and fabrics. 'You look... well, you look gorgeous. And a date is a great distraction from the trouble we're in.'

'I should've said no, but—'

'No, you shouldn't have.' She handed Mallory the glass. 'I'm glad you said yes.'

Mallory drank the entire glass of water in a few thirsty gulps.

'Slow down or you'll need the toilet, maybe at the most inopportune moment.'

Mallory handed her the empty vessel. 'Do I look all right?'

'More than all right; he'll be blown away.'

Penny's mobile went and when she saw it was Carlos she sent it to voice mail.

'Ignoring him?' Mallory asked.

'He was here last night.'

'No way. Booty call?'

'Felt that way. He wasn't happy I didn't stay at the hotel with him overnight. I told him there's a lot going on right now but he doesn't get it, he doesn't understand that this is our family and it's in trouble.'

The phone in the shop went again and that call Penny answered.

She came back to Mallory who'd sat down on the stool next to one of the machines, another half-drunk glass of water in her hand.

'That was another call in response to the press coverage. This time a local saw the article in the newspaper and contacted a friend who has been looking all over London and not found what she wants in the way of a wedding gown. She's going to give this place a go. Can you believe it?'

'It's amazing. And Rose will think so too, eventually.'

'You're being very nice about my mother, your aunt, considering she almost stopped your parents being together.'

'I really do think Rose's heart was in the right place when she did it.'

'You're very kind. I mean, imagine if there hadn't been a Gigi and Hector, there would be no you. That would be terrible, unimaginable. The world would have been less bright, at least for me.' She noticed a look pass across Mallory's face that she didn't recognise. 'What have I said wrong?'

'Nothing, honestly.'

'There's something...' But then she understood. 'You must really like him. You really are nervous. And here I am running on and on. You need to go, don't be late for your date.'

'Can I use your bathroom before I go?'

'Told you you were drinking too much!' Her voice followed after Mallory who was already heading for the washroom facilities.

Penny turned her attention to the shop and when she turned around it wasn't Mallory coming up behind her. It was Rose. She'd emerged from her hiding place at long last.

'Hey Mum.'

Rose came and stood beside her daughter, both of them able to see the back of the dress in the window, and it was a good couple of minutes before she spoke.

'I can remember every stitch,' said Rose. 'I remember taking every measurement, the feel of the fabric and how beautiful Gigi looked every time she put it on.'

'It's a stunning gown.'

'We never thought we could do it. But we did.'

A voice came from behind them. Mallory. 'Mum was a beautiful bride.'

Rose turned. She looked at Mallory properly rather than scooting off like she usually did if they crossed paths. 'I'm very sorry for what I did, or almost did, to her and Hector.'

'You were young, the both of you were. I'm only sorry you

two have gone so many years angry with each other and not in contact. I know Mum has struggled with that.'

Rose nodded. 'Me too.' She cleared her throat. 'I'll go back up to the flat. I'm ready to talk, Penny, when Michelle gets here to look after the shop.'

'Okay.' Penny shared a smile with Mallory and when Rose had left she lifted up her hands, her middle fingers crossed over each index finger.

'Now you go have your date,' Penny urged when Mallory didn't look like she was going to budge. 'Don't keep him waiting.'

'Are you sure I look all right?'

'You look perfect. And remember, he's seen the goods already.'

Mallory left laughing, which made Penny smile.

She had a feeling that things were going to be just fine.

* * *

Penny waited for Michelle to take over and then went upstairs to the flat. Rose had already made the tea and Penny took her cup over to the sofa.

She didn't wait for Rose to start. She wanted to apologise first and foremost. 'I'm sorry that we went about things in a way that has hurt you, Mum. I know you're angry.'

Rose nodded. 'The thing is, I know why you both did it. And you're right, without a big nudge I don't think either of us would have made the move and tried to talk through what happened all those years ago.' She paused. 'As painful as it was, it was still good to see Gigi. She looks really well despite...'

'Losing Hector? Yes, she does. She's coping.'

'Hector was the love of her life.'

'He was.' Penny sipped her tea and when neither of them said anything else she told her mother, 'Gigi isn't happy, Mum. She's lonely. And I think you are too.'

'I'm fine, don't you worry about me.'

'But I do. So does Stephen. We know that you adore the shop, we also know you're struggling and both of us realise you've missed your sister ever since she left.'

'I tried to make a life without her. At first I was angry with her, then upset, then I'd get furious all over again. I think her leaving and taking the dress made me even more determined to make the shop work, to prove myself, to show that I had something too. But I never got over the pain of losing my sister to a man, the pain of our family splintering.' She looked embarrassed at her next admission. 'She must have hated me knowing I'd never passed her Hector's letter.'

'I'm not sure whether hate is the right word. But she would have been angry.'

'I really thought I was doing the right thing.'

'Tell me what happened, Mum. In your own words.' She already knew a lot of this from Mallory's talk with Gigi, but she wanted to hear it from Rose. 'How did Gigi meet Hector, how did they go from strangers to Gigi leaving her family behind?'

Rose started at the first day when Gigi lost her scarf and a man – Hector – came running towards them with it. Her sister had been smitten from that moment on.

'I was her alibi when they met up in London,' said Rose. 'I didn't mind too much, I spent hours in the haberdasheries, I was in my element. But I was still very worried about my sister. One day I stayed behind in the village and arranged to meet Gigi at the station after she'd been to London. I planned to lie low so our parents would never know and that was when I managed to get talking to a film crew.' Rose smiled. 'It's a great story.'

And she told it while Penny listened to every word. It sounded exciting, for both sisters, to have their dress worn by someone famous in a movie in the local village.

'I thought about hiring the dress out after that,' said Rose. 'I told Gigi that it could earn us even more money. I said it would help us save for one day starting up our own shop. I don't think I wanted to admit to myself that my dreams might not have been my sister's.'

'It sounds like you were the one with the passion for the bridal industry.'

'I have loved every moment of it,' said Rose. 'But now I'd like you to.'

'What do you mean?'

'I've been talking with Michelle. She loves her job here but has stopped wanting to run her own shop; she doesn't want the business side.'

'And you think I do?'

Rose shrugged. 'I'm not sure. But perhaps it could be good for you to have a change of scene and pace. You and Michelle seem to be making it work.'

'And you'd retire if the two of us took over?' Penny hadn't expected Rose to go from not talking to her to suggesting she be the one to take over the business, or at least part of it.

'I would.'

Penny felt an immense sense of relief hearing her mother say that, and something else... excitement. The same feeling she would've got once upon a time on a big project for a major corporation.

Penny remembered the two phone calls she'd had. 'Did you read my texts?'

'I did. And I'm impressed. I have no worries leaving the shop in your hands. Business will boom and I'll get to witness it with a cup of tea in hand and perhaps the odd visit to the shop downstairs for a chat with customers.'

'You sound really on board with the idea.'

'I am. But the question is, are you?'

'It's a big move, Mum.'

'Is that a *no*?'

'It's not a *no*, it's a *let me think about it*.' Penny smiled. 'Yours and Gigi's dress got new customers calling the shop and making plans to visit, that's quite something, isn't it?'

'It is. And I suppose I should say thank you for making it happen.'

Penny wasn't expecting her to do anything of the sort. 'Maybe in time you might.'

'Hmmm.'

'The dress really is absolutely stunning you know.'

'Gigi looked after it all these years.'

'It's not too late for you two to talk.'

'She'll never forgive me for my part and I'm not sure I can forgive her for taking the dress. I planned to use it to open the shop, to put it in the window just like it is now.'

Penny thought for a while. 'Perhaps this is even better. Perhaps this way the dress has created a bit of drama by appearing in the window after all these years.'

'Maybe you're right.'

'One caller asked whether the dress was for sale, if it could be tried on—'

Rose gasped. 'Please tell me you said no.'

'Of course I said no. I told them it's just on display, that's all.'

'I can imagine a *Cinderella* scenario, with the ugly sisters competing for the dress.'

Penny grinned. 'That's exactly what I was thinking when I was asked.'

'Gigi wouldn't want anyone trying it on. And neither would I.'

She waited a beat. 'You were nice to Mallory earlier.'

'She seems wonderful. You two have grown close.'

'She's my cousin, she's family, and she's my best friend as you know. She feels more like a sister which is why I feel your pain that you lost yours. I can't imagine losing Mallory.'

When the phone upstairs rang Penny picked it up after five or six rings, which usually meant whoever was in the shop was busy. 'Hello, Rose Gold Bridal, how may I help you?' Penny had been answering the phone up here like that ever since she was old enough to take phone calls. Sometimes it wasn't a customer but Rose had taught her, Stephen and Albert to be prepared.

'Customer.' She mouthed the word to her mum and then dealt with the call about opening times at the weekend. They should soon get less of those calls because a website would give the customer the pertinent information.

'Do you know why I called it Rose Gold Bridal?' Rose asked her the second she hung up the call.

'I assume because your name is Rose and Rose Gold is beautiful.'

'Almost, but not quite. Rose was, of course, for me, but Gold was because Gigi's middle name is Goldie.'

'I never knew that. And you used it even though you had fallen out and were angry with her?' She was surprised but now she knew, it showed that her mother hadn't ever forgotten the special relationship she'd once had with her sister.

'Deep down I was sad more than I was angry. Gigi was such a big part of the very first wedding gown that I ever made, or partly made, and I wanted to honour that.'

When the phone went again, this time Rose offered to answer. She asked the caller to hold and covered the receiver with her hand. 'You go down to the shop, Penny. Let Michelle know we're both still alive. She knows all about my idea that the pair of you run the place by the way.'

'Now why doesn't that surprise me?'

'Talk it over, see what you both think.'

Penny left her mother to take the call and smiled all the way back down the stairs, ready to talk to Michelle. She might have known her mother had already set things in motion. When she got an idea, she liked to see it through.

And as she and Michelle discussed how this new business arrangement might work she hoped that the special dress in the window wasn't only going to bring in new business but that it would eventually help Rose and Gigi find a way to put the past behind them.

She knew that was what Mallory wanted too.

28

MALLORY

If Mallory thought waking up in a cottage in Saxby Green was out of the ordinary, then waking up in a hospital bed took on a whole other dimension.

One minute Mallory had been finishing up a wonderful date with Will down by the river, and the next, she felt odd, like she wasn't really there at all, and then the ground suddenly got a whole lot closer as she lost consciousness.

She came round to Will at her side, ambulance sirens in the background. She was put onto a stretcher, then she was looking up at the inside of the moving ambulance and at paramedics monitoring her on the way to hospital. She drifted in and out. She wanted to go to sleep, for this all to be a dream. She wanted to be back there on the riverbank with the wonderful man who was interested in her.

She looked across the hospital room now. She was on a ward. Curtains were drawn around the patient in the bed opposite. Instead of her beautiful floaty summer dress she was wearing a hospital gown. The make-up she'd applied carefully, the hair she'd styled gently, making sure the scar from the biopsy was covered the way it usually was, would all be ruined by now.

'I've squeezed oranges to make juice.' It was the first thing Will had said to her when she met him on the riverbank this morning beside the public barbeques that nobody else was interested in pre-9 a.m. 'And now I've made myself sound like an idiot.'

'You haven't at all.' Maybe he was as nervous as she was. By the looks of things he'd arrived nice and early to set up. On top of a picnic blanket was a tray table upon which there was a carafe of juice, plates, cutlery, and napkins.

'I sound like I'm seeking approval for my juicing skills,' he said.

'You don't. And I love juice.'

He took in the sight of her when he got over his awkwardness at the conversation and oddly it felt more intimate than the day he'd seen her emerge from the water completely naked.

'You look beautiful,' he said.

'You look pretty good yourself,' she told him and meant it.

They had bacon, sausages, eggs cooked in a skillet, cooked tomatoes on the vine along with fresh sourdough. The breakfast feast was cleverly done, delicious and Mallory could barely move afterwards she'd eaten so much.

'We'll grab a coffee while we're at the café, it's only polite.' Will secured the hamper once they'd loaded everything back in and put it in the boot of his car. They'd been sitting on the riverbank a while as they ate and the skillets were cool, the food more or less gone, and they both needed to use the toilet if they were going to take a walk as Will had suggested.

The time together had flown by and Mallory had quite forgotten the reason she'd come to the village, the truth she hadn't yet shared. On this day she felt like a woman, a normal woman with a future ahead of her and perhaps even a man she might share it with.

With their coffees in hand after they used the facilities in the café, they headed back down the riverbank to the wide path that ran alongside it before it narrowed the further you got away from town. Mallory jumped when a swan leapt out of the water a little too close for her liking.

She stayed behind Will.

'It's not going to attack you,' he said.

'I don't trust them. They're serene and beautiful on the water, but not when they're out.' She walked fast enough that they left the swan in their wake and she recalled the story of how she and Penny had met.

'So your cousin saved you from a swan.' It was just about wide enough on the path to stay walking side by side. 'That's true friendship.'

'Have you got a close friend? Men aren't always like that, I guess.'

'Some are. I have a few friends, some closer than others. I've known some since school. Others I met later, like Joel. We met playing pool one night at the pub, I helped him out with some furniture he needed for his flat, we've been mates ever since.'

'I've not met him properly, but he seems keen on Penny.'

'We haven't talked about her. At least not yet.'

'Maybe he'll mention her soon.'

'I'll let you know.' He grinned.

'I consider myself a late bloomer when it comes to friendships, to be honest.'

'How so?'

'I didn't really gel with anyone at school, neither did Penny, so I think we found each other at the right time. I've made friends at work – one in particular, Sasha, she's wonderful. But

Penny has been my best friend for a long time. Knowing she was my cousin when we met made us curious about each other and it went from there.' She cleared her throat when her emotions almost took over with words that were so simple and yet at the same time were anything but with what was looming on the horizon. 'We were eighteen when we met, Penny and I. More than thirty years ago, which makes me feel really old. Which I am.' She laughed. 'I'm fifty. How old are you? I don't think I've asked.'

'Three years older than you. So that makes *me* definitely old.'

Will had commitments mid-morning so they turned and began making their way back towards the riverbank that would lead up to the street.

He took her empty coffee cup from her and threw it into the bin they were coming up to along with his own. 'I'd really like to see you again.'

She hadn't thought this through. You never went into a relationship assuming you were going to end up with that person, but there was always the possibility.

She didn't have the luxury of the dream, which made her feel as though she couldn't say yes.

'I'm only in the village for a short while,' she said.

'Why does that matter?'

She didn't answer, not until his hand found hers and she slipped her fingers between his.

'Will, I really do like you, but believe me when I say this: you don't want to get involved with me.'

He stopped then, faced her and grabbed her other hand, his fingers absentmindedly rubbing against hers. 'Are you a serial killer?'

'No.' She laughed. 'If I was, I'm hardly likely to admit it, am I?'

'Probably not.' He grinned. 'Are you running from one maybe?'

'Definitely not.' She laughed again. He had a way of making her feel at ease and he had no idea how much she needed it.

'Do you have a secret husband you haven't mentioned? A weird habit you think I won't like? A family who won't approve of me and my furniture fetish?'

'No secret husband. Thankfully I never married Jilly's father as he was never really on the scene. He wasn't interested in being a dad. He was a bit of a loser as it happened. I don't think I have any weird habits although you could try asking Penny that one. And I'm pretty sure if anything, your furniture fetish only enhances your appeal. My mother would approve.'

He tipped his head down, their faces so close she could feel the warmth of his skin. 'Then what could be so terrible to make me not want to do this again?' He didn't say that *this* meant a breakfast, he simply pressed his lips against hers and took her breath away.

When he pulled back they stared at one another. 'Am I in trouble for doing that?'

She shook her head. She kept hold of one of his hands and carried on walking along. They were back to the riverbank that led up to the bend in the high street.

And that was it, the moment her truth caught up with her. She'd had another seizure and woke up here in the hospital.

Will came in and sat on the edge of her bed. 'How are you feeling?'

She managed a weak smile. 'I'm okay. But I feel a bit stupid for collapsing like that.'

'It was a bit of a dramatic way to get out of a date, although it backfired because I got in the ambulance with you.'

She slotted her fingers between his when he picked up her hand.

The doctor hadn't been in to see her when she was awake yet. She knew that much. 'Have they told you anything?' Was it out of her hands? Would everyone know what was going on with her already? Had she messed this up by waiting so long to tell the truth?

But he shook his head. 'I'm not your next of kin. I admitted I barely knew you. I should've said I was your fiancé, then I might have found out all of your secrets.'

She held up her left hand. 'I don't see a diamond so you're out of luck.'

When she coughed, her mouth dry, he lifted the cup of water with the straw from her tray table near the bed and helped her take a sip.

Mallory laid her head back down on the pillow. 'Has anyone contacted my mum?'

'I've tried – you'd told me she was staying at the pub. I've called her there but she's out; they even gave me her mobile number when I said it was an emergency, but no answer. I'm working on it.'

'Thanks. You barely know me and you're doing all this.'

'Happy to. Would you like me to call Penny?'

'I think I need to see my mum first, if that's okay. But then I'd love Penny to come too. I could call her.'

'You rest, leave it to me. Once your mum has been in, I'll get Penny.'

She was struggling to keep her eyes open. Just like her first seizure, this one had left her spent and wanting to sleep the nightmare away.

But before she let herself give in to the exhaustion she remembered he'd had an engagement that morning. 'Did I make you miss your meeting?'

'I asked Dad to go. He went there in a taxi, said he was more than capable. One of the advantages of being a family business is that we tend to be pretty flexible doing one another favours. He's slowed down a lot but still likes to be involved.'

Mallory realised she'd closed her eyes when Will paused for a while.

'Sorry,' she said, opening them again.

'Don't be sorry, just get well.'

She gulped. She couldn't even promise him that.

'Why don't you rest? I'll go out into the corridor and try getting hold of Gigi again.'

She mumbled her agreement. Or at least she thought she did.

Mallory had known the time was fast approaching when she'd have to tell the truth. She just hadn't expected it to be so far out of her control. This latest seizure meant she had to do it now, and she needed it to be before Jilly came back from her camping trip. Everyone needed to be strong, coping in whatever way they could to make this easier for Jilly. Because her daughter was the biggest worry of all, and she wouldn't be here forever to protect her.

She must have drifted off because when she woke up Will had gone.

And so she closed her eyes again, giving in to the need to rest.

29

GIGI

Gigi couldn't see Penny in Rose Gold Bridal although she was standing a good fifteen metres away, in a position that would enable her to take one step out of view if she saw Rose's daughter, but in a position where she could see the dress.

She'd thought of the dress as *her* dress ever since she realised Rose had betrayed her and hidden the letter. Taking it had been revenge, but it had also been what she'd wanted all along. She hadn't told Rose that every time they worked on it, every time she put it on, she could see herself exchanging vows with the man she loved. And it was hardly surprising because Rose had never wanted to hear much about Hector, hear Gigi's dreams about sharing her life with him some day. She'd been jealous, Gigi was sure of it, but Gigi had also hoped that the jealousy would pass and her sister would be happy for her. Now it seemed she wasn't jealous at all. Instead she'd been worried about her sister and the man she wanted to spend her life with, concerned that she was going to turn her back on her family.

But it still hadn't been Rose's choice to make.

Gigi remembered the day she returned from London and Rose met her on the platform. Her sister told her a movie company were going to pay them to borrow the dress and part of Gigi had seethed at the thought of someone else wearing it but she wasn't daft, her half of the money could go towards the new life she and Hector dreamed of. It wasn't all bad.

But then she got sick. She didn't get to see the filming although she didn't care too much about that. All she really cared about was that she hadn't managed to get to London to see Hector for so long with her mother confining her to the house. She was panicked that he would think she was never coming to him again.

And then she'd found the letter.

She'd been furious. And she felt she had no other option than to leave Saxby Green and her family for good. Her mother in particular was never going to accept Hector. She knew her mother well enough to know what she thought of *those* people. *Those* people were people who weren't British born and bred, *those* people had come from other lands, *those* people looked different and talked different. Gigi longed to introduce the man she loved to her family but she knew deep down that as soon as she did there was a high possibility of her closing herself off to her family forever. So she had nothing to lose by making the decision to leave sooner rather than later.

Hector's family were wonderful to them. They accepted Gigi, gave her a roof over her head. It had been sad to say goodbye to them when they left London but she and Hector had each other. They got married – her in the dress of her dreams and Hector standing beside her, devilishly handsome in a dark suit with a rich cream handkerchief in the breast pocket.

Gigi had contemplated taking the dress back to Saxby

Green after she was married and she might well have done had she not been holding on to so much resentment at Rose hiding the letter. And Rose was talented, she could make another dress. She had the design sketched out after all – why not make another and pretend it was the dress worn in the movie?

With that thought, Gigi had held on to the dress but she knew the real reason that it wouldn't be returned was more that she didn't want to face Rose again; she didn't want to go back to the sister who'd betrayed her.

Gigi turned away from the shop. She'd seen enough for now.

She wasn't quite sure what she wanted to do with regards to the dress, how she really felt about Rose and whether she would try to speak to her properly, but she did know she wanted to talk to Mallory again.

She walked back to the pub and climbed the stairs to her room. She was going to call her daughter, she hated tension between them. She wanted to tell Mallory that she understood why she'd done it, that without the dress making its way to Saxby Green Gigi most likely wouldn't be here in the village right now. And she wanted to tell Mallory that her dad would be proud of her, that she was helping him get his second wish.

When she went into her room, her phone, which she'd left here on charge, was ringing.

Good. Hopefully it was Mallory, perhaps she'd get her here for dinner at the pub. They did wonderful food. And it would be nice, just the two of them, before Jilly was back in the village. They could talk, really talk, about everything. And perhaps Mallory might know how Rose was feeling, have some suggestions at where the pair of them might go from here.

But it wasn't Mallory.

A man on the other end identified himself as Will

McGregor and told her what had happened. 'Mallory collapsed down by the river,' he said, 'she's in the hospital, she seems fine, the doctors are running tests—'

She didn't let him get any further. 'I'm on my way.'

* * *

'My daughter Mallory Templeton was brought in,' Gigi told the harried ward clerk at the main reception in the hospital.

'One moment.'

I don't have a moment. But she kept that thought to herself. It was no use getting angry with anyone here, she knew from Mallory and her tales of the hospital she worked in that they were all doing the best they could despite enormous pressures.

The nurse didn't take too long to tell her where her daughter was and as Gigi made her way towards the lift and up to the appropriate floor before following the complex network of corridors, she wished Hector was at her side. She wished she still had his support, she was so lost without it.

When she found the right ward and the right bed, Mallory was asleep and Gigi took a seat on the chair quietly so as not to wake her.

She watched her daughter, this beautiful girl she loved with her whole heart. The day she was born Hector had been at work. He'd only just made it to the hospital on time before Mallory arrived screaming into the world minutes after he got there. And from that moment he doted on their daughter. Like many fathers, he was worried he wouldn't know what he was doing but he'd taken to parenthood easier than Gigi had – she blamed all the hormones surging around her body, but really he was calmer, more practical, and able to keep Mallory that way all through teething, the terrible twos and even the tumultuous teens. And then when Jilly came into their lives, Pappy Hector had forged the same sort of relationship with his granddaughter.

Gigi reached a hand out to stroke Mallory's hair the way she used to like when she was a young girl, but she withdrew her hand before it made contact, not wanting to disturb her.

Mallory had put them through the wringer over the years, as all daughters, maybe all children, did at some point. She'd been good at school but after that, fell into a relationship with a boyfriend who was known to local police for suspected burglary, not the sort of person they wanted their daughter involved with. She'd moved out with him too, caught up in the excitement of it all, his promises he would likely never keep. Hector had gone to bring her home and even though Mallory never said it, Gigi could tell when she got out of the car with all her belongings that night, that she had needed rescuing. Mallory had focused hard on getting into nursing after she came home and succeeded. She'd got her own place, continued to work hard, but then got together with Jilly's father. He wasn't a terrible person, but he wasn't exactly present, and Gigi and Hector had felt somewhat relieved when he'd walked away, disinterested in being a dad. Mallory chose to raise Jilly on her own and Gigi and Hector could see their daughter was the happiest she'd ever been.

'Nobody will ever look at me the way Dad looks at you,' Mallory had told her when Jilly's father was out of the picture.

'Oh love,' said Gigi. 'Your dad is rather special, but there's someone out there for you too.'

Mallory shook her head. 'I'm going to be a mum, that's my focus for now.'

'One thing at a time,' Gigi had told her.

At Mallory's bedside, Gigi looked around for a doctor but

nobody seemed to be coming their way. That had to be a good sign, didn't it?

She wondered what had made Mallory collapse in the first place – was it perhaps the heat of the day? The humidity could wreak havoc, especially at Mallory's age. When Gigi was in her late forties and early fifties, menopause had come knocking and with it a whole load of weirdness. She remembered telling Hector rather tearily one day to stick with her, hang in there, she knew she wasn't much fun to be around with the night sweats that saw her changing sheets and her nightwear more than a few times, the mood swings, the vertigo that had been terrible for a while.

Perhaps that was it – vertigo.

Gigi remembered it was Will who had called her at the pub. They'd been together – now he was a man unlike the others her daughter had been involved with over the years. Gigi liked what little she knew of him, and she knew his family were kind too.

Mallory stirred and Gigi reached out, stroked her hair the way she'd been longing to do since she arrived.

'I'm here, Mallory. It's me, Mum.'

Mallory tried to sit up but didn't quite manage it.

'No, no. You stay there. Don't try and move on my account.'

'Could you put another pillow underneath my shoulders?' she croaked.

Gigi did the honours. 'Better?'

Mallory smiled. 'I can see you properly now.' She reached out and held her mother's hand. 'Mum...' Her bottom lip quivered.

'I'm here.'

'Mum... there's something I need to tell you.'

* * *

Gigi was in a daze when she left the ward. The doctor had been in and delivered the same information Mallory had except with a lot more medical jargon. But it all meant the same thing in the end, didn't it?

Gigi hadn't wanted to leave but Mallory needed to rest and Gigi needed to absorb the information without her daughter seeing the utter terror on her face. It wasn't going to help her and what she wanted more than anything was to be there for Mallory.

Gigi saw Will in the corridor. He'd been hovering there the whole time Gigi was with her daughter and he offered to take Gigi back to the pub in Saxby Green.

'Does Will know?' Gigi had asked her daughter after Mallory told her she had an inoperable brain tumour.

Mallory shook her head. 'Not yet, but I'll tell him.'

Gigi had put her head on Mallory's bed and cried, this time Mallory shushing her and reaching out her hand to stroke her mother's hair.

Will talked while he drove her back to the village, he told Gigi about the breakfast he'd made, how he was going to do it all over again when Mallory was better.

'That's a lovely idea,' she said, looking out of the window so he couldn't read her expression, her devastation that such a simple thing as a date was perhaps out of reach.

Mallory liked Will, she'd admitted that too, but she'd said it wasn't fair on him to get involved when she wasn't going to last forever.

That phrase had set off a fresh new batch of tears both from her and Mallory this time. They'd held each other, gripping on for dear life, and when Mallory said that Jilly didn't know, that she was here in the village to get her ducks in a row, Gigi had smiled at the memory of Hector using that expression.

And then her heart had broken all over again that poor Jilly would have to learn of this devastating diagnosis, that her time with her mother would be cut short.

'Thank you for bringing me back.' Gigi toyed with the handles on her handbag on her lap as she sat in the passenger seat of Will's car.

'You're welcome. We're almost there.' He turned left, into the high street and past the sign welcoming them to the village.

Gigi clutched her bag tighter. 'If it's not too much trouble, can you drop me off somewhere else?'

'Sure. Where do you need to go?'

She looked out of her window at the river as they continued on their way. They passed the seating area and the barbecues beyond where Mallory must have collapsed.

'I need to go to Rose Gold Bridal please.'

30

ROSE

Rose heard a knock at the door to the flat. She expected it to be followed by Michelle opening the door and calling out a hello because that was what she normally did. But Rose only heard a second knock.

She came out of the kitchen, along the hallway and opened the door to find Gigi on the other side.

Her sister opened her mouth but nothing came out. Tears streamed down her cheeks and she was so distraught it reminded Rose of the twelve-year-old whose goldfish had died, the fourteen-year-old who'd cried when she got her period because the pains were so bad, or the fifteen-year-old who'd failed her maths test and thought her parents were going to go mad.

But she wasn't the same Gigi any more, was she?

This Gigi had run away, left her behind, taken the dress that belonged to the both of them.

She moved back a few steps and Gigi came inside. Rose closed the door behind her and without a word she went back into the kitchen, filled the kettle and took out two mugs.

'I assume you still drink tea,' she said.

'Yes please.' Gigi's voice shook. 'Milk, no sugar.'

Rose kept her focus on the ritual she carried out numerous times a day. And when she was done she took both mugs into the lounge and set them down on the coffee table she'd bought at discount from the McGregors.

She waited for Gigi to say something. She looked terrible and Rose felt her sympathies come out for the sister who had come back into her life. It hadn't all been Gigi's fault, what happened, because what Rose had done was something she'd never forgiven herself for, not really, even in the times she told herself it had been out of love for her sister and her family.

Rose left her tea where it was, on its coaster. 'Gigi, are you here to talk?'

But she shook her head. 'It's Mallory.'

'Mallory?' Not what she'd been expecting.

'She's in the hospital.' Rose had no opportunity to ask why because Gigi delivered the blow without waiting. 'She collapsed, she had some sort of seizure, she has a brain tumour, they can't take it out. She's going to die.' Her staccato speech shared the cruel facts in rapid fire.

Rose shifted from her sofa to the one Gigi was sitting on. She sat by her side, and the more Gigi sobbed, the closer she got until she was holding her sister's hand and then she took Gigi in her arms, swaying gently, comforting her for the first time in years.

'I wish it was me,' Gigi blubbed. 'I wish I could take away her pain, do this for her.'

'It's what every mother would do for their child.' Rose sniffed back her own tears. To think a dress had been the most important thing, what had come between two sisters, when in the grand scheme of things a dress didn't matter at all.

'I should've known something was wrong. I assumed she was going through the menopause, that she just wasn't quite herself. I thought she might have vertigo – that happened to me a lot when I was her age.'

'My menopause left me feeling like I was on a roller coaster – the carriage coasting along happily one minute and then the next, derailed,' said Rose. 'Nothing prepares you for it.' She wished, not for the first time, that they'd had each other through those difficult years, to laugh with about it, to reassure each other that it would settle down over time if they were lucky.

'Nothing has ever prepared me for this. Oh, if Hector were here, it would break his heart.'

Rose sat and listened. There wasn't anything she could say that would make this better.

'I should've realised the other day when she fell in the street. It was the day I arrived, I thought she'd been clumsy, rushing around and just lost her footing. How did I miss something as big as this?'

'Because she kept it from you,' said Rose. 'And she would've had her reasons.'

'She told me that's why she came here. It wasn't only because she wanted to honour her dad's last wish and have us talk, it was more than that. She wanted everyone around her so that she could get us all prepared. This monster has taken up residence in her head, Rose, and I want to rip it out with my bare hands.' She spoke through gritted teeth, her anger mixed with sheer devastation, her fists clenched as though she wanted to go into battle.

'I'm sure you do,' said Rose.

'Did you know that Mallory is a nurse?'

'I did know that. Penny told me once.'

'She's so wonderful at her job. She's always been kind, caring, able to listen to people's problems. She never lets us listen to hers.'

'So it's in character for her to keep this from you,' said Rose. 'You can't blame yourself for not seeing it, Gigi. She seems a determined young lady; it sounds like she's thought about the best way to tell everyone but was caught out today.' She prompted Gigi to drink some of her tea and Gigi obliged.

'I'm sorry to just show up like this. I was on my way to the pub to get some space, to let Mallory rest while I fell apart. And then, in the car, I found myself desperate to see you and I asked to be dropped off here.'

'I'm glad you came.'

'Really?'

'Really. Those girls of ours knew better than us this time around, didn't they.' Her bottom lip wobbled; there was so much emotion, not only for Mallory but for their history, their lost years. 'I was so angry with Penny when I knew what they'd done. I mean I always wanted the dress back, but they forced our hand a bit.'

'I was furious at Mallory too.'

A smile formed for Gigi, a smile that Rose returned as she said, 'They made us take the leap into one another's lives again. They thought we were worth it.'

'Do you think we are... worth it, I mean?' Gigi asked.

'If you'd asked me that when I first saw the dress and then saw you then I might have pushed away any notion of ever sorting things out. But now? Yes, I do think we are worth it. We let it go on for so long.'

'So many years,' said Gigi.

'I was angry you left.'

'I was furious you hid the letter.'

They both spoke over one another with, 'I'm sorry.'

'I'm especially sorry I ran away like that,' said Gigi. 'I had to get to Hector so he wouldn't think I didn't want him any more. I knew Mum would stop me if she got wind of what I was planning, or at least she'd try to, so I made a snap decision.'

'I wish you'd confronted me about Hector's letter when you realised what I'd done,' said Rose. 'Then I would've told you why I did it – I was worried that you'd be disowned by your family and the people in the village, I was worried Hector wasn't going to look out for you, but mostly...' She cleared her throat. 'I was worried about myself and how I'd manage without you. I feel terrible. I don't deserve your forgiveness.'

'Hard luck, because you're getting it. As long as I can have yours.'

'Gladly.' Rose choked back a tear, sniffed it away and took hold of her sister's hands. 'It's been too long. Tell me Hector was as good to you as I think he was.'

A smile crept across Gigi's face. 'He was always good to me. Leaving with him, falling in love, might have seemed fast to other people but it wasn't to us. It was joyful, wonderful, and all the opposition we faced made us stronger and more determined to make it work. Rose, I wasted a lot of time being angry at you over the years, and it was Hector's dying wish – one of them anyway – that you and I talk.'

'He wanted that even though he knew I hid his letter and almost ruined things for the both of you?'

'I told you, he was a good man.'

'I wish I'd got to know him more.'

'Me too, but I can tell you everything you want to know.'

'I'd really like that.'

Rose made them another cup of tea and brought over some Welsh cakes while Gigi told her all about Hector, the struggles, the place they lived when they were first together, their wedding, having Mallory. And in turn Rose told Gigi all about meeting Albert, opening the shop and then the arrival of Penny and then Stephen.

'Do you like the name of the shop?' Rose asked. Gigi hadn't mentioned it.

'It's wonderful.' And when Rose carried on smiling, she realised. 'Gold... as in Goldie?'

Rose nodded. 'Rose Goldie Bridal wouldn't have sounded right but Rose Gold Bridal was perfect. And you were with me to make the dress that started it all off, I wanted to honour that.'

'I'm incredibly flattered.' She began to smile. 'Whatever happened to Helpful Harriet, our mannequin?'

'She retired a long time ago. Probably what I should've done as well.'

Gigi smiled. 'I'm glad our girls found each other despite our estrangement.'

'Me too. They're so close.'

Gigi hesitated before telling her sister, 'I'm sorry I didn't share with you what I was thinking, that I didn't necessarily want a shop as badly as you did. I should've been honest.'

'I probably wouldn't have listened. I had the idea in my head, then charged on with it, you know what I'm like.'

'I'm pleased for you, pleased you made it work.'

'It's been a labour of love.' Perhaps over the years she'd been so blinkered by her anger that she'd remembered it the way she had wanted it to be – a dream shared by her sister – rather than what it actually was, her dream. 'What time are you heading back to the hospital?'

'I'll go for the evening visiting session.'

'So you have a bit of time?'

Gigi nodded.

'Then let me make you something to eat – you need to keep your strength up for Mallory.'

In the kitchen she made them both a sandwich and after that she made two rather large decadent hot chocolates with solid dark chocolate and fresh heated milk – who cared that it was summer, they needed it.

As they ate and drank they talked more about their daughters, their memories of the both of them over the years, the hard times, the good times. They talked about Albert, Rose's marriage, Stephen and his life in America. They even talked about the movie, the fact that neither of them had ever watched it.

All the while the sadness about Mallory lingered on the surface but it felt good to help Gigi have a moment before she'd be back at the hospital once again.

'Maybe some day we could watch the movie with our daughters,' Rose suggested.

Gigi smiled. 'I'd really love that.'

Rose thought of something. 'You told me that Hector's wish for us to talk was one of his wishes. Does that mean he asked for something else?'

Gigi grinned. 'He only went and sent me on a cruise around the Mediterranean... Mallory pulled out at the last minute, now I know why, so I went on my own.'

'What was it like?'

'Actually it wasn't as bad as I thought it would be.'

'I've always thought about going on a cruise, I just never had the time with the shop.'

A look passed between Gigi and Rose and Rose wondered whether maybe they'd go together some day. Was it ridiculous to hope for such a thing? The shop had taken her time and her money; she'd never regretted it, but perhaps there were other things in life now. And with everything that was happening with Mallory, Gigi might need to get away at some point. She might need her sister.

But she'd put a pin in the idea for now.

And perhaps Gigi would too.

31

PENNY

Penny waited in the queue at the bakery to pick up some pastries for morning tea. She'd take the goodies back to the shop for her and Michelle who was holding the fort with Rose still upstairs.

As she waited she thought about her mother and the fact she'd finally opened up about what happened. Surely it was a real step in the right direction for her and Gigi.

As she walked back to the shop once she had her pastries she thought about Michelle. They'd been talking quite a lot about their plans for the shop and the more they'd talked the more excited Penny found herself getting.

'You're a natural with this place,' Penny had told her earlier as she picked up the broom to sweep the offcuts of material out from beneath the table where Michelle had been working on another stunning gown. 'I think we could make a good team.'

'I think so too. When do you think you'll be able to decide what you are definitely doing?'

'Soon.' And unlike when Carlos had asked her to make a decision about them moving in together, this felt very different.

This felt significant, this was something just for her, something she might well need.

'You know, if we get many more calls in response to the dress in the window, we might need one or two assistants,' said Michelle.

'I think you might be right.'

After they had yet another phone call from someone who had seen something online, Penny checked Facebook. Not much had happened on there apart from an additional handful of comments and shares of the local newspaper article about the wedding dress and the movie. On the shop's Instagram account however, it was a different story. Not only had random people shared, liked, and commented on the post with the press write-up, Norma Monroe's daughter had shared it with her hundreds of thousands of followers!

Penny pushed open the door to Rose Gold Bridal, ready to brandish the bag of pastries and eat them while she and Michelle talked more about how this running the shop as a joint venture might work. But when she saw Will McGregor waiting inside with a look on his face that told her he wasn't there with good news she passed the bag of pastries to Michelle with a murmur of 'morning tea'.

'It's Mallory,' he said. 'She's in the hospital. I can take you there, we'll talk on the way.'

Michelle was on it already. 'I've got things here, you go.'

Penny went to grab her bag from the back room and met Will outside. She climbed into the passenger seat and fastened her seatbelt, too scared to ask what was happening.

'She collapsed down by the river,' he said without prompting. 'The doctors have been doing a lot of tests.'

'What sort of tests?'

'No idea. I haven't asked her, I just wanted to be there for her and to check she was all right.'

'Does Gigi know?'

He nodded. 'She's been in to see her already. She's up in the flat talking to Rose.'

'She's what?'

'She's been up there for a while.'

Penny might have been excited that the two sisters were together were it not for Mallory being in the hospital. She wondered whether they were yelling at each other or talking properly.

When they arrived at the hospital Penny thanked Will and leapt out of the car. She ran, she didn't stop to think whether he was parking up to come inside as well or whether he was heading back to the village.

Penny at last found Mallory's ward and over at her bedside was happy to see her friend smiling at her and awake. She was going to be fine.

'You had me worried.' Penny hugged her and then stood, holding her hand. 'Haven't we had enough drama lately?'

'Sorry, thought it was my turn for the spotlight.'

Penny wondered how much effort it had taken Mallory to smile at her when she arrived because already she'd stopped doing it and she really didn't look well at all.

Maybe she was drowsy, perhaps she was hopped up on medication.

'What sort of tests are they running?' Penny asked. 'Have you had any results? Was it dehydration? A dodgy breakfast barbecue – because if it was the barbecue I will personally see to it that Will McGregor avoids another breakfast date and sticks to a traditional dinner.'

She perched her bottom on the side of the bed.

A nurse pulled back the curtain Penny had drawn across. It didn't afford much privacy but it was better than nothing. 'I can come back,' she said.

'Thank you.' Mallory smiled at the nurse but the second she left she looked on the verge of tears once more.

'Mallory, what is it? You're scaring me now.'

'I collapsed because I had a seizure.'

'A seizure? That must've been really scary. Are they giving you medication to stop it happening again?'

She clasped Penny's hand, looking at their fingers entwined together and then she looked at Penny. 'I was already on medication but it wasn't quite right.'

'What do you mean already on medication? You never said.'

She locked eyes with the woman she'd known for more than three decades. 'I had a seizure once before. There was never a course with work. When I told you that was what I was doing before I came to the village, I was in the hospital having a biopsy.' She waited as Penny tried to catch up. 'I have a brain tumour.'

Penny put a hand across her mouth, choking back a sob. 'No.'

Mallory's voice wobbled. 'Yes.'

'And you've known all this time? Since you came here to the village? Why didn't you say anything?'

'I knew I'd have to in the end. I was trying to work out how.'

'I could've helped you, supported you. Wait, is that what the wound on your head really was?'

'Yes, that was from the biopsy. They had to take a little piece of it to determine what type of tumour I have and what they can do about it.'

'So they'll remove it.' Penny breathed a sigh of relief. 'They'll take it out and then you'll get back to normal.'

A single tear tracked its way down Mallory's cheek. She gripped Penny's hands again. 'They can't remove it because of its location. And it's grade 3. All I can do now is have the chemotherapy and radiotherapy. I'm scheduled to start all that soon and it's hoped that those treatments will give me as much time and as much quality of life as possible.' Mallory didn't look away. 'They can't fix me, Penny.'

'How...?'

'How long?' Mallory's voice broke when she said, 'I don't know.' And now Penny dissolved into tears. 'It could be years if I'm lucky.'

Penny's tears continued to fall. 'And if you're not?'

Mallory shrugged.

Penny felt as if her steady world had begun floating around in an abyss and she had no idea where she would end up. She couldn't lose Mallory, she couldn't lose her cousin, her best friend.

Penny sniffed, her tears in free fall. 'I'm sorry...'

'Because you're making this all about you?' Mallory was grinning. 'Oh Penny, I love you, you cheer me up when there isn't much to smile about, and I want you to keep doing that. Because it's going to get harder. A lot harder.'

Penny was nodding. She took a tissue from the box on the side cabinet, wiped beneath her eyes where her mascara was sure to have run. Her insides churned, her breath caught. 'What about Jilly?'

'I haven't told her yet. I wanted Mum to know, then you.'

'Gigi is with Rose.'

Mallory gave a nod of satisfaction. 'Well, our plan appears to be working, doesn't it?' She cleared her throat. 'My diagnosis is the reason I was so keen to come here to Saxby Green. I had my doubts about taking the dress but I knew it would get Mum down to the village and that you and she would be in the same place so that I could gather my team. I sound a bit like you, managing a project.'

Penny couldn't talk. Mallory was smiling – how could she smile when she knew what she knew? When this thing in her head was taking over and changing her life forever?

Penny bent her head to rest on Mallory's shoulder. 'Whatever you need, I'm there for you.' She let the tears come some more before she sat up.

'I need to get things in place for Jilly, Penny. I want her to have people around her. She'll have Mum, but what I really want is for her to have you.' She lifted her shoulders as if asking for this favour, this favour of gargantuan proportions.

'Of course. I said I'll be there for you, whatever you need. I'll do anything at all.'

'I want you to think really carefully about this, Penny. Jilly will need someone all the more if I die sooner rather than later.'

'Don't say that.'

'Penny, I can't ignore this.' She looked upwards, frustration and emotion lacing her voice. 'I've been doing that for too long already. This...' She gestured at herself in the bed, in the hospital. 'This wasn't supposed to happen. I have an appointment with my specialist in a couple of days. He might well have adjusted my medication and it could've prevented this latest seizure. It might have given me time to tell you all what was going on before you had to see it for yourselves. I wanted you and Mum to know before I told Jilly after her camping trip.'

But what sounded like well-prepared sharing of information came to a halt and instead Mallory's voice broke and great heaving sobs came from her as the enormity of it all hit her at full force.

Penny held her, rocked her, comforted her. It all made sense now – the dress idea, the long stay in a quiet village with a teenager, the headaches, the tiredness, the not seeming herself.

The same nurse as before eventually reappeared and did the observations Mallory would've done a thousand times herself on patients.

'You're the patient now,' said Penny when the nurse left them alone again. 'I know what you're like, you like to help people. I wish—'

'I'd prefer to be the one doing the helping too, but I wouldn't wish this on anyone. It's scary, downright terrifying.'

'You seem calm.'

'Believe me, I haven't been this way the whole time. The seizure has left me tired today and time over the last few weeks has given me the chance to attempt to get my head around it.' She harrumphed. 'My head... that's the whole problem.'

Penny held her hand until she was ready to talk again.

'I've done a lot of yelling, Penn.'

'You, yell? No, can't imagine it.' She was snuggled next to her friend's side, the only place she wanted to be right now.

'I swore, threw things. It's so fucking unfair. I screamed at the top of my lungs and talked to the tumour – asked it why it couldn't grow somewhere else and give the doctors a hope in hell at removing it.'

Penny sat up. 'What about a second opinion? You must have contacts from work, know of other doctors you could see, one of them must—'

'Already done that.' Mallory pulled her back down next to her. 'It's the same verdict.'

As the waft of the food trolley permeated the ward, Penny thought about Gigi. 'Your mum must be in pieces.'

'She's devastated.'

'Will Jilly go to live with her, if...' The words were trapped inside, her voice unable to let them out.

'If I die? Maybe. If she's eighteen she could stay in the house, but...'

'I could take her.'

Mallory turned her head to look Penny in the eye.

Penny ran a hand across Mallory's cheek to remove the tear that escaped. 'It's what you want, right? We put it in our wills.'

'I never thought we'd ever need the clause.'

'Me neither. But now we might do. And I meant it when I agreed back then, and I mean it now.'

'It's a big ask.'

'I haven't changed my mind. You'd do it for me, and I'll do it for you.'

'You really mean it?'

'Yes, so stop asking. I absolutely will, no question.'

'What about Carlos? Your job?'

'Just you leave all that to me.'

They hugged each other until Penny got cramp in her calf. She leapt off the bed theatrically and hearing Mallory laugh felt so very special today of all days.

When Mallory was taken off for another scan Penny left the hospital so her cousin could get some rest before Gigi came back.

It was only when she went to the bathrooms before she left the hospital that Penny dissolved into sobs. She'd cried in front of Mallory, but not like this.

She cried until there was nothing left.

An Uber took her back to the shop and there was no hiding her emotions from Michelle. She told her what was going on and Michelle hugged her tightly.

'You go upstairs, take a bath, try and relax a little bit.'

Michelle turned at the sound of the bell tinkling above the doorway and in a lower voice suggested to Penny that if she hung around she'd scare the customers.

She was right. When Penny got upstairs, one look in the mirror in the hallway at her panda eyes from where her mascara and eyeliner had run, a red nose which was never flattering, and a puffiness from all the emotions gave her away.

But she couldn't have a soothing bubble bath. How could she when Mallory had a life-altering, or was it life-limiting, diagnosis?

She'd thought she was all cried out but the tears came again the second her mother emerged from the lounge and opened up her arms.

She fell into her embrace and cried like never before.

32

PENNY

Penny wanted to save Mallory, to pay for her to go abroad and get a treatment that would get rid of the tumour. But that was never going to happen so she'd have to settle with whatever else she could do to help, no matter how small.

'I'll make us some tea,' she said when Mallory sat down on the sofa in the lounge in the flat above Rose Gold Bridal.

Mallory had come out of hospital yesterday and had been ordered to take it easy. Gigi had given up her room at the pub and moved her things into the cottage so that Mallory wouldn't be alone but today Penny had asked her to come to the flat for the day. She'd told Gigi she would be able to keep a close eye on her and give her a change of scene. She could help Michelle in the shop when necessary, let Mallory sleep if she needed, and keep her company when that was what she wanted. She'd told her aunt all of that with her arm around her and had added that they were family. They were there for each other.

Penny hovered at the door to the lounge and watched Mallory. The colour was back in her cheeks, she was more relaxed, and her smiles seemed more genuine. Mallory had told her that in some ways, apart from the constant fuss, it was a relief that some people now knew the truth because hiding it had been exhausting.

When Mallory looked up because Penny still hadn't disappeared to make the tea, Penny said, 'I've got scones with jam and cream, or I can warm up some lentil soup, or—'

'Stop fussing.'

'I'm sorry, I'm doing exactly what you didn't want.' Mallory had explained on the phone last night that when none of them knew about her tumour they'd let her lead a normal existence, and they had to keep doing that to a certain extent or she would go insane.

Mallory patted the sofa next to her and Penny went to sit down.

Mallory took her hand. 'I know I'll need looking after a lot more at some point, but I'm not there yet. Save your efforts for down the line.'

'I'll try my best.'

'Thank you.'

'When's your appointment with your specialist?'

'A few days' time.'

'And I'm allowed to take you to it, right? You're not going to tell me that's too much fuss.'

Mallory smiled. 'I wouldn't dream of it.'

'Are you sure you're not hungry?'

Mallory pulled a face. 'Actually, I am a bit. I'll pass on the cup of tea in exchange for food.'

'Soup it is then, and a roll. Wholemeal or white?' She stood up, ready for action.

'Wholemeal please, with butter.'

'Yes, ma'am.'

Once they were sitting on the sofa, trays on their laps, bowls of comforting soup in front of them, Penny told Mallory about the conversation she'd had with her mother that morning. 'Mum told me that she and Gigi have been talking about the house they grew up in. They've been laughing about things they did all those years ago. They're actually getting on well together.'

Mallory dipped a piece of roll into her soup. 'For two sisters who haven't spoken in almost sixty years I think we might have pulled off a miracle.'

'I wish—'

'Do not say anything about miracles for me.' Mallory didn't look at Penny when she spoke, she kept her focus on her soup. And Penny knew she was going to have to stop herself before she spoke many times over from this day on. Mallory shouldn't have to absorb and process her grief, her upset, she had enough to deal with. And she had to be there for Jilly too.

Mallory looked up. 'Hey, do you think if I didn't have a brain tumour they might be angrier at us?'

Penny smiled at the attempt at humour. 'It's a possibility. Maybe that's why we got off quite lightly in the end.'

'The emergency forced them together. I'm glad Mum came to Rose.'

'Me too. I suppose if there was no love there in all these years, there wouldn't have been anger either. They would've both moved on and never looked back.'

'Do you think they're getting on well making pie in the kitchen at the cottage?'

'Let's hope so.'

Both sisters were tentatively taking steps in a new direction.

And soon it would be time for Mallory to do that too. The next step was to tell Jilly, which Penny knew was weighing heavily on Mallory's mind. If she thought about it too much, thought about Jilly's face crumpling when her mum delivered the devastating news, she wouldn't be able to function. And she had to, for Mallory's sake.

Mallory had shared some details of the treatments she'd be undergoing to try to stop the bastard tumour in its tracks. The treatment was going to be lengthy, tough and probably the hardest thing she'd ever done. But it could give her more time. And she desperately needed as much time as possible with those she loved. It was what anyone wanted, wasn't it?

When her phone rang Penny left Mallory resting on the sofa, the remote control for the TV within easy reach, and went into her bedroom.

She'd been ignoring Carlos's calls all morning and she couldn't do it any more.

Things had changed. She'd changed.

'Hey,' she said when she answered.

He wasted no time getting straight to the point. 'You're not going to move in with me, are you?' She'd always liked that about him and right now it was probably for the best because since Mallory had shared her news she'd known exactly what she had to do. She just hadn't had the guts to do it yet.

She felt the air go out of her lungs. 'I haven't been fair to you.'

'No, you haven't.'

'I'm sorry. I didn't think I'd feel like this when I came to the village from London, and now with Mallory and everything she's facing...'

'How is she?'

'Doing well under the circumstances.' She'd messaged him

the gist of what was going on yesterday but they hadn't talked about it until now.

'This is about more than Mallory, isn't it? You don't want the life you had here, the life you had with me.'

'No, I don't.' Again he'd got to the point and she was thankful for that. She waited for her eyes to well up but the tears didn't come. Maybe she was all cried out after the hospital drama or maybe they would never have been there anyway. 'We worked when we were both in London. I promise I wasn't pretending.'

'I know you weren't.' She heard a deep sigh down the phone. 'Take care of yourself, Penny.'

And that was it. Done.

She found Mallory flipping through television channels but she switched the TV off when Penny went into the lounge.

'Me and Carlos are over,' she said as she sat down.

'Wow. That was...'

'Quick,' Penny finished for her.

'Are you okay?'

She turned her head to look at Mallory. 'More than okay. I'm almost relieved. Since I came here I've realised we're not meant for each other. I've not been here long, but it's been long enough to realise that I've changed. I was changing before I left London but it took coming here to really see it.'

'You didn't break it off with him because of Jilly, did you?'

Penny sat bolt upright. 'No, of course not.' Although she had been dreading telling him that she would be taking Jilly in when the time came, that she might be looking after a teenager again, because Carlos and kids definitely didn't mix. 'I did it for me. And the fact I'm not devastated tells me something.'

'You know what you need?'

Penny smiled. 'Some of that Ben & Jerry's ice-cream in the freezer? I bought that for you, you know.'

'Go get it, Penny.'

Over a tub of chocolate fudge brownie Penny switched the talk from her love life to Mallory's. 'What's going to happen with Will? Have you seen him since the hospital?'

She shook her head.

'May I ask why not?'

'How can I, Penny? I've got an expiration date.'

'We've all got one of those.'

'Except mine is coming at me at a speed I'd rather not think about.'

'He was incredibly strong at the hospital. You could see he was worried, but he didn't pry, he didn't demand to know what was going on. He got Gigi to see you, Gigi here to see Mum, he waited for me and brought me to you. He sat by your bed for hours. Has he called since? Stopped by?'

'He was at the cottage this morning. I was lying on the sofa and pretended to be asleep.'

'You didn't! I think if anything, he deserves some time to talk to you. Give him that much.'

'I know I should.' She laughed as their spoons clanked together in the ice-cream tub.

'How was the breakfast date anyway, before you ended up at the hospital? I haven't even asked you.'

'It was great. He's the kindest, most wonderful man I've ever met.'

Penny could see how much it hurt Mallory that she wasn't letting herself go with her feelings. 'You left out the word hot.'

'And that.' Mallory grinned.

'Did you kiss him?' A heap of chocolate fudge brownie ice-cream hovered on Penny's spoon.

When Mallory nodded, smiling, Penny squealed. 'I knew you would. Mallory, *talk* to him.'

'I have so much to deal with. There's Jilly, I have to tell her, be there for her. Then there's chemotherapy, radiotherapy. Did you know I'll likely lose my ability to taste much at all with chemo? Some patients say food ends up tasting like cardboard.'

'Then eat more of the ice-cream.' She pushed the tub Mallory's way. 'Make the most of it.'

But Mallory didn't dive in for more. 'I can't go through all that and start a new relationship. For a start I'll look like crap – that's fine if I'm with someone who's known me for years, but it's no way to start out, is it? I'd say he'd have to hold my hair back for me to be sick with the after effects of chemo, but I likely won't have any hair.'

'Imagine how much you'll save on haircuts.'

'Good job I love you, you know.' But it did the trick. She was laughing and Penny wanted to bottle up the sound and cherish it forever.

'Mallory, he's been at your side at the hospital, he knows something is going on. And I'd almost bet money that he won't be going anywhere when he finds out the truth.'

'Maybe.'

'Don't you want him there for your good days? You'll have some, you know. Just tell me you'll think about letting him in.'

'Okay. But maybe not for a while.'

Penny sighed. 'He's besotted by you, remember, has been ever since you emerged naked like a goddess.'

'Will deserves to be free. He should find someone else while he still has time.'

'Shouldn't he be the judge of that?'

'Maybe.' She leaned her head on Penny's shoulder. 'Jilly will be back tomorrow.'

Penny would drop the subject of Will for now, but not for ever. She wanted Mallory to grab at every possible chance of happiness and something told her that Will was one of those.

'Jilly will come back to the cottage,' said Penny. 'And you'll tell her. And it will be awful. But she will have me, she has Gigi, we are all here for the both of you.' Penny kissed the top of her head. 'Any time you need us.'

33

MALLORY

Gigi had helped Mallory pack up her things from the cottage, ready to go home earlier than planned. Penny would drive her and Jilly back to Marlow this evening once the truth was out, and their lives would never be the same again.

Mallory felt nauseous, her stomach churned as she waited for her daughter.

Penny had gone to pick up Jilly from the train station and she'd bring her back to the cottage. Mallory couldn't wait to hear all about the camping trip but she knew the whole time she was listening she would be thinking about having to deliver a terrible blow right afterwards. She had no choice.

She hovered at the window looking out to the street, waiting to see Penny's car come in to view. Gigi had left her to it, Mallory wanted to do this on her own. And Gigi would spend the day with Rose to leave Mallory and Jilly to process this together. It was a comfort to know that her mother was with her sister today – after all this time they had each other again, neither of them would be lonely if they leant on each other when they needed to.

And Gigi would definitely need her sister for what was coming.

As they'd packed up Mallory's things earlier, Gigi had told Mallory off for worrying about her.

'I can't help it, Mum. Nothing would please me more than to see you happy again. Well, aside from blasting away my inoperable brain tumour that is.'

'It's not a joking matter, Mallory.'

'Oh Mum, if I don't joke, I'll cry and I'll wallow. And I don't want that to be the way you all remember me. Please...' When her mum took her hand she told her, 'Some of us don't get to live to a ripe old age. I'm fifty, in many ways I'm lucky. I've seen enough in my job to know that. Make the most of every day you have. Please. Promise me.'

'I promise.' And she'd turned to carry on packing up the clothes from the chest of drawers but Mallory knew she was trying to hide her tears.

Mallory stood at the window for nearly fifteen minutes but then, sure enough, Penny's car came in to view and her daughter climbed out of the passenger side.

Jilly talked ten to the dozen after they hugged hello and Penny left them to it. She talked animatedly about pitching the tent, cooking on a tiny little gas stove, the rabbit that had hopped right up to her tent one morning and frightened the life out of her when she unzipped the canvas about to emerge.

'The tent got a bit too hot when it was really sunny,' she said, devouring the fruit cake Mallory had given her alongside a glass of milk.

Mallory watched her daughter, listened to her tales, embraced all of it. This reminded her of Jilly's early school days when they'd come home and do this same ritual with milk and a snack and talk about what had happened that day, good or bad.

'I've brought a lot of dirty washing back.' Jilly popped the last of the piece of cake into her mouth.

Mallory reached out and took her daughter's hand. 'That can wait. I need you to sit here for a minute. There's something I need to say.'

Jilly slumped back against the sofa. 'Is this about school? It's not term time yet. I've said I'll try harder, that I'll be better. I won't ever vape again. I mean it.'

'This isn't about any of that.' She held Jilly's other hand too. She wouldn't cry, she couldn't right now, she had to get this out and stay strong for her child who was about to face the unthinkable.

'Jilly...' She could do this. She had to. 'One day when I was at work I had a seizure, I lost consciousness. They ran tests and they found out what was wrong.'

This was horrible. Worse than she thought. If she could keep the words in and never have to do this she would.

'Mum... what's wrong?'

Her bottom lip wobbled. 'Oh Jilly. I'm not all right, and they can't fix me, not properly.'

And the rest spilled out, inelegantly, all the medical facts and alongside the layman's terms that made it all so much more real. She didn't know her prognosis, but there were estimates and Jilly had wanted those.

And by the time she'd finished telling her daughter everything, neither of them could stop crying.

* * *

Mallory had no idea how long she'd sat there rocking Jilly in her arms, soothing with her words that she knew probably made no sense. How could she say it was okay, that everything would be fine, when it was all lies?

It was what you did though, wasn't it. As a parent you wanted to take away your child's pain and right now Jilly was hurting more than she ever had before. Mallory had had both of her parents in her life for so many years, she was lucky. Jilly didn't have her dad, she'd lost her pappy, and now this.

'I would never have left you and gone camping if I'd known,' Jilly sobbed. Her tears had soaked Mallory's shoulder, her cheek, her hair.

'Of course you would and of course you should, Jilly. I wanted you to go camping. I want you to have a normal life. This doesn't change that – well it does, but not completely. I need to see you carrying on, don't you see? Otherwise it'll break me before anything else does.'

Mallory pressed her forehead gently against Jilly's. They'd done this when Jilly was little, and Jilly would always open her eyes first and begin to giggle while Mallory was still savouring the skin-to-skin contact.

It was Mallory who opened her eyes first this time.

She got up and went over to the sideboard and took out the memory book she'd been working on from the bottom drawer.

Jilly sniffed as Mallory opened up the first page to a photograph of Jilly as a newborn, eyes tightly shut, in Mallory's arms.

'That was the day I brought you home from the hospital.' She waited for Jilly to read the words next to it, words that said her daughter's name, weight and the way Mallory felt having a baby of her own.

Jilly turned the page to a photograph of her with food all

over her face and the biggest grin, and Mallory's handwritten comment that it had been like feeding time at the zoo. She laughed at that one, and the one of her in a graduation gown, aged four, graduating nursery.

'Your nursery teachers thought it would be fun.' Mallory shoved aside the nagging realisation that she might not get to see another graduation. She needed to think of the now, the time they had.

Jilly flipped to the next page and the next, memories over the years – her first day at school with Pappy lifting her into his arms to comfort her because she didn't want to go in. There was the photograph of the spaceship birthday cake for her sixth birthday when she'd been obsessed by space, the piñata the day she turned eight years old, a picture of her at a funfair, sandwiched between her grandparents on the Ferris wheel Mallory had refused to go on.

'I was happy to be the photographer,' Mallory reiterated now.

'I didn't really like it either,' Jilly admitted, sniffing away her tears. 'But I told Pappy I did because he loved them so much.'

'I never did understand his love for them.'

They had a good giggle at the photographs of Pappy Hector and Grandma Gigi attempting to do the limbo at a cricket club family day. 'I thought Pappy was much better than Granny Gigi,' said Jilly, 'but don't tell her, will you.'

'I wouldn't dare.'

One of Jilly's favourite photographs was of the year Mallory took her to Lapland to see Father Christmas. 'All my friends were so envious. It was magical.'

'Did you still believe that year?'

Jilly's eyes widened. 'You mean he isn't real?' But when she laughed Mallory joined in. 'It was so much better when I did believe.'

'Christmas is magical as a kid, it was the same for me.' And it would be magical for Jilly's kids, but Mallory couldn't let herself be swallowed up at the thought that she would most likely not be around to meet them.

'Did Pappy do the footprints in the hallway like he did for me every Christmas Eve?'

Mallory cleared her throat, bit back tears. 'He did. I loved it. I'd try and walk in those footsteps, my feet so much smaller than the big boot prints.'

As they progressed through the album and it got closer and closer to the present day with photographs of Cedella, then of Penny, Penny and Jilly making the pizza the other night, a picture of Mallory with Jilly when they hadn't realised they were being photographed, the lightness of mood was overtaken by a more sombre one.

Mallory closed the book and set it on the table.

'Did you make this because you're going to die?'

The harsh word, the reality, hit Mallory again hearing it on her daughter's lips. She didn't think she'd ever get used to that. 'I did. Remember the album Pappy made? Well, I loved that so much, it was what gave me the idea.'

'Can we keep adding to it?'

'For as long as we can.' She put her arm around Jilly and pulled her close and she felt her daughter's shoulders lift and fall again, the tears coming once more.

'One foot in front of the other,' said Mallory. 'One day at a time.'

'I don't want you to be sick.'

'Jilly, neither do I. I promise if I could do anything to

change this, I would. I want us to keep doing normal things for as long as we can – like taking Cedella for a walk, baking cakes, having Christmas and fighting over the last mince pie.'

'We do do that.'

'I know, and I want to do it again, every year. Do *not* feel sorry for me this Christmas and insist I have it.'

Jilly's face paled. 'But—'

'And don't say it could be my last Christmas. It could be, but I may have a lot more. Let's stay positive even though it feels impossible. I have to have hope, Jilly, and I can't do that without your help.'

She clung tighter to her mum. 'I'll do it for you, I promise.' But she sat up again. 'I wish I had two parents and then...'

'The other one could step in when one was no longer here.'

Jilly's head dropped. 'I shouldn't say that, should I?'

'You can say anything to me, Jilly. No secrets, not any more.'

'I'm scared. If something happens to you... or rather *when* it happens, I could end up like Skye, she hasn't got anyone looking out for her. She's all alone and she says she doesn't know what she would've done if it wasn't for you. You got her away from a boyfriend who wasn't very nice to her, a flat she hated living in. She's really grateful.'

'She reminded me of myself at that age,' said Mallory. 'And Jilly, I'm sorry you don't have another parent in your life. I want you to be surrounded by love, but it can come from other places. You have Granny Gigi, you have Penny.'

'I like Penny.'

'She loves you. And she'll take you in, she'll look after you, she'll become your guardian.'

'If I'm still young when it happens, you mean.'

Mallory nodded. 'She'll be there for you for whatever you

need, she's promised me that. It's something we agreed many, many years ago for each other.'

Jilly's eyes filled with tears.

'Jilly, if you want to find your father, then I can help with that. It's your right, I won't be hurt.'

'Was he horrible to you? My father?'

'What? No. Disinterested is the best description, or irresponsible.'

'I always wondered whether you'd protected me from some awful truth.'

'How long have you been thinking that?'

'Only off and on. But I decided I didn't want to know. The man, my father, will never be my dad, not like Pappy was yours. Pappy was more of a dad to me than some stranger who was never interested.'

'Your pappy loved you to pieces.'

'I miss him.'

'Me too. You know, when I was Skye's age, way before I met your father I had a boyfriend like Skye's. But I also had Pappy Hector and Granny Gigi in my corner. It's why I really wanted to help Skye. She has nobody to stand up for her, to that boyfriend of hers. Do you know Pappy Hector confronted my boyfriend and until then I don't think I'd ever seen your Pappy so menacing.'

'But Pappy was a teddy bear.'

'To those he loved, he was. But not if you hurt someone precious to him.'

'I'm glad you helped Skye. I like her.'

'Me too.'

'Does she know about your tumour?' Jilly asked.

'No.'

Jilly digested her answer. 'Will you tell her?'

'I expect so.' She kissed Jilly on the temple. 'She'll be a good tutor for you as well as a friend. I think it's a much better idea than having me try to teach you, don't you?'

'To be fair, Mum, you're a bit out of touch with the curriculum.'

They were still talking about school, about Jilly's enjoyment of textiles and perhaps putting her focus there eventually, when Penny came through the door to the cottage cautiously, most likely wondering what she would be walking in to. They'd agreed she should stop by after a few hours to give Jilly a chance to talk to Penny and ask any questions she might have.

Jilly noticed Penny hadn't come empty-handed. 'What's in the bags?'

'Chinese takeaway,' said Penny with a smile. 'Anyone interested?'

'I'll get the plates.' Mallory was up before either of them could argue and she gave them a couple of minutes before she came back into the lounge with plates and cutlery and some paper napkins she'd found in the drawer. She knew she was right to do so when she saw Jilly lean her head against Penny's hand on her shoulder, and they pulled apart when Mallory came back in.

Mallory had to allow them to get closer. They already meant a lot to each other, but they'd be leaning on one another a lot more soon. And rather than it making Mallory completely sad, it offered a modicum of relief.

'Help yourselves before it gets cold.' Penny boomed the instruction and Jilly was first to dig in to the selection – roast pork and beansprouts, Szechuan chicken, mushroom rice.

Normality.

Real life.

Moments of enjoyment.

This was what Mallory wanted and needed for now.

Mallory broke open her fortune cookie and read it out loud:

These are the best days

It brought all three of them to tears and yet it couldn't be a more perfect sentiment.

34

MALLORY

One year later

Mallory's eyes glistened with happy tears as she looked in the mirror. Wearing the gown that her mother had worn to marry her father, the gown that her mother made from scratch with Aunt Rose, the gown that had brought them all together as a family, she was more than ready to marry the man she loved.

Will McGregor.

A whole year had passed by since Mallory had shared her diagnosis with those closest to her. She had endured the rigours and horrors of chemotherapy, radiotherapy. She'd almost lost her mind going through that, especially knowing that none of it would cure her. None of it would change the final outcome. On some days she'd wanted to go to sleep and never wake up again but scans every few months told her that for now the tumour was stable, it hadn't grown.

Mallory hadn't returned to her job at the hospital but once her treatment was done and she was feeling a bit more human, she'd volunteered with a brain charity to support other patients.

She'd found it a therapy for herself at the same time, she'd learned a lot, but mostly she'd drawn strength from everyone she was surrounded by and by helping others it had helped her to help herself, to see the good things amongst the more sinister, to take each day at a time. And she no longer tried to hide her symptoms, something that had been so hard to do. These days she could take her medication with other people around, she said when she needed to rest, she let herself be looked after even though it went against her natural instincts most of the time.

Will had never given up on her. Mallory had refused to see him or take his calls for a while, her focus had been Jilly and then getting home to start her treatment. But following the chemotherapy and radiotherapy, months after she left Saxby Green, when she'd been sitting at home and her energy had begun to return, she'd answered a call without checking who it was. Will had been on the other end of the line. He'd asked to come and see her, and she'd agreed. Hearing his voice that day had been like a magic spell, grabbing at her heart and making it full again.

They'd met on a bench on the Thames River walk – Skye, who was by then her lodger as well as Jilly's tutor, had walked slowly down there with her while she walked Cedella and she waited until Will showed, giving Mallory instructions to call her as soon as he left.

He seemed unsure when he approached and after Skye left them to it, Mallory gave him a smile she realised he'd been waiting for. Hoping for.

'I like it.' He pointed to her headscarf, a fancy multi-coloured one Gigi had made for her at Rose's shop. Her mother had wanted to be there at the hospital for all the treatment sessions but Mallory had let Penny and Sasha handle that part.

She'd insisted Gigi keep Jilly company and spend time with Rose back in Saxby Green.

That was the thing when you had a terminal diagnosis – you could get your way a lot easier than ever before, and Mallory had cheekily decided to milk it by making her own rules.

'I'm glad you called,' she said to Will as they watched the river float lazily by.

'I'm glad I called too.'

She hadn't wanted him to see her with a bald head covered in a scarf, she hadn't wanted him to see her weak, but the way he looked at her now was the same way he'd looked at her by the river the day of their date and she'd never felt more special, more worthy.

She smiled at him again. 'Do you want to take me for breakfast?'

'I'd love to.' They got up and he waited for her to take his arm. 'Let's try to make it less dramatic this time though, shall we?'

'Deal.'

Since that day they'd started to see each other regularly, with Will coming up to Surrey mostly. Occasionally Mallory had headed down to the village with Gigi escorting her and timing it with a visit to Rose.

One weekend when Will arrived at the house as usual, he'd whisked her away for a long weekend on the Devonshire coast. Jilly had stayed behind with Skye, who had become more like a sister to Jilly than Mallory ever would've imagined. They even fought occasionally like siblings, but when one or the other apologised Mallory would have to turn away so they couldn't see the emotion it evoked. Mallory had a feeling that Skye would be in her daughter's life for many years to come. They'd both be there for each other.

Walking a stretch of the coastal path hand in hand that weekend, Will had stopped to admire the view.

Next to him Mallory closed her eyes, undeterred by the wind that had done its best to stop them coming this far. 'I love the sound more than anything... the crash of the waves, the seagulls.' She opened her eyes when he didn't answer.

Will still had hold of her hand but instead of standing by her side he was down on one knee.

A box, with a diamond solitaire ring set into a velvet interior, was open in his hand.

'Mallory—'

'Yes!'

'I haven't asked you yet.' He laughed.

Tears spilled down her cheeks; she hadn't even realised until the salty tang reached her lips.

'Mallory...' Will, strong, handsome, kind and gentle Will who had come into her life right when she needed him to was going to ask her a question she never ever thought she would get to hear from any man let alone one as special as him. 'Mallory, will you marry me?'

She sank down onto her knees in front of him, wrapping her arms around him, saying over and over, 'Yes, yes, a thousand times yes!'

He spoke softly into her hair as he held her. 'You're stuck with me now.'

'For better or worse.'

He pulled back and slipped the diamond onto her ring finger. 'Always.'

As they'd walked back the way they'd come, the lure of hot chocolate made with real chocolate and a cosy open fire to curl up beside, just the two of them on the last night before they left their love cocoon, he told her he'd asked Jilly's permission before he popped the question. He hadn't asked Gigi, nor Penny, but Jilly he had spoken with. And Jilly had been over the moon.

And now their day was here.

The door to the bedroom in the McGregor property in Saxby Green opened and in came Gigi wearing a periwinkle blue suit with matching hat Rose had said would take someone's eye out if she wasn't careful.

Gigi put a hand to her chest. 'Your dad would be so proud if he could see you now. And that dress…'

'It's perfect, Mum.'

Gigi blinked back her tears. 'Absolutely perfect.' She smiled. 'Ready?'

'I've never been more ready.'

35

ROSE

Rose watched Penny stop at the hall table and pick up the bouquet that she'd hand to the bride. Dressed in a strapless jade gown Rose and Michelle had worked on together in record time to be ready for the big day, Penny looked happier than she had in years. Getting away from London and her stressful job suited her down to the ground.

'Penny, you look beautiful,' said Rose.

'So do you, Mum.' Penny kissed her on the cheek. 'Now off you go, outside, before Mallory and Gigi come down those stairs.'

'Okay, bossy.' But she was glad Penny was using those skills away from the boardroom these days.

Mallory had asked her Aunt Rose to come to her wedding, and Rose had almost burst into tears as she gladly accepted the invite. Gigi was back in her life, Mallory and Penny were a huge part of it, Jilly too. Rose had handed the shop over to Penny with Michelle as the dressmaker, but she didn't want for anything these days. Michelle let her consult about dresses whenever she felt the urge; neither Michelle nor Penny minded her hanging around in the shop, it was the best of both worlds.

Rose smiled at other guests as she went outside in the McGregors' garden to take her seat. She and Gigi would soon be off on a two-week cruise around the Caribbean and over the next few days they were going to make lists of what to pack, carry on making plans for their adventures.

Gigi had enticed Rose with the idea of a cruise when she'd told Rose all about the first one. It sounded very different to what Rose had ever expected. It didn't sound like you needed to leave the boat if you didn't want to. There were shows on board, pools to swim in, a garden to relax in, and restaurants at your fingertips.

Rose had also managed to find the Norma Monroe movie for sale online and ordered the DVD to come through the post.

She and Gigi had watched it twice with Mallory and Penny, they'd admired their part in the making of a film – an actual film! – and then once it finished they'd talked about those days, the days of two sisters working together on a project for a competition but instead of it being painful to recall, there had been nothing but love and fondness. Because those good times had always been there, they'd just been buried beneath rubble for a long time.

Of course Hector had been a topic of conversation many times and Mallory and Gigi had insisted they cook a Jamaican banquet for Rose and Penny when they came to visit for the weekend.

'It's a part of Mallory's heritage,' Gigi had said. 'And Jilly's.'

'What's that one, Gran?' Jilly was about to spoon out the food from a dish in the centre that Gigi hadn't named. Everything else had been identified – perfectly golden dumplings, brightly coloured peppers with pasta, spicy jerk chicken, and a rice and pea dish, but this one's introduction she had bypassed as she brought it over to the table.

'Gigi?' Rose prompted when Gigi said nothing in response to Jilly.

'Why don't you try it first,' Gigi suggested to everyone.

'No, no way.' Penny shook her head when the dish came her way. 'What is it?'

'You're going to have to tell them,' said Mallory.

'Very well,' said Gigi. 'It's goat curry.'

A roar went up – a refusal from Jilly, a hard no from Penny. And Mallory was laughing so hard it started everyone else off.

Rose had reached for her phone and taken a picture and that picture was in the album Mallory was continuing to make for Jilly. It had captured Jilly, her mum at her side, Penny and Gigi, all their happiness, as if this moment was all that mattered.

Perhaps that was the key. To treasure the moments, to not think of what was coming.

Be happy for now.

As Rose sat waiting for the wedding to begin she thought about the sister she had back in her life after all this time thanks to their meddlesome daughters.

She couldn't be more proud of the both of them.

The music started and everyone seated stood up, ready to see the bride making her way down the aisle.

36

GIGI

Gigi walked proudly towards the congregation, across the grass, the view of the river beyond at the foot of the McGregor property. Mallory had her arm, she walked steadily, which Gigi knew was the thing that had worried her daughter the most. She had good and bad days, some days her balance was worse than others, but Gigi had assured her she wouldn't let go of her, she wouldn't let her fall, they'd get her down that aisle to marry the love of her life.

When Will had brought Mallory back from the Devonshire coast and her daughter told her the news Gigi had cried.

'They're tears of joy, I promise.' It was only a small lie – she was happy, but it also reminded her that for this pair they would only get a snapshot of the time they deserved to have together.

But Mallory didn't seem to be thinking that way at all. Gigi didn't know how she did it – her spirit, her positive approach, her strength over the last year was to be admired. And her approach forced everyone around her to stay strong. Her tumour hadn't grown over twelve months thanks to the brutal treatment regime which Gigi had wished she could do for her daughter, and Mallory's symptoms were relatively under control; she managed the all-too-frequent headaches, some confusion, the recurrent muscular weakness and unsteadiness. Gigi felt the dread pool in her stomach every time Mallory had a check-up at the hospital, followed by relief when the tumour was said to be stable.

Gigi had been in the village with Rose when Mallory had returned from her trip to the coast that day and Mallory had wanted to go into the shop, see whether Michelle had anything that would fit her. She was so excited.

Will took himself off to meet a friend and left the women to it. Inside Rose Gold Bridal, Mallory made a quick call and told Penny to get there now. She was renting the same cottage Mallory had stayed in until she found somewhere of her own to buy. Her son had returned from his travels and had started a new job so he was living in her apartment in Notting Hill. Penny was loving running the shop with Michelle and how different her life was compared to how it had been before, and she had dedicated her time to Mallory as much as possible and to Jilly when she needed the support.

Mallory went through some of the gowns on the rack while she waited for her best friend. 'They're all so beautiful.'

Rose told her which she'd made, talked about shapes and sizes Mallory might like.

Penny was there less than two minutes later. 'I was in the café.' Panicked, she must have run she was so out of breath.

Mallory raced over to her. 'It's good news.'

'What? Tell me!'

She held up her hand to reveal the ring. She hardly needed to add, 'I'm getting married!'

Gigi watched them squeal, hug each other. Penny wanted to

know everything about the proposal, she gasped at the ring, she hugged her cousin again.

'We don't have long,' Mallory told them all. 'I won't be able to get a gown made, but there's something here for me, right?'

Rose took charge. 'When is the wedding?' She was no longer the owner of Rose Gold Bridal but she kept her hand in.

'This Friday,' said Mallory.

You could've heard one of those sequins from the box out back drop in the silence.

Everyone knew why it would be quick, but nobody said a word until Rose took Gigi's hand. 'I have an idea.' She looked at her sister and Gigi knew exactly what she was thinking.

'She's about your size,' said Rose.

'In my dreams.' Gigi grinned. 'My size back in the day, yes.'

'Mum... Rose? What are you two plotting?'

Gigi took the reins. 'We want you to wear our dress. *The* dress.'

'It would mean the world to us,' said Rose.

Mallory looked over at the dress, on the mannequin once again. They'd taken it off display for a while – it had brought a lot of custom for Rose Gold Bridal, demand that had kept Michelle on her toes. Michelle had eventually recruited an assistant, her niece, who had got up to speed quickly and at Easter they'd put the dress back on the mannequin to coincide with an interview in the press given by Rose and Gigi about the history of the shop. It was a part of a feature on Saxby Green to appear in the national press because of the village's surging popularity – a popularity Gigi hoped wouldn't change too much around the local area – and so the dress had gone back on display and had been photographed to be included with the piece.

Mallory's voice caught when she asked, 'You really both want me to wear it?'

'Darling, yes,' said Rose.

'Do you really think it'll fit?'

'Only one way to know,' said Penny who was already clambering into the window to lift out the mannequin.

Between them they gently eased the dress off the doll and Penny carried it to the changing room for Mallory. 'Try it on, no time like the present.'

While Mallory was in the velvet-curtained fitting room, a rope sash holding the material to shield her from view and Penny ensconced inside as well to help her friend, Gigi's phone pinged.

She peered at the screen. 'Oh my golly... it's him.'

Rose squeezed closer to read the message too.

A month ago Gigi had taken up swimming at the local leisure centre and in the café afterwards, as she was waiting for a cappuccino, a man had come up to introduce himself. The man, Patrick, had been swimming in the lane next to her, he said, although without her glasses she didn't recognise him. He'd asked to join her at her table given there were no others spare; she agreed, and they'd spent a very pleasant hour talking. Ever since then they'd bumped into each other regularly and a week ago she'd shared her phone number.

'He wants to meet up,' said Gigi aghast.

Rose smiled with glee. 'I hope you're going to say yes.'

Mallory stuck her head out of the curtain. 'Mum, do you have a date?'

'Well, I...'

Mallory's head disappeared again and Gigi could only assume Penny had pulled her back because she heard her niece say, 'would you get your butt back in here so I can do you up!'

'Do I say yes?' Gigi asked Rose, although clearly not quietly enough that their girls didn't hear.

'Hell yeah!' came the joint response from behind the curtain.

That was followed by Mallory hollering, 'Go for it. Life is short, Mum!'

She was right of course. Life was sometimes so painfully short. All of them knew that all too well.

Gigi continued their walk in the McGregors' garden now, between the rows of chairs, her daughter on her arm, smiling faces all around them, the bridesmaids walking up ahead, the groom waiting.

It was time for Mallory to step into a new life.

And Gigi was so very happy for her.

37

PENNY

Penny reached the beautiful wildflower arch holding her bouquet of sunflowers, ranunculus, dahlias and daisies that matched Mallory's and Jilly's. Surrounded by the scent of the same blooms that cascaded up and over the arch and with the jetty where Mallory and Will had first met as the backdrop, the day was perfect.

The story about how Will and Mallory first met had been shared by Will during one of his and Jilly's father-figure-and-daughter bonding nights – the name they'd both given to the weekly evenings they spent just the two of them. Jilly had realised she'd overheard Penny and Mallory talking about it a year ago when they'd come to the village for the summer, but she'd closed her ears to the full story because it involved her mother naked. Now she loved teasing Mallory about it.

Jilly was very taken with Will, she loved him being in their lives. The pair looked after Mallory when she needed them to, they gave her space when that was what she wanted, and Jilly, despite everything she faced and still had to come to terms with, was the light in Mallory's life and never faded.

Will and his best man, his friend, Joel, stood on the opposite side to Penny and Jilly came to stand with Penny as they'd rehearsed yesterday. Penny nudged her and smiled down at this beautiful girl in a matching dress to hers with the flawless skin and radiant smile just like her mother's. Jilly had come in to the shop every time she visited the village and was getting more and more on board with the idea of a career in dressmaking. It was early days for a teenager of course but the passion was there, Penny could see it in her eyes every time Jilly asked Michelle a question, every time she watched her work on the sewing machines. Gigi might not have opened the shop with Rose all those years ago but it looked like the future might well involve not only Penny from Rose's side of the family but Gigi's granddaughter too. And she had a feeling the story of the wedding dress and the two sisters would keep being told for years to come.

The weather was at least dry today and nobody seemed bothered about the bruised clouds up above. In fact, Mallory had said earlier that they added to the mood and allowed the jar candles Mrs McGregor had used to make a pathway shine even more. They'd been standing at the top window, watching everyone Mallory loved gathering in the one place for her big day. She'd knocked on the glass when she saw Sasha and Sasha had waved up to her and Penny. Penny had got to know Mallory's nursing friend a lot over the last year and although Penny tried to be there for Mallory whenever she needed her during treatments, scans, any check-ups, when it was Sasha who was the one to go with her best friend, Penny knew she was in safe hands.

As the music sounded from the speakers, Penny's gaze locked with Joel's. Since Penny had been renting in the village she'd been getting to know the handyman a lot more. She'd called him one evening when she couldn't get a window to open at the rental place and the rental agency hadn't answered her call. He'd accused her of making excuses to get him on his own, told her she should get it over with and just ask him out.

She hadn't – at least, not yet – but when he smiled her way now, she thought that perhaps when the wedding was over and the happy couple went on their honeymoon to the Lake District she might just agree to something more than the friendship they had already.

Penny's focus shifted as Mallory got closer. She wasn't sure she'd ever seen a bride look more breathtaking.

When Mallory had stepped out of the fitting room in the shop that day wearing the dress that had brought them all together in the village there hadn't been a dry eye amongst the women. It had fit almost perfectly. And once they pulled themselves together, Gigi and Rose had flown into practical mode and fussed around Mallory, pinning, talking, bossing her about. They'd fitted the veil, they'd talked bridesmaid dresses, cakes, flowers. Penny had gone into planning mode right afterwards too, and the first thing she'd done was called Jilly and told her she was coming to get her, and she would stay at the flat with her.

She sneaked a look at Jilly standing next to her beside the wedding arch and Jilly was still beaming. Nothing was going to extinguish that smile, her happiness for her mum.

This was a good day.

And she knew at least one or two photographs would be added to the memory book.

The wedding was small, as the bride and groom wanted, and because it was such short notice, the McGregors had had the perfect excuse not to invite extended family and all their acquaintances. Mallory had whispered her relief to Penny, saying that if they'd given a few months' notice they might well have had in excess of 250 guests.

As the vows were exchanged, Penny doubted she was the only one mesmerised by this pair. They were so in love, it didn't matter that their forever wouldn't be as long as other people got, they had each other for now, and that was their focus.

When the celebrant pronounced Mallory and Will husband and wife, a cheer went up and they had their first kiss as a married couple.

A whistle that almost deafened Penny came from Jilly.

'Where did you learn to do that?'

'Will taught me.' And then she nudged Penny. 'Joel is looking at you. He's very good looking for an old man.'

Penny burst out laughing. 'He is not old!' She was still smiling when she looked across at him. He was still looking her way, but a rumble from the skies had everyone looking upwards because the rumble left no doubt that the storm on the forecast they'd tried to avoid by having the ceremony earlier than planned was coming.

It was a matter of mere seconds after the rumble that the heavens opened with an incredible downpour.

Mallory's laugh was the loudest of all as Will scooped her into his arms and ran towards the house.

Gigi and Rose both had their phones. They didn't care about getting wet, they were taking pictures to capture every single thing about this day.

Jilly ran ahead, Penny following in her wake, struggling, like most of the other women, to run in heels, on grass!

The next thing she knew she'd been scooped up into Joel's arms. 'Will clearly knows what he's doing, thought I'd follow suit.'

And rather than protesting, she let herself feel safe in his arms and admitted that yes, he was good looking, and yes, she did want more than a friendship with him.

And she intended to tell him just as soon as they were out of the rain.

38

MALLORY

Mallory had spoken to all of their guests and had already said goodbye to Sasha, who had to get back home to work the night shift at the hospital. She'd been an absolute rock through this and Mallory knew how lucky she was to have all these wonderful people in her life.

Will had already moved in with Mallory, basing himself in Marlow, and travelled to and from the village for work. It wasn't ideal but until Jilly finished her studies, it was the best all round.

Mallory came back from the bathroom – using the toilet wasn't an easy task wearing a wedding gown and took her longer than it should – and hovered for a moment watching Jilly talk to Skye. They were growing close and she couldn't be happier about that. Skye had cried when Mallory told her her diagnosis but she'd insisted that she would be there for whatever she and Jilly needed. And Mallory had no doubt about that. She and Will had overheard Skye one day comforting Jilly and in those moments Mallory had listened and let them be there for each other. It was what she'd wanted all along after all, for Jilly to be surrounded by people who would help her through this when the time came.

The official photographs were done, they'd cut the cake that Rose and Penny had made, and now they moved into the centre of the drawing room to have their first dance as Mr and Mrs McGregor.

Mallory felt safe and content as she put her arms up and around Will's neck. His hands fell to her waist and there was no need to say a thing.

As they danced, she caught a glimpse of Jilly talking with a young lad who had helped do a wedding video. She hoped he was good enough for her daughter, but she wasn't the only one looking out for Jilly, she had a village now.

She noticed Penny and Joel, their bodies so close together that they may as well get it over with and kiss each other already. Penny's whole world shouldn't be watching out for Mallory and Jilly, which was what she'd been doing for most of the past year. She deserved to find her happy too.

Gigi and Rose were giggling about something as they both reached for a canapé. They'd found each other again and Rose had even persuaded Gigi to agree to meet Patrick outside of the leisure centre's café. They were good for each other, those women, just like her and Penny, just like Skye and Jilly.

Here in Will's arms, surrounded by everyone she loved, Mallory was happy.

She didn't know how many tomorrows she would have. All she knew was that she was going to spend the rest of whatever time she had left surrounded by love and security, and enjoy the little things in life. Because it was the simplest things that meant the most.

'How about we sneak off for a walk down by the river?' Will whispered.

'I'd like that.'

The rain had stopped and when they reached the water's edge they stood on the jetty, the river continuing to flow past in the way it had always done.

In Will's arms Mallory closed her eyes. 'I love you, Mr McGregor.'

'I love you too, Mrs McGregor. For always.'

She smiled. It sounded so right.

And when she opened her eyes she couldn't believe what she was seeing – six ducks swimming past, all in a row.

* * *

MORE FROM HELEN ROLFE

Another book from Helen Rolfe, *The Year That Changed Us*, is available to order now here:

www.mybook.to/YearChangedUsBackAd

ACKNOWLEDGEMENTS

This was an emotional story to write and I am enormously grateful for all the help I received with my research. It is this research that enabled me to portray an accurate picture of what it might be like for Mallory on this life changing journey.

Helen Bulbeck is the Director of services and policy at Brainstrust UK. Helen's help enabled me to keep Mallory's story realistic with regards to the type of tumour she has, the symptoms and the likely prognosis.

Bridget Dowty is the communications lead at Brain Tumour Support UK. In our email exchanges, as well as answering my many questions, Bridget explained that as an organisation they are constantly working to raise awareness of brain tumours and the impact they have on so many people. Bridget went on to say that having characters accurately portrayed within works of fiction could play a very important part in doing that. Bridget, I really hope I've done that with Mallory's story in this book.

Lucy Wilkinson is the support services manager and client liaison at Brain Tumour Support UK. Lucy works with patients, families and friends impacted by a brain tumour diagnosis and she helped me keep my story on track with regards to the type of tumour Mallory has and when her treatment would start.

Helen, Bridget and Lucy, thank you once again for your time, your kindness and your generosity.

Thank you as always to my husband for his support on a

daily basis – I wouldn't be a full time author without having him in my corner and encouraging me all the way. He didn't let me give up in the early days and I'm forever grateful for that!

A big thank you to my fabulous editor Rachel Faulkner-Willcocks. This book came with my biggest edit yet! With a lot of work and Rachel's incredible insight and expertise I hope we've managed to bring an emotional yet uplifting story to readers all around the world. Thank you also to the entire team at Boldwood Books, in particular my copyeditor, Candida, my proofreader, Rose, and Jenna for her marketing and social media expertise.

Much love,

Helen x

ABOUT THE AUTHOR

Helen Rolfe is the author of many bestselling contemporary women's fiction titles, set in different locations from the Cotswolds to New York. She lives in Hertfordshire with her husband and children.

Sign up to Helen Rolfe's mailing list for news, competitions and updates on future books.

Visit Helen's website: www.helenjrolfe.com

Follow Helen on social media here:

instagram.com/helen_j_rolfe

ALSO BY HELEN ROLFE

Heritage Cove Series

Coming Home to Heritage Cove

Christmas at the Little Waffle Shack

Winter at Mistletoe Gate Farm

Summer at the Twist and Turn Bakery

Finding Happiness at Heritage View

Christmas Nights at the Star and Lantern

New York Ever After Series

Snowflakes and Mistletoe at the Inglenook Inn

Christmas at the Little Knitting Box

Wedding Bells on Madison Avenue

Christmas Miracles at the Little Log Cabin

Moonlight and Mistletoe at the Christmas Wedding

Christmas Promises at the Garland Street Markets

Family Secrets at the Inglenook Inn

Little Woodville Cottage Series

Christmas at Snowdrop Cottage

Summer at Forget-Me-Not Cottage

The Skylarks Series

Come Fly With Me

Written in the Stars

Something in the Air

Standalones

The Year That Changed Us

The Best Days of Our Lives

BECOME A MEMBER OF

THE SHELF CARE CLUB

The home of Boldwood's book club reads.

Find uplifting reads, sunny escapes, cosy romances, family dramas and more!

Sign up to the newsletter
https://bit.ly/theshelfcareclub

Boldwood

Boldwood Books is an award-winning fiction publishing company seeking out the best stories from around the world.

Find out more at www.boldwoodbooks.com

Join our reader community for brilliant books, competitions and offers!

Follow us
@BoldwoodBooks
@TheBoldBookClub

Sign up to our weekly deals newsletter

https://bit.ly/BoldwoodBNewsletter

Printed in Great Britain
by Amazon